Praise for Lia Farrell

THREE DOG DAY

4 Stars: "Three Dog Day is a wonderful cozy mystery, and a great addition to a lovely series. It is sure to offer a lot of entertainment for mystery fans."
—Cyclamen, Long and Short Reviews

TWO DOGS LIE SLEEPING

"Another fantastic whodunit from Lia Farrell. This series is now one of my firm favorites and I'm really excited to see where she takes the series next."
—Cozy Mystery Book Reviews

"The story is told from several points of view—Mae's, July's, Ben's, and others—and each point of view adds greatly to the story. Not only do the different viewpoints bring more information to light, but more characters are developed and the reader is drawn into the lives of a number of them. And through it all, there are a number of dogs who add even more charm to a delightful cozy mystery. This is the second in the Mae December Mystery series and I have read the first as well. The books stand alone just fine, but my choice would be to read them in order so that the growth in some of the personal relationships can be fully savored. Mystery readers can't go wrong if they take a trip to Rosedale, TN, to meet Mae December and the entire cast of *Two Dogs Lie Sleeping*."
—Cyclamen, Long and Short Reviews

"A mix of drama with some comedic moments (well, there are dogs; and a four-year-old), *Two Dogs Lie Sleeping* is an enjoyable read. You really want to know how Mae and Ben get along; if Dory will move up in the police and if Mae's sister will—at last—get over Tom Ferris and make peace with her husband."

—I Love a Mystery Reviews

"The dog days of summer have never been quite like this. From its opening with a single gunshot on a sultry August evening to its satisfying conclusion, Lia Farrell's tale of greed and murder explores a compelling range of human (and the odd canine) relationships with an intriguing cast of characters and an imaginative plot. Fast paced, multilayered, and thoroughly enjoyable."

—Kathleen Hills, author of *The Kingdom Where Nobody Dies*

ONE DOG TOO MANY

"The author has worked carefully on the setting so that I really did feel as if I were a part of this rural town and I could picture the scenes as well as the people. Character interactions and the descriptions of daily life definitely ring true, and the characters seem to be very real. Fans of the cozy mystery will certainly enjoy adding Mae December to their list of charming detectives."

—Long and Short Reviews

"A lively tale with plenty of twists, turns, and unexpected situations to satisfy the most ardent cozy mystery lover. The story is told in several voices, including Mae, Sheriff Ben, and Detective Wayne, with Mae's best friend Tammy piping in occasionally, giving the tale several viewpoints of the mystery. Farrell's additional cast of characters are fun folks to get to know, and the setting of the Tennessee countryside is

charming. Animal lovers will enjoy the interaction with Mae's kennel customers, and fans of whodunits will love figuring out the intriguing plot as the story moves along .... A fine introduction to what promises to be an exciting series to follow."
—Sharon Galligar Chance, Fresh Fiction

"The story is a combination of police procedural, rocky romance (at least two of them), and a stroll through the world of dogs. Even for readers who don't find canines especially appealing, this novel—written by a mother/daughter pair— still has its charm. The plot is fairly straightforward, the major protagonists are believable, and the perpetrator's motives are quite understandable."
—John A. Broussard, I Love a Mystery

"A tidy little mystery peppered with likeable characters, interesting back stories, and lots of canine lore. *One Dog Too Many* is an entertaining book to read on a lazy day."
—Mary Marks, *The New York Journal of Books*

5 Thumbs Up: "What a great start to a series. This debut novel contains exactly all the right ingredients needed to make a perfect cozy mystery.... Through a crisp writing style the authors bring their characters not only to life, but has them serving sweet iced tea to the reader as they progress through this book, and in this way it I found it very easy to connect with them and establish a relationship; even their gossip made me feel included in their everyday lives."
—Cate Agosta, Cate's Book Nut Hut

"With an equal mix of charm and intrigue, Lia Farrell has created a twisty tale of murder and wagging tails."
—Jane Cleland, author of The Josie Prescott Antiques Mysteries

FOUR DOG'S SAKE

FOUR DOG'S SAKE

SAKE

A MAE DECEMBER MYSTERY

LIA FARRELL

Seattle, WA

Camel Press
PO Box 70515
Seattle, WA 98127

For more information go to: www.camelpress.com
www.liafarrell.net

Cover design by Sabrina Sun

Four Dog's Sake
Copyright © 2016 by Author

ISBN: 978-1-60381-246-7 (Trade Paper)
ISBN: 978-1-60381-247-4 (eBook)

Library of Congress Control Number: 2015950164

Printed in the United States of America

For Ruth, beloved mother and grandmother.

She walked in beauty all her life.

———

Also by the author:

One Dog Too Many

Two Dogs Lie Sleeping

Three Dog Day

Acknowledgments

——

W<small>E WISH TO</small> acknowledge and thank all the usual suspects from our publication team: Catherine Treadgold, Publisher and Editor-in-Chief, Jennifer McCord, Associate Publisher and Executive Editor, Sabrina Sun, graphic artist at Camel Press, and our agent Dawn Dowdle from Blue Ridge Literary. Detective Lieutenant Robert Pfannes of the Ann Arbor Police Department has helped us throughout the Mae December series in writing about subject interrogation. We would also like to thank Dr. Robert Stuart, Chief Medical Officer for Aurora Healthcare in Wisconsin. We are indebted to him for his clinical insights that provided medical expertise to our character Lucy Ingram, M.D. Any mistakes are ours and not his. Lastly, we are grateful to Will Schikorra, our webmaster extraordinaire.

Prologue

———

THE WIDOWER KNEW he was running out of time. *I won't live to see another summer.* The fluids were building up in his aging body as the congestive heart failure progressed. His wife and daughter were already gone. His two sons, both unmarried, would soon be all that remained of the family. If his daughter had lived past her college years, he'd probably have grandchildren to give the big house some life, but complications from diabetes had taken his little girl too soon. His wife had never really recovered from the loss.

I need to talk with the boys, he thought, and phoned his younger son. Chester agreed to come out that afternoon. The old man mentioned that he also wanted to see his eldest son.

"I'll get ahold of Rick, Dad. We'll see you in a few hours."

"Thanks, Chester. Better come after three thirty. My massage therapist will be here from two to three today."

After saying goodbye, he spent some time reviewing his investments and making a few notes. Last week, he had changed his will. He knew Chester wouldn't give him any trouble about it, but Rick was likely to kick up a fuss. His oldest son wouldn't want anything from the estate going out of the family. Shaking his head, he stood up and leaned heavily on the desk until he felt steadier. He went upstairs to his bedroom. After taking off his clothes and putting on a bathrobe over his underwear, he opened his wife's rosewood jewelry case that still sat atop her dresser. Selecting a necklace with a garnet cabochon pendant, he put it in his pocket and went back downstairs to await the arrival of Brooke, his massage therapist.

The doorbell rang at one forty-five, and the old man ushered Brooke Piper in with a smile. Brooke had blonde hair that she wore in one long braid. She always made him feel better, and not just physically. He was a realist and knew that he was in danger of becoming a cliché—the rich old man in poor health who falls for the pretty young woman—but he didn't really care. He knew his life was almost over, but Brooke was just starting out, and he wanted to help her, if she would let him.

They talked for a while as she set up her table in the spacious formal living room, and then she gave him his massage. Afterward, she folded her table up and took it out to her car while he wrote her a check. Brooke came back through the front door and took the check with a big smile.

"That's more than you need to pay me, you know."

He nodded, suddenly shy. "I know. I want you to have it." He paused. "And this." Before he lost his nerve, he took the necklace out of the pocket of his robe and pressed it into her hand.

"Thank you, Mr. Willis, but I can't accept this."

"You most certainly can. I'm old and sick and giving you this little trinket makes me happy. And how many times do I need to ask you to call me Leonard?"

She looked uncertainly from his face to the glittering gold and garnet necklace in her hand, a small frown creasing her forehead. "Well, thank you very much, Leonard. I need to get to my next appointment, so I'll see you on Thursday." With another smile, she was gone.

Leonard watched her drive away before he closed the door. Feeling a little lightheaded, he sat down on the brocade sofa. Looking up at his smiling wife, flanked by their boys and holding baby Jillian in the family portrait that hung over the mantel, he felt a sudden pang. God, he missed Corinne. Had he done the wrong thing, giving her jewelry away on a whim?

"No," he said out loud in the empty room. "I can't take any of this with me and the boys will just have to understand."

Chapter One

———

Mae December

MAEVE MALONE DECEMBER, known to friends and family alike as Mae, glared at her very pregnant best friend, Tammy West. How was it even possible that a woman who was days away from delivering her first child could be kicking her butt in barre class? Tammy seemed to be in even better shape now than before she got pregnant, sporting the perfect basketball of a belly and full breasts without an ounce of visible fat anywhere else. She had persuaded Mae to come to barre— an extremely demanding, ballet-based exercise class—to stop herself from "blimping out" and to help Mae get in shape for her upcoming wedding to Rose County Sheriff Ben Bradley.

The instructor, a goddess of physical perfection named Camille, complimented Tammy on her form.

"Beautiful relevé, Tammy."

Her friend gave her an angelic smile in the mirror they were both facing. No compliments were forthcoming for Mae, who continued to struggle with her relevé—a move that required standing on your toes with heels in the air, as though you were wearing three-inch stilettos. The class was almost over, thank God. She could get an iced coffee and take a cold shower. Tammy probably had world domination on her calendar after this, Mae thought, and gave her friend a little grin.

"Great work this morning, ladies. Please clean your mats before you go, and remember to hydrate. It's going to hit ninety-five by noon today." Camille turned off the music and left the studio.

Mae and Tammy wiped down their mats with the sanitary spray and paper towels provided by the studio. Walking outside, Mae lifted her thick, wavy, blonde hair off her sweaty neck and looked at the sky, white with the haze and humidity of a July morning in Rosedale, Tennessee.

"What are you doing the rest of the morning?" Tammy asked as she lowered herself carefully into the driver's seat of her sporty blue convertible and applied lip gloss. She fluffed her short, silver blonde hair and donned her sunglasses before turning the key in the ignition.

"Mama wants me to go to Atlanta to look for my wedding gown, but I think you're about to have this baby any minute," Mae said. "I don't want to be four hours away when you go into labor. I have some kennel chores to do, of course. Mainly I'm looking forward to getting out of these sweaty exercise clothes. What about you?"

"Finishing touches on the baby's room and shopping for an SUV with Patrick later today." Tammy's smile faded for a second. "I'm trading this car in—just not practical for a mom to drive—but I'm going to miss it."

"Send me some pictures of the nursery when it's done, okay?" Mae had painted a mural above the crib as a gift to Tammy and her husband Patrick—a fairytale woodland scene, complete with a cottage surrounded by baby animals.

"I will, and thank you again for that beautiful mural. Patrick just needs to install the light fixture and put the rods up so we can hang the curtains and it's done. Have a good day, Mae-Mae. See you in class on Tuesday."

Tammy sped off with a wave and Mae climbed into her Explorer and cranked up the air conditioning. *I bet she's in the hospital by Tuesday, not back here in class.*

After stopping for an iced coffee and picking up dog food and groceries at Kroger, Mae drove home to the restored, historic farmhouse she now shared with Sheriff Ben Bradley, her fiancé who had moved in with her in March, and her three dogs: Tallulah, a black pug, and Titan and Tater, her two Welsh corgis. In addition to running a boarding kennel, Mae also did dog training and bred the "porgi," a corgi/pug cross. Titan and Tallulah were the parents of her original litters, but they were retired and she was waiting until Tater was a little older to breed her.

She had planned to breed Tater to a friend's male, an apricot pug, but had also been thinking about the number of people who were interested in non-shedding breeds. She could breed Tater to a friend's white poodle and begin a new line of corgi-poos. Maltese and bichons were other options, since both were non-shedders. She had plenty of time to investigate the possibilities.

Ben was at work today, and the one-hundred-year-old house on Little Chapel Road was quiet when she walked inside. Her three dogs were asleep, sprawled in various patches of sunshine in the living room. Mae put the groceries away and went upstairs to her bathroom, where she peeled off her sticky exercise clothes and stepped into the long-awaited shower. She luxuriated in the cool water streaming over her hot skin, reflecting on all the changes in her life over the last two and a half years.

Mae was months away from marrying Noah West—the brother of Tammy's husband Patrick—when the talented young songwriter had been killed in a car accident. Before he died, Noah and Mae had purchased the farmhouse she lived in with the proceeds from his first hit song, "Calendar Girls," written right after he and Mae first met. Inspired by her name, he'd ended the song with the line, "and I saved the best for last, Miss December."

The year after Noah died was still a bit of a blur. A talented artist, Mae had stopped painting, focused on her dog breeding and boarding business and spent a lot of time with Tammy West, née Rodgers, and Noah's younger brother, Patrick. Her two friends had consoled and supported her through the worst of her grief—falling in love with each other in the process.

Then one early spring morning over a year ago, Mae found her neighbor Ruby Mead-Allison's dead body while walking one of her boarding dogs. Sheriff Ben Bradley had suspected Mae of being involved in Ruby's murder, but quickly dismissed the notion. Although Ben had initially resisted her efforts to help him identify Ruby's killer, he had recently succumbed to her wishes to be involved in his work life and named her a consultant to the sheriff's office. One other momentous thing happened during their investigation into the Mead-Allison case—Ben learned that he was the father of young Matthew, who had turned five in the spring, and was now a major part of their lives.

Mae shut the water off. Wrapping a towel around her hair, she paused to look in the mirror before wrapping a larger one around her body. She was looking less curvy and more toned, so the damned class was working. She looked down at the ruby engagement ring sparkling on her left hand. The ring—two hands holding a crowned heart inset with a ruby—was a Claddagh, a traditional Irish engagement design that signified "With these two hands I give you my heart and crown it with my loyalty." Mae smiled, thinking about what Ben had said when she shared her fitness goals with him.

It was Valentine's Day, right after Tammy and Patrick's wedding reception, and he'd just proposed. "I love your curves, Maeve Malone December. Please don't lose all of them, okay?"

By then they'd solved a total of three murder cases together. Lately things had been much quieter at the Rosedale sheriff's office. Mae found a loose blue and green sundress and put it on. Unable to face a blow dryer on such a steamy day, she left her curls to air dry and went back downstairs to fix herself some lunch. It was a good thing Ben hadn't had to deal with any big cases lately, she thought. He had enough to do with his campaign to be reelected Sheriff of Rose County in November.

Chapter Two

—

Dr. Lucy Ingram

O^{N THE FIRST} morning of July, Lucy Ingram got up at nine and turned on the coffee maker. She looked out her kitchen window while the coffee perked, seeing her neighbor Mae's old farmhouse across the street at the top of a hill. They both lived on Little Chapel Road, a historic lane that wound through a leafy valley in Rosedale, Tennessee. Lucy poured herself a cup of coffee, taking it into the bathroom with her.

When she got out of the shower, Lucy checked her beeper to be sure she hadn't missed a call. She towel-dried her long brown hair, French-braided the top and then gathered the braid into a low pony tail. She dressed in lightweight black leggings, a white blouse, and her most comfortable shoes. The shoes had a removable anatomical foot bed—a shock absorbing system necessary to ease the long days on her feet. She quickly put on facial lotion and lipstick. Her twelve-hour shift in the emergency department started at eleven.

It was Sunday, but Lucy had been in the emergency business for over a decade. Weekends and weekdays had become either "shift" or "non-shift." ER work depended heavily on the season. In winter it was usually sick kids, which occasionally necessitated trips to the chapel. She was not a religious woman in the conventional sense, although whenever she lost a patient she visited the chaplain. He always smiled gently when he saw her, calling her one of his "strays." She hoped she wouldn't have to see him today.

Summer brought out the weekend warriors. There would be ankle sprains, back pain, cuts, and broken bones. July was also the month when clueless first-year interns from the university hospital in Nashville rotated onto her service.

Driving into the parking lot at Rose County General at 10:40 a.m., she grabbed a clean white coat from the backseat of her car and threw it on. She walked quickly into the emergency bay door, said hello to one of the young ambulance drivers, and went to the nurses' station. Her favorite assistant, Channing Soldan RN, looked up and smiled.

"Boy, are we in for it today, Dr. Lucy," she said. "We have not one, not two, but three first-year interns here. I've already called the med school asking for one to be shifted to the Peds ER. There was a woman vomiting all over the patient waiting room. I sent her back to bay two." Channing sighed. "I hate the barfers; they're worse than the bleeders. And we have a patient for you in bay four." She consulted her notes and read, "Chester Willis, age forty-one. Practically sliced his leg off clearing some woods on his father's property. I diagnosed him as FTF." Channing's mouth curved in a grin. FTF was a common acronym for "failure to fly," used to describe patients who fell from a roof, a balcony, or out of a tree.

"Why's he an FTF?" Lucy asked.

"There was a tree the patient's father wanted taken down. It was blocking his view. The patient climbed up in the tree and was cutting off a limb above him when the branch he was standing on gave way. Chainsaw lacerated his leg on the way down." Channing rolled her eyes. "He's pretty flirtatious for a guy bleeding all over. Trying to avoid a Darwin Award, I'd say."

The Darwin Awards were a tongue-in-cheek designation for foolhardy individuals who improved the gene pool by getting killed before they could procreate. Lucy shook her head whenever faced with people who took ridiculous risks with their bodies.

"Let's go patch him up. What've you done already?"

"Cleaned the wound and put on a temporary dressing."

Lucy pulled the curtain to the side of bay 4 and took a look at her first patient of the day. "Mr. Willis?" she said, holding out her hand. "I'm Dr. Ingram. Took a tumble, did you?" He was tall and slim; she guessed over six feet. He had shiny black hair, dark eyes, and despite the pain furrowing his brow, a nice smile.

"Sure did." He gestured to the long gash on the calf of his right leg.

"Let me take a look," Lucy said, gently removing the dressing. "Ouch. What's the pain now on a scale from one to ten, ten being the worst pain you ever felt?"

Willis grimaced and said, "An eight. I thought chainsaws were supposed to shut off when you dropped them. Turns out not all of them do."

"I'm going to have to stitch that up. And I don't want you moving around while I'm working on you, so I'm going to give you some lidocaine injections, okay?"

"Thank you," he said gratefully. "I'm diabetic, if that matters."

"Not for this," Lucy said. The wound was about six-inches long, and she put little pinprick injections of lidocaine along both sides. The lidocaine would numb the skin so she could suture it shut without the patient feeling pain.

An intern wearing a short white coat opened the drape to the examination bay. The length of the white coat in the medical profession indicated the stage in training of the person. Blazer-length coats designated medical students. Longer, thigh-length coats were worn by interns, residents, and fully licensed physicians—called "attendings" in the jargon of the hospital. The girl's nametag read Emily Thompson, MD. She should have been wearing one of the longer coats. Obviously Emily hadn't gotten the memo. The girl was tall and willowy with dark eyes. At close to six feet, she towered over petite Channing Soldan, who had blonde hair often streaked with a color to match her scrubs and an irrepressible sense of humor.

"Dr. Ingram, this is Dr. Thompson," Channing said. From the slightly surprised look on the intern's face at Channing's calling her "doctor", Lucy realized that Emily Thompson must have just graduated from medical school. While she was a long way from being fully trained or licensed, courtesy demanded she be introduced as "doctor."

"Nice to meet you, Dr. Thompson. This is my patient, Chester Willis. As you can see, he incurred a laceration from a chainsaw." Turning to Mr. Willis, Lucy said, "Dr. Thompson is a first-year intern here. Do you mind if she joins us?"

"Not a bit," Chester said, smiling at the pretty Dr. Thompson, who gave him a small nod in return.

Lucy consulted her notes and looked up at her patient. He seemed to be in good shape physically, and despite his painful injury was alert and pleasant. She looked at the intake form that read IDDM.

"Tell me about your diabetes, Chester. You're insulin dependent?"

"Yes, Type one. According to what I've been told, I'm a *brittle* diabetic. Apparently my blood sugar level often shifts very quickly from high to low and back."

"Tough to manage," Lucy said. "What do you take?"

"I take thirty units of long-acting and ten units of short-acting insulin every day. I was going to get one of those insulin pumps, but my father isn't well, and I just moved back home to take care of him. My mom died several years ago. Once things settle down, I'll go in for the pump. Supposedly they work pretty well."

"They do. I'm sure you've been told this, but any alcohol or recreational drug use is not good for you." Lucy looked intently at Mr. Willis.

"Yes, I'm no fun at parties," he said with a rueful shake of his head. Grinning at Dr. Thompson, he added, "It makes it tough to ask a good-looking woman out for a drink. I usually have to stick to coffee."

"Good man," Lucy said. "I'm going to send you to X-ray first, to be sure you didn't chisel off any bone fragments. Dr. Thompson, would you please accompany Mr. Willis and then bring the X-ray and the patient back to this bay?"

When Chester and the intern returned and the X-ray showed no bone chips, Lucy bent to the task of stitching up Mr. Willis. He hadn't cut any tendons or ligaments so it was a straightforward repair. Emily leaned forward to observe Lucy's small, careful stitches. Lucy asked if she would like to finish up and tie off the suture at the end of the repair. Emily said she would and did a decent job.

"So, you're the primary caregiver for your dad? That can be pretty stressful," Lucy remarked to Chester.

"I love the old man. He depends on me, and it's pretty much mutual."

"What's his medical problem?" Emily Thompson asked.

"Congestive heart failure," Chester said. "He's had it for a number of years now, and the meds he's been taking aren't working so well anymore."

"How are your spirits holding up? Long term caregivers have a tough job," Lucy said.

"I'm doing okay. I just moved in with him a few days ago, once I noticed how fast he was going downhill. It's going to be very sad for me when he goes, but we're enjoying each other's company for now. He's had an interesting life, and I'm learning a little more about his early years."

"Well, don't forget to take care of yourself, too. You need to eat well and get plenty of sleep," Lucy told him. "And it's good to exercise from time to time, although maybe not by cutting down trees." She gave him a knowing grin.

When the laceration had been bandaged, Lucy gave her patient a prescription.

"The scrip I just handed you is for Vicodin. Don't take more than one of these tonight. You can have one tomorrow morning and again in the evening and the same the following day. I wrote the prescription for five tablets. If you can't control the pain with these, you can add a couple of Tylenol each day. If that still doesn't do it, you'll have to come back. You can have your family physician re-bandage the wound in three days and remove the dressing in a week." Lucy smiled at Mr. Willis.

"Thank you, Doctor," Chester Willis said.

"Dr. Thompson will help you down from the examining table and find an orderly to wheel you outside." She looked at the intern. "Find him some crutches, too, please. Did you drive yourself here, Mr. Willis?"

"I did. Pain's much better now. I can drive myself home. Thanks again, Doc."

"I don't often give my phone number to patients, but here's my card. Call me if you notice the wound getting hot or red streaks coming up your leg. I'll come to the ER to check on you." Lucy shook hands with her patient.

Chester Willis pocketed the card. An orderly appeared with the wheelchair and Dr. Thompson helped him off the table and into the chair.

What's next?" Lucy asked as she and her nurse walked out of the patient bay.

"We have a D and D in bay 3," Channing laughed.

"Okay, that's a new one," Lucy said. "Define, please."

"Divorced and desperate. She comes up with these obscure pains and asks for the good-looking young male docs. This time she has a pain in her right breast. She's already asked for our sexy Dr. Alexander, but he's off today." Channing rolled her eyes.

"Well, she's going to have to make do with me this time."

Chapter Three

—

Mae December

Mae hadn't heard from Tammy since Saturday, so she went to Barre class after Ben left for work on Tuesday morning, and was in her usual spot unrolling her mat when Camille tapped her shoulder.

"Tammy's out in the car. She wants you," Camille said in a hushed voice. "I'll put your mat up; you go ahead."

"Is she in labor?"

The instructor gave a sympathetic nod. Grabbing her purse from the hook in the hall, Mae ran outside. Tammy waved at her from the window of a brand-new silver Toyota Forerunner that was parked right in front of the studio.

"Looks like you get to miss class today, Mae," Tammy said, taking an audible breath. "I'm having contractions and Patrick's not answering his phone. Can you drive me to the ER?" Tammy paled and blew out a puff of air.

Mae put a hand on her shoulder. "Sure thing. Do you want to get in my car, or should I drive you in this?"

"The infant seat's in here, along with my bag for the hospital."

She opened the door and stepped gingerly down onto the pavement. Mae walked beside her much shorter friend and helped Tammy into the passenger's seat, then walked back around to take the wheel, setting her purse on the center console.

"How fast should I drive?"

Tammy gasped and Mae saw her abdomen ripple under her snugly fitted top. "Fast, Mae," she said. "As fast as you can."

Mae adjusted the driver's seat for her longer legs, quickly fastened her seatbelt, and paused. "Can you call Ben on my phone? Just go to 'Recents' and hit his number so we can get a police escort. Tell him we'll be passing his office in five minutes."

Tammy nodded, her brown eyes huge in her pale face. "Good idea. Now drive!"

BEN'S PATROL CAR was idling at the curb when they pulled up and Tammy rolled down the car window.

"I was looking for your car, Mae," he said. He glanced at Tammy, gave a sharp nod and turned on the flashers. "Follow me." He pulled out in front of them and Mae hit the gas. The drive from the sheriff's office to Rose County General Hospital should have taken at least twenty minutes, but they were at the doors of the ER in less than ten. Ben parked right behind an ambulance and ran to Tammy's door to help her out.

"How're you doing?" Ben asked Tammy, after flashing Mae a quick smile.

"The contractions are getting closer together." She leaned against Ben, tall and handsome in his uniform. He put an arm around her shoulders and looked at Mae.

"Shut the car off and come here, Mae. I'm going to get an orderly and a wheelchair for Tammy. I just need you to hold her up."

Mae turned the car off and jumped out, hurrying to stand beside her friend, who looked like she was ready to lie down on the pavement and give birth right there. "I've got her," she told Ben, who rushed inside.

"Where's Patrick?" There were tears spilling from Tammy's eyes. "This baby's coming fast. I need him."

Before Mae could answer, Ben emerged from the ER doors with a wheelchair-pushing orderly. The two men got Tammy into the chair and the orderly spun it around and whisked her inside.

"I'll park the car and bring you the keys, Mae. You should go with Tammy." Mae handed him the keys and pulled her purse out of Tammy's new Forerunner.

"She said her bag was in here. I'll take it in with me."

Ben opened the back door, pulling out a blue satchel and Tammy's purse along with it. "Take her purse, too. She'll need her ID and insurance cards." He frowned. "Where the hell is Patrick—any idea?"

She took the purse and satchel from him and hurried toward the building, calling back over her shoulder, "I don't know. Please see if you can find him. I'm afraid he's going to miss this."

Mae didn't see Tammy in the waiting room, so she went to the ER information desk to ask where she was.

"Hi, Mae." Her neighbor, Dr. Lucy Ingram, came around the corner in her white coat. "They already took your friend up to Labor and Delivery."

"Oh dear. Is she all alone up there?"

"Don't worry," Lucy smiled, "her husband's with her. He apparently saw a missed call from Tammy and came straight here when he couldn't reach her. Guess she turned her phone off by accident."

Ben came up beside her, said hello to Lucy, and kissed Mae on the cheek. She released a big breath she didn't even know she'd been holding. "That's a relief. Where should we wait?"

"There's a waiting area outside Labor and Delivery, on the third floor." Lucy motioned toward a bank of elevators and said goodbye before opening the "staff only" door. Ben pushed the "up" button beside the nearest elevator door and took the satchel from Mae's hand.

"Let's go, Mae. I don't think we'll have long to wait."

"Let me know how she does," Lucy called back over her shoulder.

Chapter Four

—

Mae December

AT THREE THAT afternoon, Mae was still waiting. Ben had returned to work after Mae assured him that she would text him when the baby got serious about coming out. Tammy's labor had practically come to a stop by the time the two expectant grandmothers, Grace Rodgers and Sharon West, had arrived at the hospital. Grace, Tammy's mom, was walking her daughter up and down the hallway on the Labor and Delivery floor. Sharon was talking in a low voice to Patrick.

"They probably need to give her some Pitocin to get labor going again; it's not good for Tammy or the baby to have it take so long."

Patrick shook his head. "Tammy doesn't want to do that, Mom. And we've only been here for five or six hours. It hasn't really been that long yet." He looked down the hall at Tammy, who was leaning into her mother's shoulder, walking slowly but still moving. "I'm just afraid they're going to send us home if she doesn't make progress soon."

Sharon's fine-boned face was scrunched into a frown as she too watched Tammy's halting pace. "We can't have that," she said decisively. Rising to her feet, she turned to look back at Mae and Patrick. "If you two walk on either side of her and support her, maybe you can get her to walk a little faster. I'll take Grace down to the cafeteria and get her some of what passes for coffee in this place."

Mae winked at Patrick, who was already standing up. His mother epitomized the soft-spoken, gracious Southern lady, but when she decided to take charge, resistance was futile.

"Yes, ma'am, good idea." Patrick smiled at his mother. "You and Miss Grace take your time, we'll be right here." Sharon nodded and went to collect Grace.

"You know she's going to talk Grace into pressuring Tammy about the Pitocin, right?" Mae murmured.

Patrick took his glasses off and cleaned them on the tail of his shirt. "I know. I'm not sure that's a bad idea." He put his glasses back on and rolled his head from side to side. "C'mon, Mae. Let's go walk my wife."

AFTER MAE AND Patrick had gotten Tammy to walk a little more briskly for a while, she came to an abrupt halt and bent forward, digging her fingers into her husband's arm. Tammy gasped and shuddered, letting go of Mae and sagging toward Patrick on the exhale. She straightened up slowly. "Take me back to the room now," she said, in a demanding tone Mae had never heard from her best friend before.

"Are you sure, honey? Seems like the walking is starting to work—"

"Yes I'm sure! Don't argue with me."

Patrick gave Mae a wide-eyed look above Tammy's head. "Okay, okay. Let's get you turned around then."

"Are you actually going to stand there and patronize me, Patrick Daniel West?" She practically spat her husband's name. Turning away from him, she grabbed Mae's arm and moved purposefully toward her room. "Let's go, Mae," she barked. "This is all *his* fault anyway."

"I'll go find her nurse, Mae." Patrick raised his eyebrows, mouthing the word "transition" at her behind Tammy's back. Mae was excellent at reading lips, but she didn't know what he meant. She gave Patrick a blank look.

"Just go." He sighed. "I'll explain later."

TAMMY'S NURSE, ERICA, had gotten her settled back into bed and asked Mae to leave so she could examine her. Mae resumed her seat in the waiting room and texted Ben that the baby was still ensconced. Patrick went into Tammy's room but was back out in a few minutes, taking the chair across from Mae. Grace and Sharon hadn't returned from the cafeteria yet.

"How's it going in there?" Mae asked.

"Erica confirmed that she's in transition, moving into a more active phase of labor. That's why she's so irritable." Patrick leaned back, stretching his long legs out in front of him and his arms above his head. "She's still not very dilated, though. It's gonna be a while."

"That happens when dogs go into labor too," Mae told him. "They get agitated and snappish before they really get down to business. I guess it's just natural."

Patrick grinned. "I dare you to go in there and tell Tammy that right now. She'd love to hear how natural this all is. And I'd like her to insult someone besides me."

"No way. She's a little scary at the moment. I've witnessed a lot of puppies coming into the world, but dogs can't insult you."

Grace and Sharon got off the elevator and Erica emerged from Tammy's room and approached the group. "I've got the monitors hooked up and everything's going well with mother and baby," the young, dark-haired nurse told them. She nodded at Grace. "Tammy would like her mother to come sit with her for now, and I'm going to track down the doctor."

Sharon put her hand on Patrick's shoulder. "Why don't you

and Mae go get something to eat and take a break? I'll text you when the doctor shows up, or if anything changes. If you want anything decent to eat or drink, I'd suggest leaving the hospital."

"No. I don't want to be very far away if Tammy needs me," Patrick said. "Even if she just wants to cuss me out some more."

His mother laughed. "When I was in labor with Noah, your dad said I used words he'd never heard before. And he was in the Army! Apparently I was quite derogatory about his ancestors as well, but I have no memory of that myself."

Afternoon slipped into evening. Ben texted Mae to let her know that he'd gone home after work to change and check on the dogs and that everything was fine at the house. She replied with a quick thanks, took the elevator down and walked outside to call him.

The warm, humid air felt good on Mae's skin after spending hours in the air-conditioned hospital. She looked up at the purpling sky with its scattering of stars and took a deep breath. The lemony scent from the blooms of a nearby magnolia tree filled her with a sudden sense of well-being. She called Ben and heard a cellphone ring from the sidewalk in front of her. The outline of a tall man walking toward her coalesced into her fiancé. She clicked the "end" button and ran to Ben.

"Did you just hang up on me?" he teased, wrapping his arms around her.

She smiled up into his face. "Yup. I saw a cute guy walking in from the parking lot and decided I'd rather talk to him than the sheriff."

He shook his head, releasing her from his embrace. "What a hussy. How's Tammy doing … everything all right?"

Mae took his hand, and they walked back toward the hospital entrance. She filled Ben in on all the events of the day as they made their way back up to the Labor and Delivery waiting area and found chairs near Sharon and Grace. Patrick, who had been readmitted to his wife's room several hours before, came out and visited with them for a while.

Mae leaned her head on Ben's shoulder and closed her eyes. It seemed as though only a few minutes went by, but when she opened them again it was 11:15 and Tammy's nurse was standing in front of Patrick's chair.

"It's time, Dad." She told him. He leaped to his feet and followed Erica. Everyone else got up and followed Patrick toward Tammy's room. Patrick opened the door and walked in without a backward glance. Erica smiled at the four of them as she held the door's edge. "It won't be long now, folks. You can stand right here in the hall. Just don't block the way of anyone who needs to get through." She too went into the room, and the door closed behind her.

Some time went by and Mae heard her friend start to scream. *I wish Tammy had agreed to pain medication.* She squeezed Ben's hand and looked at Miss Grace, who had visibly paled. Sharon bit her lip and winced. Without a word, Tammy's doctor hurried past them and into the room. When he opened the door, the screams got louder.

Ben put his hand on the back of Mae's neck and rubbed the tight muscles there. "It's almost over," he whispered, and she nodded. The screaming had stopped and Mae leaned close to the door. There was a tiny, crowing sound and her eyes filled with tears. She stepped away from the door just as Erica stuck her head out.

"He's here and he's perfect," she said, beaming at Grace and Sharon. "Congratulations! You have a beautiful, healthy grandson."

Chapter Five

—

Sheriff Ben Bradley

O**N THE** 4**TH** of July, Sheriff Ben Bradley glanced around the historic downtown of Rosedale, Tennessee. As expected, it was thronged with flag-waving kids, dogs in patriotic bandanna collars, and adults with damp brows. The parade was about to start and the digital display at the bank read 2:47 p.m. and 98.4 degrees.

Carrie Allen, the avid reporter for Channel 3 News, had appeared out of nowhere.

"Good afternoon, Sheriff." The heavily made-up brunette stuck a microphone in Ben Bradley's face. "How's your reelection campaign going?"

Ben straightened his shoulders and smiled into the camera. "It's going well. I think my record as sheriff of Rose County speaks for itself."

"I'm surprised to hear you say that, Sheriff Bradley," a man's voice drawled from the crowd. Ramsey Tremaine ambled over, inserting himself neatly between Ben and the reporter. Unlike Ben, who was sweating in his uniform, Ramsey looked cool and unruffled in a seersucker suit and star-spangled bow tie. He was also wearing a straw fedora, which Ben thought was a bit much.

"Hello, young lady." Mr. Tremaine flashed Carrie Allen and the camera a wide grin before dimming it a little in Ben's direction. "If you're running on your *record as sheriff*, my victory is a foregone conclusion."

Ben's face grew even hotter at Ramsey's grandstanding tactics. "What would you even know about law enforcement?" he asked, glaring at his opponent.

"Obviously you don't consider members of the legal profession part of law enforcement," Tremaine said grimly.

"Well not the *enforcement* part anyway," Ben replied stiffly. Ramsey was a top-notch defense attorney with Babcock, Woolsey and Tremaine. He had tangled with Ben on numerous occasions, trying to prevent criminals from serving the time Ben thought they deserved.

"Perhaps you've forgotten that I served as assistant district attorney for five years prior to joining the firm," Ramsey said.

"Now, now boys," Carrie purred, her brown eyes gleaming. "Why don't you both shake hands? We'll get a good shot for the five o'clock news."

"May the best man win." Ramsey Tremaine stuck out his hand and Ben took it with an extra-firm grip.

"The best *law* man, not *lawyer*." Ben narrowed his eyes at his gadfly of an opponent. "Please excuse me; I have to get back to work."

THE 4TH OF July parade had begun. Two dark-haired women waved at him from across the street, and he quickly walked over before the marching band got any closer, seeing Suzanne December, Mae's mother, and Mae's sister Julia Powell, who everyone in the family called July.

"Happy Independence Day, Ben. Is Mae here somewhere?" Suzanne December asked. Along with July, she was flanked by

Olivia, July's seven-year-old blonde daughter. The three were appropriately garbed in red, white, and blue. Little Olivia's blue eyes sparkled when she looked up at him. "Hi," she said and waved the small flag she held.

"Happy Fourth of July, ladies. Y'all look very pretty today. Mae's at the hospital visiting Tammy and her baby right now, ma'am. Where're the men in the family?"

"At Zana and Papa's house, lighting stuff on fire," Olivia informed him solemnly.

July laughed. "Fred and the twins are helping Daddy set up for a home fireworks show tonight. We got out while the getting was good. What did Tammy and Patrick name the baby? Did you get to hold him? How much did he weigh?"

July and Suzanne were looking at him with identical expressions, eyebrows raised and smiles bright and interested. Ben shook his head.

"They hadn't decided on a name when we left the hospital last night. I thought he would be born on the third, but her labor slowed down and he ended up being the first baby born on the fourth at Rosedale General."

"First babies usually take their time," July said.

"I don't know how much he weighs, but he looked awfully small to me," Ben went on with a grin. "Has a big voice though. Definitely enough volume to get his parents' attention."

Suzanne and her eldest glanced at each other and then back at Ben. Before either could ask another question he didn't know the answer to, he said, "Well, enjoy the parade. I need to circulate a little and keep an eye on things."

" 'Bye, Ben," the women chorused, and Olivia gave him another wave of her flag.

IT WAS CLOSE to midnight by the time the final glittering display of Rosedale's fireworks had faded into the hot summer darkness. Most of the people had left, although a few stragglers remained. Ben was still on duty and saw an ambulance coming slowly down Main Street.

"Out of the way," he motioned to the few who remained. "Let them through."

Families pulled their little ones back to the sidewalk as the ambulance driver stopped next to Ben and put the window down. Ben hurried over.

"What's wrong?" he asked the young black man at the wheel whose name tag read Zack Randall. "Why aren't your flashers on?"

"The patient didn't make it."

Ben put his hand on the driver's shoulder. "Heart attack?" he asked with a frown. "Someone with a bad ticker get startled by the fireworks?"

"No, it wasn't a heart attack," the EMT in the passenger seat said. "Younger guy, diabetic. We're taking him in to Rose County Hospital so they can pronounce him DOA, but there's no rush. He was gone before we got out of his neighborhood."

Ben sighed. "All right, take it slow then. We don't need any additional casualties tonight." The driver nodded and put the window up.

Ben watched the ambulance drive away.

Chapter Six

———

Dr. Lucy Ingram

A s the last hours of July 4th evaporated in the busy emergency room, Dr. Lucy Ingram worked like a besieged general fighting off an unending wave of injuries. Wednesday was normally her day off, but holidays were often an exception—especially those as potentially dangerous as Independence Day. It was nearing dawn on the 5th when the relentless pace slowed enough that she could go off-shift. Two of her colleagues had come on to man the barricades. She took the elevator up to the office reserved for attendings to do their patient notes and email, pulled off her white coat, and laid it over the back of a chair. There were several cubicles in the room with computers and dictation equipment, but the space was devoid of charm. Lucy wanted to check her email before she left the hospital; then she would sink into bed for a long, lovely sleep.

She flipped through her emails, noting several from retail sites. She would have to unsubscribe from those soon or they would become relentless. Among the shameless solicitations that had somehow slipped through the hospital's firewall, there was a message from Dr. Estes, the coroner and ME for Rose County. He was known throughout the hospital as prickly and difficult but excellent at his job. Most of the staff doctors called him an ice man and said that he had no feelings, but Lucy knew better. She was on to his little secret.

It had started some time ago when Dr. Estes emailed her with information about one of her patients who ended up in the morgue. The note said she might want to contact the victim's family and suggested she attend the funeral of the young man, a runner who died from a coronary. She did, and on that warm summer morning two years ago was surprised to see Dr. Estes standing by the grave. As the family dispersed after the ceremony, Lucy walked up to him.

"Good morning, Dr. Estes," she said quietly. "Thank you for letting me know about the funeral."

"Thought you might want to be here," he said brusquely. "I noticed you were the one to pronounce him dead."

"And if I might ask, why are you here?" Lucy asked gently.

"He was so young," he replied, looking off at the hills in the distance. "Should've had his whole life ahead of him."

That was all there was to the interaction, but whenever Dr. Estes issued one of his blistering invectives at staff incompetence on grand rounds, Lucy smiled to herself, knowing he only did so because he cared so much about the patients.

ON LUCY'S COMPUTER screen the message from Dr. Estes read, "Chester Willis, 41, Caucasian, DOA July 4th. Cause of death: drug or insulin overdose, probable suicide."

"What the hell?" Lucy said aloud. She shared the office with other doctors, but there was no one else there in the wee hours to hear her outburst. Something about this wasn't right. She checked her tablet computer for her notes on Chester Willis' visit for the chainsaw injury. There it was: "Brittle diabetic, no known history of alcohol or drugs. Knowledgeable about his condition." She had spent over twenty-five minutes stitching Chester up, during which he displayed no signs of depression. He was the last guy she would have suspected of being a suicide risk.

She quickly wrote an email to Dr. Estes saying she had some questions and would be stopping down to see him about Chester Willis. As her finger was about to hit "send," she hesitated, knowing that the email might come across as challenging the ME's declaration on nothing more than her intuition. She had no evidence, but her gut said that something was very wrong about Chester Willis' cause of death.

She knew that patients lied to her, putting on a front to hide depression or saying they were not drinking or doing drugs when they were in fact using. *But not Chester Willis.* He had been looking forward to his remaining time with his father. She had seen insulin injection marks on his thighs when she stitched up his injury, but they were in a tight pattern— as diabetic injections should be. Chester had worn a short-sleeved shirt and shorts to the ER, and Lucy hadn't noticed any needle marks on his arms, where recreational drug injection marks would typically show up. Baffled, she hit "send" on the email and then quickly called her boyfriend—Wayne Nichols, Chief Detective of Rose County.

"Nichols," his sleepy voice said.

"Wayne, it's Lucy. Sorry to wake you. Just getting off shift. Something's come up and I want to talk to you about it."

"Okay," he yawned.

"I had this patient the other day; his name was Chester Willis, a diabetic with a deep leg laceration. He was fine when he left here and then came in DOA yesterday. I got Dr. Estes' report on email. He listed the cause of death as a probable suicide, caused by drug or insulin overdose. It doesn't fit. Chester was the primary caregiver for his ill father and knowledgeable about his diabetes. Plus, he didn't use recreational drugs. I've got a bad feeling about it. Could you drop by my house this morning?"

"Sure thing," Wayne said. "I'll see you later."

WAYNE KNOCKED ON Lucy's door at 9:00 Thursday morning. It was already over 90 degrees outside. Lucy answered the door, still wearing her short cotton nightshirt. "Come on in. I didn't make coffee. It's just too hot outside." She yawned, still trying to get herself fully awake. "But I'm making pancakes."

When they had polished off blueberry pancakes and fresh strawberries, Wayne looked intently at Lucy. "Did you talk to Dr. Estes about your patient yet?"

"I did. I asked him if there was any chance the man's death was caused by someone else giving him an insulin overdose."

Wayne's eyebrows went up. "I imagine he wasn't too pleased to hear that question."

"He wanted to know what evidence I had for my suspicions. All I could tell him was that I spent nearly half an hour stitching Chester up and that he was upbeat, flirted with my intern and was committed to being the caregiver for his father. He wouldn't have killed himself. His father was depending on him. The upshot is that Dr. Estes is waiting on tox screen results, but he's grudgingly agreed to take another look."

"Good work, Lucy. Thanks for the pancakes." He smiled and reached across the table to take her hand. After planting a kiss on her palm, he stood up. "Gotta get to work. Let me know what you find out."

"I will," Lucy said, pensively. "I don't suppose you would look into this for me, unofficially?"

Wayne shook his head. "Sorry, hon. I know how important your patients are to you, but without any evidence, my hands are tied. If you turn up anything conclusive, then I definitely will."

Lucy nodded. He kissed the top of her head and left the

kitchen. Moments later, she heard the sound of his Harley leaving the driveway.

As she walked down the hall to her bedroom, Lucy was deep in thought. She put on some lightweight khaki pants and a sleeveless blouse. Looking in the mirror while she brushed her long brown hair and put on her favorite silver earrings, she wondered why Chester Willis' death was bothering her so much. She went back through her interaction with Chester point by point. Maybe she was wrong. He was a single guy, committed to caring for his dying father. Maybe it suddenly got to be too much and something happened that led him to kill himself.

"No," she said aloud, shaking her head. "No matter what, Chester Willis wouldn't kill himself."

Suspicion was growing deeper in her mind. If somebody had driven Chester Willis to suicide or murdered him, she had to know who … and why.

Chapter Seven

—

Mae December

Mae tapped on the door of the hospital room. Opening it, Patrick said in a low voice, "They're both sleeping. Come with me to the cafeteria. I need some caffeine."

"I can tell." Mae took in Patrick's appearance—dark hair standing on end more than usual, clothes the same as yesterday, blue eyes bloodshot, and face in dire need of a shave. "I have a better idea," she said. "Why don't you go home, grab a nap, food, and a shower? I'll be here when they wake up."

He rubbed his hand over his face and nodded. "You relieving me of duty, Mae?"

"Yes." She smiled and gave his shoulder a light push. "Go on home, get some rest and food before you fall over. I've got this." He nodded, smiled, and gave her a quick hug before he walked away.

Mae opened the door a little wider and tiptoed in. The room was dim and Tammy was sound asleep in her hospital bed. The baby, wrapped up like a burrito in his bassinet, had his eyes squeezed shut as well. Mae closed the door behind her and sat down quietly in the chair beside the bed to watch over them until they woke up.

She almost dozed off herself, tired after being at the hospital most of the day yesterday and up late the previous night for the fireworks. Ben and all his employees had worked well into the night, and he had crawled into bed with her sometime after two in the morning, his hair smelling of smoke. He'd still been dead to the world when she left the house this morning. Her fiancé had the day off, so she would catch up with him later.

"How long have you been here?" Tammy croaked. She'd lost her voice during labor and it was not quite back yet.

Mae glanced at her cellphone. "Almost an hour. I sent Patrick home, and I've just been relaxing here watching you and your son. He hasn't made a sound."

Tammy reached for the Styrofoam cup beside her bed and drank from the straw. "We've picked out a name, did Patrick tell you?"

Mae shook her head. "He was sleepwalking, barely said a word." The baby made a little crowing sound. "Should I hand him to you?"

"Yes, please."

Mae picked him up carefully. His eyes were midnight blue in his little red face. Cradling him to her, she breathed in. He smelled heavenly. Tammy used the button to raise the head of her bed and reached for her child.

"Hello, Noah Bennett West. Did you have a nice nap?"

Mae blinked back tears. "That's perfect—Bennett for your dad and Noah for Patrick's brother."

"Patrick's father's middle name was Noah too, so it's really for all three of them," Tammy smiled at her. "We're going to call him Ben."

Smiling at her friend, Mae felt her heart flood with joy. "He's a beautiful baby. And I love his name." The two women sat quietly in the dim hospital room, listening to Noah Bennett make his infant sounds.

Their moment of perfect peace was interrupted by a tap on the door.

"Come in," Tammy called.

A gray-haired nurse in pink scrubs bustled in and turned on the lights. "How's baby doing?" She looked down at him. "Wide awake, I see." She turned to Mae. "I need to check on mom and baby, if you could step out for a moment. Hopefully you can go home soon, Mrs. West, if everyone's in good shape."

Mae stood up. "Of course. I'll be back in a little bit. Do you need me to bring you anything, Tammy?"

"Just my waistline," she said with a laugh, her eyes glued on her son's face. "This little man seems to have made it disappear."

Mae found a chair in the waiting area down the hall and checked her phone for messages. She had a voicemail from her mother, who wanted to set a date for shopping for Mae's wedding dress in Atlanta. There was also a text from Ben, wondering when she was coming home. Ben's son, Matthew, was spending the night with them and Mae needed to pick up some groceries and get back to the house. Much as she wanted to, she couldn't spend the entire day with Tammy and baby Noah Bennett.

She called Ben and left him a voicemail saying, "I'll be home in an hour or so. When Patrick gets back, I'll leave the hospital. Love you." Then she tried her mother's number. Suzanne answered on the third ring.

"Hi, Mae," she said. "When can you get free to go to Atlanta?" As usual, Mama got right down to business.

"I've got one more place I want to look here before we plan any out-of-town shopping trips. One of the nurses told me about it when I was here yesterday—it's a vintage store that she says has some beautiful wedding dresses. Can you go with me another time?"

"Of course, sweetheart. How's the baby today?"

"He's so adorable. They named him Noah Bennett." Mae got a little catch in her throat. "They're going to call him Ben."

"That's a great name. I love it. Can't wait to meet him. Call me tomorrow and we'll make a plan. 'Bye, hon." She was gone.

Mae found a website that had all kinds of cute birth announcements. After the nurse left, she went back to Tammy's room. She pulled up the website on her phone and showed Tammy a few examples.

"If we take a picture of him with your cellphone, we can create your birth announcements and order them today. We can have them shipped to your house."

Tammy and Mae spent an hour happily taking pictures. The announcement would say "With love and fireworks we welcome Noah Bennett West: 8 pounds 3 ounces, 21 inches, born on the 4th of July, 2014." After Patrick showed up looking much refreshed, Mae said goodbye to the new family and went on her way.

Chapter Eight

———

Sheriff Ben Bradley

TODAY WAS A big day for Matthew Bradley. The first thing Ben saw when he opened his eyes that morning was his fully dressed five-year-old son in shorts and a Batman T-shirt. The second thing was the bedside clock, which read 6:13 a.m.

"Are you getting up now, Daddy? It's time to go get my puppy!" Matty declared in a loud, excited voice.

"Sssshh, it's still early," Ben whispered, sliding out of the big four-poster bed he shared with Mae. She made an inarticulate sound and rolled away from him.

"Where're your pants?" Matty asked in a slightly quieter voice. Ben pulled on jeans and a T-shirt before shepherding his son out of the room, closing the door quietly behind them.

"Why don't you sleep in pajamas?" Matty said, continuing his line of questioning. "What does Miss Mae wear in bed? It looked like she was naked!"

Ben pulled milk and apple juice from the refrigerator. "We didn't wear pajamas last night because it's so warm outside." *Hope he doesn't tell his babysitter about us sleeping in the nude, or anyone else ....* "Grab yourself a box of cereal out of the pantry." He got out a plastic cup, a bowl, and spoon, poured apple juice and set everything on the kitchen table.

"Can I pour the cereal and milk?" Matthew looked up at him, blue eyes bright and light brown hair curling exuberantly.

"Just the cereal, buddy. I'll pour the milk." Ben added milk after Matty poured half of the cereal box out on the table, getting some into his bowl in the process. He put the milk and juice back into the fridge, scooped the runaway Cheerios back into the box, and opened the kitchen door to let the dogs out. Tater, Mae's young female corgi, was the first to rush outside, followed by Tallulah, the small black female pug. The older male corgi, Titan, lollygagged around the kitchen before making his way out the door into the backyard. Ben shut the door.

"Can I go out with them, Daddy?" Matthew asked around a mouthful of Cheerios.

"Finish your breakfast and we'll go together." Ben poured himself a cup of coffee and took a sip. Mae always set the timer on the coffee maker, adding fresh water and putting coffee in the filter before she went to bed, and Ben was particularly grateful for the caffeine fix at this early hour.

"I'm eating fast, because I need to pee," Matthew informed his father. "Mommy won't let me at her house, but we can pee outside at Miss Mae's, can't we?"

Ben nodded. Matty dropped his spoon, took a swig of juice and ran outside, leaving the door wide open behind him. Ben finished his coffee and followed his son out into the warm sunny morning.

Mae was leaning against the kitchen counter with coffee mug in hand when they trooped back in. She wore yellow athletic shorts with a black tank top. Ben kissed her cheek and she gave him a sleepy smile.

"Good morning, Matty," she said, looking down at Ben's son.

"You're black and yellow like a bumblebee," the observant little boy pointed out. "Did you remember that we're going to get my puppy today?"

"How could I forget?" She laughed and shook her mop of yellow curls. "We're supposed to be there by ten, so we'll get in the car in about two hours, okay? In the meantime, I need another cup of coffee before I check on the kennel dogs. Do you want to help me with my chores?"

"Yes, I'll help you."

"I'll get food and water for the inside dogs, babe." Ben said. "You and your assistant can get started out in the barn."

He watched them go with a grin. Matthew was chattering away to his fiancée whose outfit did remind Ben of a bumblebee, just a little.

ALL MATTHEW HAD wanted for his fifth birthday was a puppy, a basset hound puppy to be precise. Ben admitted to Mae that he had fostered the choice of breed because he once owned one himself. Some days he still missed Buttercup. There was something ridiculously appealing about their appearance. Descended from the bloodhound, they were used for hunting and as companions. They were peaceful, well-behaved dogs, and their brown eyes had a soft, sad look. Shakespeare described the breed as having "ears that sweep away the morning dew." The combination of short legs, a low stocky body, and long ears made Ben smile whenever he saw one.

Little Matt had worn down his father and his mother, Katie, with ceaseless pleading. Mae, of course, had needed no persuading. The three adults had agreed that the pup would travel between their houses, accompanying Matthew. When Matty's birthday came around on March 25th, they had been unable to find a litter of bassets nearby. The puppy they were picking up today had been born early in April, so she was twelve weeks old and ready to go to her new home.

Ben fastened Matty into his booster seat in the backseat of

the truck and put a towel-lined box beside him for the pup to ride home in. Mae and Ben sat in front, with Ben driving. As the truck pulled out, Ben's fiancée turned in her seat to smile at their backseat passenger, whose excitement had reached a fever pitch.

"We're on our way, Matty. Slow as a herd of turtles but a whole lot better looking," she said, and he gave a delighted laugh. "What do you think you're going to name your puppy?"

Matthew's eyes met Ben's in the rearview mirror. "How do you pick a dog's name, Daddy?"

"Well, some people wait until they see the puppy, and that gives them an idea. Or you could name her after something you really like."

There was a significant pause before his son spoke again. "Then I'm going to call her Cupcake," he announced. "Because cupcakes are my favorite thing."

Ben glanced at Mae and they shared a smile.

"I think that's a wonderful name," Mae said.

"How much longer, Miss Mae?" he asked, as he already had several times.

Mae consulted her watch. "Not too much longer now." She reached back and held Matthew's hand for the rest of the ride.

THEY ARRIVED AT a small brick ranch house that was over the Rose County line at the end of a quiet, residential street. A short, heavyset woman wearing glasses and a housecoat opened the door. She looked to be in her late sixties, and she held her hand out to Matthew.

"I'm Dorothy Midgett," she said. "You must be Mr. Matthew Bradley."

Matty took her hand and gave a solemn nod. Dorothy smiled at Ben and Mae. "Well, y'all come on in. My last beautiful baby is sleeping in the kitchen." She gestured down the hall and they followed her into a time capsule of a squeaky-clean, sixties era kitchen at the back of the house. A playpen stood on the avocado green linoleum in the center of the floor. Mae, Ben, and Matthew all peeked over the edge.

"Oh my goodness!" Mae exclaimed. "She's adorable."

Ben bent down. Gently picking up the long-eared puppy, he deposited her, still sleeping, into Matthew's arms.

"She's pretty heavy, Matty. Don't drop her," Mae said. She and the boy gazed raptly at the puppy.

"Her fur is so soft. And she smells so sweet," Matty said, lowering his little nose to the puppy's head. "She's so warm!"

"There's just something about a boy and a puppy, isn't there?" Dorothy smiled in approval at the little pair.

Ben gave Dorothy Midgett a check; she gave them a bag of food and a copy of Cupcake's pedigree. Then she watched from her front porch as they ensconced the puppy in her box and buckled Matthew into his booster seat. As Ben backed out of the driveway, they all waved at Mrs. Midgett. Ben was alone in the front seat. For the return trip, his fiancée Mae had chosen to sit in the backseat, where she and Matty were both petting the puppy.

"Remember the *Dumbo* book, Matty?" Mae asked. "The one about the little elephant whose ears were so long that the other elephants were mean to him? Turned out his ears were like wings that he could use to fly."

"Do you think Cupcake can fly?" Matty asked. His son's eyes reflected in Ben's rearview mirror were wide as saucers.

"Maybe in her dreams she does," Mae told him gently. Cupcake slumbered on.

Chapter Nine

—

Chief Detective Wayne Nichols

WAYNE WALKED OUT to his pickup truck just after 6:20 in the morning. It was muggy and warm already. As he opened the door and climbed inside, he answered his ringing cellphone.

"Hi, Lucy."

"Hey. Dr. Estes is taking his second look at Chester Willis this morning. Do you want to come and join us?"

"Sure thing. What time?"

"Can you come now? Dr. Estes is an early morning guy. He's already started. It's the morgue entrance off ambulance bay two."

"On my way."

Driving to Rosedale County General, Wayne let his mind drift. His truck could virtually drive itself to the hospital, where he had spent many hours interrogating hospitalized patients, helping guard dangerous felons who were having surgery, and talking with family and friends of victims of crimes.

He thought about Lucy and felt a little grin tug at his

mouth. Things were going well for them. He really hoped this relationship would endure. He knew Lucy wanted him to look into Chester Willis' death, suspecting it was a homicide. He was not averse to bending the rules when they were closing in on a perp, but he was going to wait this one out until they had more than just Lucy's intuition.

Lucy was standing on the ambulance dock, wearing a long white coat. She waved when she saw him, and a little breeze caught her shiny brown hair.

"Since Dr. Estes started already," she said, walking up to the truck as Wayne pulled into a parking area reserved for officers of the law, "we need to hurry."

LUCY OPENED THE swinging door to the morgue to see Dr. Estes picking up a bone saw. He switched it on. Lucy called out, "Dr. Estes."

The ME switched off the machine and nodded to Lucy. He saw Wayne and frowned.

"Detective, what's your business here?" he asked, his voice pinched with disapproval.

"Dr. Ingram asked me to attend," Wayne answered, quietly standing his ground.

"I'm not in the habit of having law enforcement present unless the patient succumbed to foul play," Dr. Estes said sternly.

"Dr. Ingram suspects this one was murder." Wayne kept his voice low and his body posture relaxed. "I'll leave if you wish, or I can stand back against the wall." He gestured to the bank of stainless steel drawers, each containing a dead body.

"Just don't get in my way," Dr. Estes said crisply and turned back to his work, dictating as he began. "Dr. Hector Estes, with Dr. Lucy Ingram present and Wayne Nichols, Chief Detective for the Rose County Sheriff's office, observing, conducting second postmortem examination on the body of Chester Willis. The current time is 6:53 a.m. on July seventh. Initial cause of death was probable suicide, caused by drug or insulin overdose."

Dr. Estes cleared his throat and continued, "Chester Willis' body was brought to the morgue close to midnight on July fourth. I first examined him early on the morning of July fifth. Checking his hospital records and noting that he was an insulin-dependent diabetic, I suspected his death was caused by an insulin overdose. Then I checked the ambulance driver records. The patient's father had told the EMTs that Mr. Willis displayed symptoms of fatigue, irritability, and confusion just prior to the father calling 911. He was also sweating profusely— all symptoms of too much insulin. By the time the EMTs got to the house, Chester Willis was slipping into a coma. He died fifteen minutes later." Dr. Estes paused and looked at Lucy. "As you are aware, Dr. Ingram, some biologic processes continue after death and insulin is quickly metabolized in the blood. Mr. Willis' levels were negligible at postmortem."

"Did you see any unusual injection sites?" Lucy asked.

"There were no additional injection marks that I saw at the first autopsy. Mr. Willis' body displayed the usual rotational pattern of insulin injections on his stomach and thighs. Since there were no injuries, bruises, or ligature marks, I was faced with a conundrum. If Chester Willis didn't die of an insulin overdose, he must have died from another cause, possibly a drug overdose. For someone less expert than myself, the investigation would have ended there."

Lucy cast a quick amused glance at Wayne who nodded imperceptibly.

"To rule out other causes of death, I sent samples from the stomach and intestines to the toxicology lab for the drug screen. To eliminate a case of poisoning, I sent blood samples to the poison control laboratory. There were no indications of poison and no recreational drugs in Chester Willis' system, leaving me with the cause of death as suicide. However, I was still troubled by the patient's symptoms of insulin toxicity. Your email coincided with my own thinking."

"So, despite finding no detectable insulin in Mr. Willis' blood, you continued to think that Chester Willis killed himself by way of an insulin injection," Lucy said, thoughtfully. "What made you think that?"

"Following your phone call, I did some additional research. As I'm sure you're aware, for many years there was a belief that insulin was the perfect weapon to use to kill someone because it was supposedly undetectable after death." Dr. Estes looked meaningfully at Wayne. "Although insulin levels virtually disappear as soon as a person dies, today there are highly sensitive and precise methods for measuring insulin in the body postmortem. The test involves measuring the uptake of radioactive glucose by muscle tissue incubated at body temperature for several hours in a flask containing the patient's blood serum. The rate of glucose uptake is directly proportional to the amount of insulin present in the incubating fluid. We found a high level of insulin using that test. I knew then that the patient had died of an insulin injection, but there was nothing to say that Mr. Willis didn't inject himself. Therefore, my original listed cause of death …."

Wayne's concentration drifted away from Dr. Estes' droning voice explaining the intricacies of testing bodily fluids. He looked closely at Chester Willis' youthful body lying on the table. He was in good shape physically, tall and slim. He had taken care of himself, and it couldn't have been easy with the diabetes dominating every aspect of his life. Wayne's focus was brought back abruptly when Lucy spoke.

"But I'm of the opinion that Mr. Willis wasn't depressed and would never have given himself an overdose of insulin or any other drug deliberately. And he wouldn't have accidentally used too much insulin—he was quite knowledgeable about his dosages. Are you saying that my intuition was off base?" Lucy asked. Her voice was low, in keeping with Dr. Estes deadpan delivery, but her body posture had changed, grown more rigid. Her shoulders were high. Glancing at Wayne, she took a deep breath and lowered them.

"In fact I'm not," Dr. Estes said. He paused and they both waited silent and motionless for his conclusion. "I took another look at Mr. Willis after your call. I began early this morning before your somewhat *late* arrival." He gave Lucy a sidelong glance. "I found a single injection site under the toenail of the big toe on the right foot. Please observe," he said as he lifted Mr. Willis' right leg. Lucy leaned forward. Dr. Estes pulled out a penlight from his pocket and shone it carefully under the slightly curved nail of the big toe of the right foot.

"I see it." Lucy looked up. "I also see that the stitches I put in to close the gash on his leg are intact. If he had given *himself* an overdose by placing an injection under his toenail, he would have disturbed my stitches."

"I agree, and I see no rational reason why Chester Willis would have chosen to inject himself in that location. I congratulate you, Dr. Ingram. Your instincts would do a bird dog credit. I'm changing the death certificate to manslaughter."

"Not quite correct," Wayne said, and Dr. Estes and Lucy looked at him. "Chester Willis' death was premeditated felony murder."

"Indeed, Detective." Dr. Estes almost smiled. "Just wanted to see if you were paying attention."

After thanking the coroner for letting him observe, Wayne exited the morgue along with Lucy, leaving Dr. Estes to his arcane analytic pursuits.

"*Now* will you look into this?" Lucy asked.

"You bet," Wayne said, noting the tingling feeling that always came at the beginning of the hunt for a killer. He needed to get to the office. The staff meeting would be starting, and after that, he and Ben Bradley, sheriff of Rose County, with the help of their deputies and Rob Fuller, the new detective in the office, would begin the tedious gathering of evidence that would in time point to Chester Willis' killer.

Chapter Ten

—

Chief Detective Wayne Nichols

WAYNE GRABBED A cup of black coffee in the staff room and was walking to the conference room at the sheriff's office when his cellphone rang. He glanced at the number. It was Lucy.

"Did you miss me already?" Wayne teased.

"I've only got a minute. Turns out my timing was impeccable. I returned to the morgue after you left to see if the tox screen had come back. It had and was negative, except for normal levels of prescription meds. But I learned something else. Dr. Estes said that the Main Street Funeral Home came for Chester Willis' body on July 5th. The family wanted to have him cremated. It was incredibly lucky I asked the ME to take another look, because he refused to release the body. If Chester had been cremated, every bit of evidence would've been destroyed."

"Lucky, indeed. Sorry, the staff meeting is about to start. I'll call you later." Wayne clicked off the phone and walked down the hall lit with fluorescent lights that shone off the old tile floor. Ben Bradley, Sheriff of Rose County, was in his accustomed seat at the head of the table. Dory Clarkson, former longtime office manager, now investigator, sat next to Cam Gomez, their newest deputy. Deputy George Phelps and Detective Rob Fuller were taking their seats. Wayne crooked a finger at the sheriff, who rose and came to the conference room door.

"What's up, Wayne?"

"As of this morning's second postmortem on Chester Willis, Dr. Estes has officially changed the cause of death on the death certificate. It's murder."

"Hold on a minute. This is Lucy's patient we talked about who had a chainsaw laceration on his leg? I thought the cause of death was suicide caused by drug or insulin overdose."

"Correct, but the injection was intentionally given—by his killer."

The two men stood in silence in the hallway, hearing the cheerful voices of their staff asking to have the donut box passed and teasing each other. Ben stepped out in the hall and closed the door behind him.

"I talked to the ambulance driver when he came through the parade route on July fourth," Ben said. "His lights weren't on because he said the patient died on the way to the hospital. It must've been Chester Willis. How do you think we should approach this one?"

"With kid gloves. Lucy told me that Chester's mother died a few years ago and Chester moved home to take care of his dad. He's in very poor health—congestive heart failure."

"Good Lord, the poor man," Ben said, his brow furrowing. "And the timing couldn't be worse. Another murder, just as my reelection campaign is about to get underway. I'd like to keep this one quiet, at least until you and I get a chance to go see Mr. Willis senior."

"I agree."

When Ben and Wayne walked into the room, Rob was teasing George. "So with that gut of yours, it must've been hard to get a woman to go out with you, much less agree to marry you. Most women don't go for the type."

"I've got one at home who does," George said smugly.

"That's not what she told me when we met for a drink at the hotel bar last night." Rob grinned.

"Damn it, Rob," George yelled, slamming a hand on the table as Wayne and Ben took their seats.

"All right, Rob, knock it off. Let's get down to business," the sheriff said. "George, let's hear the list of last week's infractions in the county."

"Right." George glared at Rob before he went on, "In the last week there was one noise complaint, a medical assist that was turfed to Mont Blanc, a theft complaint which turned out to be a father who thought his son-in-law had taken money out of his wallet, two fender benders, and a complaint that somebody was driving recklessly down Main Street Saturday night. Oh, and a breaking and entering which turned out to be a false report to the police. It was Mrs. Aderholt's son, you know the kid who is …." George stopped.

"Not the sharpest knife in the drawer," Dory said, rolling her eyes.

"Okay, so nothing that needs following up, George?" the sheriff asked. The plump, redheaded deputy shook his head. "Dory, what do you have?"

Ben continued around the table getting everyone's reports. There was nothing out of the ordinary, but Wayne knew ordinary was about to come to an end. It wouldn't be business as usual again until the Willis homicide was solved.

"Thanks, everyone," Ben said when the reports were completed. "We're done, people. Except I'd like to have you stay after the meeting, Rob."

Rob Fuller, their wet-behind-the-ears detective, was instantly on the alert. Cam cast him an envious glance and Dory gave Wayne a raised eyebrow.

When everyone else had left, Rob looked expectantly at them.

"Dr. Lucy Ingram contacted Detective Nichols because she thought that one of her patients, a guy named Chester Willis—whose cause of death was originally listed as suicide—had been murdered. She got the ME to take another look this morning. Unfortunately, she was right. Dr. Estes has officially changed the cause of death to 'murder by insulin injection.' Wayne and I are going out to see the patient's father in a little while, provided he's up to seeing us. I would like you to get background on Mr. Willis Senior's financials without raising any suspicion. I'd also like to get Chester Willis' cellphone records for the day he died."

"On it," Rob nodded.

"This is to be kept quiet from the rest of the staff for now," the sheriff told him.

"Yes, sir," was his quick reply.

AT WAYNE'S REQUEST, Dory had made an appointment with Mr. Willis Sr. for the sheriff and Detective Nichols. At first, the old man said he wasn't up to seeing anyone, but under Dory's gentle persuasion he had relented. She made a note that a young woman had answered the phone before putting Mr. Willis on the line. Dory had asked her name and was told that it was Brooke.

The two men headed out after lunch. They arrived at 3271 Piney Woods Drive, an older subdivision in town, around 1:30. All the houses were either brick or stone and had large lawns and old oak trees that cast blue shadows on the crisp yellowing grass. They parked the car and walked up to the residence. Both men were dressed in suits and ties. When anyone from the office met with a bereaved family member, Ben's policy was for members of his staff to wear clothing suitable for a funeral. And this time, especially, he didn't want the old man put off by uniforms. The death of a child was the worst thing any parent could experience.

When they rang the doorbell, they were surprised to see

a good-looking young woman in her early-thirties with a long blonde braid wearing a red cotton skirt and a pale blue, sleeveless top with low-heeled sandals.

"Hello," Ben said. "I'm Sheriff Bradley and this is Detective Nichols. We're here to see Mr. Willis."

"I'm Brooke Piper. Come on in. I need you to wait just a minute, though. He's still on the table."

Wayne raised his eyebrows; the phrase "on the table" sounded medical. His confusion must have shown, because the woman said, "I'm Mr. Willis' massage therapist. I'll help him get dressed. Go on down the hall to the last room on the right. That's his office." She left the entryway quickly.

"Dory said a young woman named Brooke answered the phone when she called for the appointment. It must've been Miss Piper," Wayne said. They walked down the hall to Mr. Willis' office.

Mr. Willis entered his office ten minutes later and took a seat at his desk. He was short of breath and coughing. Wayne glanced at Ben. He hated what they were about to do to this poor man.

"Thank you for seeing us at this very difficult time," Ben said. "I'm Sheriff Ben Bradley and this is Detective Wayne Nichols. We're very sorry for the loss of your son, Chester."

"Are you here to give me your condolences?" Leonard Willis asked. His voice was rough with grief.

"Yes, sir," Ben said, "and we're also concerned about the manner of Chester's death. His doctor in the ER, Dr. Lucy Ingram, who sutured his leg after the chainsaw accident, asked the medical examiner, Dr. Estes, to review the cause of death."

Mr. Willis looked at them, his eyes dark and unreadable. Wayne wondered if he was taking all this in.

"Dr. Estes originally listed his death as probable suicide by drug or insulin overdose," Wayne said. "Dr. Ingram didn't think that was the case."

Mr. Willis looked at them. For the first time he seemed alert, narrowing his eyes. Wayne continued.

"Subsequently, Dr. Ingram talked with Dr. Estes and told him your son had not struck her as suicidal. In fact he said he was enjoying spending time with you. She didn't accept suicide as his cause of death."

The air in the room seemed to thicken as the old man processed what they had just said. Then he spoke. "I never thought it was suicide. Chester wouldn't have done that— especially without leaving me a note." His eyes glittered with unshed tears, and he cleared his throat.

"So there was no note?" Ben asked. "You're sure?"

"I'm sure. Chester had just moved back in with me. I thought we were going to have these last few months together. I have congestive heart failure. The drugs aren't working anymore and now I have nothing to live for." His voice shook. "My whole family's dead except for Rick, my oldest boy. The two kids I was closest to were my daughter Jillian and Chester." He started to cough.

"Did Chester ever give you the impression that he was having difficulties with anyone?" Ben asked when Mr. Willis' coughing had subsided.

"No, he did not," Mr. Willis said, his voice insistent. "Chester was a happy person. He got along with everyone. He told me he was going to be here for me the whole way." Mr. Willis looked away, blinking to hold back the tears. "Besides, we're Catholic. Suicide is a sin."

"That supports what Dr. Ingram thought," Wayne said. He hated what he was going to have to say next. "But it does look like he died of an insulin overdose."

"God damn diabetes. I hate the disease. My wife had it, my daughter had it and Chester had it. Rick is the only one who doesn't." The room was quiet. Nobody spoke for a few minutes. Then Mr. Willis said, "Hold on a minute. If Chester didn't overdose on his insulin accidentally, or kill himself, then what the hell happened to my boy?"

"We think somebody may have given your son an overdose of insulin purposely to cause his death," Wayne said.

Leonard Willis closed his eyes. He murmured something to himself that Wayne didn't catch.

"Can you tell us about the last day of your son's life, Mr. Willis?" Ben asked. "We need to talk to everyone he was with that day. If this is too much for you right now, we can come back later."

"No. I want to get to the bottom of this. My son Rick showed up here after lunch that day. Chester had gone over to clean the apartment he had moved out of. He got back shortly after Rick arrived."

"Was anyone else here that day?"

"Brooke was here before lunch and then I asked her to come back and have dinner with us."

"Do you mind telling us what you talked about at dinner that night?" Wayne asked.

"Before dinner I told them I was making some changes to my will. I didn't want to tell them in front of Brooke, but before she got back, I said I was leaving the bulk of my estate to the boys and something to her."

"How did your sons take that?" Wayne asked. Alarm bells were going off in his head.

"Chester was fine. Rick was teed off, but it's my money. I like Brooke and want to help her out," He sounded defensive and started coughing. When he had quelled the coughing, he said, "She reminds me a bit of my daughter, Jillian." Mr. Willis took a shaky breath.

"This is totally your business, Mr. Willis, but do you mind telling me what you planned to leave Miss Piper?" Wayne asked. "You don't have to be specific, just whether it was an object or money."

"I was going to give her my late wife's jewelry," Mr. Willis said, looking out the window at the backyard.

"Thank you. So—just double checking—besides your sons and Brooke, was there anyone else in the house that night?" Ben asked.

"There was a delivery kid who brought dinner from the club. My housekeeper Marina was here for a few hours and she stayed to wash up after dinner. Rick said his girlfriend Meredith might stop over after dinner, but if she did, I didn't see her. I went to bed early."

"We'll need to talk to all of them," the sheriff said. "We just wanted to inform you that we're going to investigate Chester's death. We want it resolved."

"Hold on, are you saying that somebody gave him this injection here at the house? Are you accusing me of murdering my own son?" Mr. Willis frowned. The shadows on his face were dark.

"No, sir, we just need to talk to everyone who saw him the day he died," Wayne told him gently.

"He must have done it to himself by accident." Mr. Willis looked confused. "It had to have been an accident. No one would've deliberately hurt Chester."

"We're pretty sure it wasn't accidental," Wayne said softly.

"What do you know that you aren't telling me?" Mr. Willis' voice was sharp with pain. "Was it malpractice? Did some doctor at the hospital make a mistake? What about those EMTs?"

"I'm sorry, sir, but Chester was dead when he arrived at Rose County General Hospital."

"Then something must've happened in the ambulance," Mr. Willis said. We was looking down at his desk, shaking his head.

"We'll be checking on that, Mr. Willis," Wayne said. "We'll be talking to everyone who was with Chester on the night he died. Was there anyone else here that night?"

"No. There was nobody—only Chester, Rick, Brooke, my

housekeeper Marina Hernandez, the delivery kid, and me." His last words were barely audible.

After confirming what Mr. Willis had just told them, Ben said, "We'll be leaving soon, but I don't think you should be alone right now. Is there someone we can call for you? Somebody who could stay with you for a few hours?"

"Maybe Brooke could stay a while. There's nobody else, except Rick. And he's got a high stress job as a stockbroker. I'll call him, but I doubt he could come until dinnertime."

Ben and Wayne exchanged a glance. "Could you hold off on calling him for a few hours? This is a criminal investigation now, and we would appreciate you not calling him yet. As soon as we talk with him, we'll have him call you. Could you give me his cellphone number?"

Leonard Willis' face was gray, and he wheezed when he gave Wayne the number. The detective entered it into his phone and thanked the old man.

"Would you like me to check with Miss Piper?" Ben asked Mr. Willis. He nodded, still coughing.

The two lawmen found Brooke Piper about to leave the house.

"Mr. Willis was wondering if you could stay with him here this afternoon until his son Rick arrives. He's just had some bad news," Wayne told her.

"Yes, certainly," she said. "I don't have any other clients today." Her smooth forehead crinkled in a concerned frown. "But what could be worse than Chester dying? What'd you tell him just now?"

"What were you doing on the evening of July fourth?" Ben asked and Brooke Piper looked at him with wide, unreadable eyes.

"Why do you need to know?" she parried.

"Because we think Chester Willis met with foul play," the sheriff answered. Brooke gasped and looked down at the floor, obviously struggling to regain her composure.

"I was here earlier in the day, and then I came back at Mr. Willis' request and stayed for dinner. I left around ten and was at home for the rest of the evening."

"Can anyone corroborate the time you arrived at home?" Wayne asked.

"Nobody, Detective. I live alone," Brooke said. Ben and Wayne exchanged a long look.

"I need you to write down your contact information, Miss Piper," Ben told her. She took a business card out of her purse and handed it to the sheriff. He glanced at it and put it in his pocket. "We'll want to talk with you again later. Please make yourself available and don't leave the area. You can go in and be with Mr. Willis now." Wayne and Ben left the house and walked out to the car.

"That girl seems quite comfortable in the Willis house, doesn't she?" Ben asked as he got in the patrol car.

It was steaming hot outside. Wayne took off his suit coat and removed his tie before he climbed in on the passenger side.

"Yep, almost like a member of the family. And she's in his will," Wayne said.

"Yes, but does she know that? And even if she does, it still wouldn't explain killing Chester."

The two men were silent the rest of the way back to the office.

Chapter Eleven

—

Sheriff Ben Bradley

RICK WILLIS APPEARED at the sheriff's office late the afternoon of the 7th. Ben was looking out the window when a tall, expensively dressed man stepped out of a dark blue BMW.

"Wayne," he called down the hall. "I think our stockbroker's here." The detective walked out of his office.

"I'll go greet him and show him into the conference room," Wayne said. Ben nodded and headed that way.

His chief detective ushered Rick Willis into the conference room and Ben introduced himself. Everything about the man exuded confidence and money—from his short, smooth, medium blond hair and golf course tan right down to his polished leather shoes. The handshake he gave Ben had been almost firm enough to hurt. They learned that he was forty-three years old and had left his father's house after ten on the evening of the fourth to watch fireworks with his girlfriend, Meredith Flynn, and that he'd been with her the rest of the night.

"Why wasn't your girlfriend with you at your dad's that evening?" Wayne asked, looking down at his notes.

"Who said she wasn't?" Rick's thick brows briefly drew together. "She came over after dinner. And what's with all the questions anyway?"

Ben pursed his lips and looked into Rick Willis' eyes. "I take it you haven't spoken with your father today?"

Rick shook his head with another frown.

Wayne and Ben glanced at each other. Ben gave the detective a slight nod. "Your dad gave us a list of people that were there that night and didn't include Meredith," Wayne said after a short pause.

Rick sighed. "He probably forgot … he went to lie down after dinner. But I still don't know why you're asking me all these questions." He gave Wayne a sharp look.

Wayne nodded. "Your brother's death has been reclassified as a homicide."

Rick Willis inhaled quickly, pressing his hand over his mouth. He paled, his tanned face turning almost gray. "Does my dad know that?"

"We told him earlier today. His massage therapist was there and she agreed to stay with him. I know that it's shocking news," Ben said.

The color came back to Rick's face. "I just bet that little gold digger agreed to stay with him," he burst out. "You should have called me. I would have come over. She's *not* family." His voice was loud in the small conference room. "I'm going over there right now, if you're done with your questions." Rick pushed the chair back. Breathing heavily, he got to his feet.

"Why would you call her a gold digger?" Ben asked the agitated man.

Rick gave a harsh bark of a laugh. "Because she is one. My dad told Chester and me that he put her in his will." His face contorted and he glanced down at the floor before looking back at Ben. "Can I please go now?"

"Of course you can." Ben handed Rick his card. "If you remember anything else about that evening, please call us."

Rick took the card and left the conference room in a rush, banging the door shut behind him. Wayne shook his head. "He was definitely upset, wouldn't you say?"

"Yeah. But more about his father giving Brooke a share of the estate than his brother's murder, I thought."

SITTING AT HIS desk early the next morning, Ben couldn't shake the feeling that Rick Willis knew more about his brother's death than he'd let on.

He stood up and walked out into the reception area at the front of the building, which was deserted. "Where is everybody?" he asked aloud.

"I'm right here, Sheriff." Deputy Cameron Gomez entered the reception area, a glass coffee pot full of water in her hand. "I'm just getting the coffee going, as you can see. What do you need?"

Cam's dark hair was pulled up in a neat twist. With her hourglass figure, dark eyes, and pretty face, she made her deputy's uniform look better than anyone should be able to. Solicitous, diligent and respectful, she arrived early for every shift and was basically a dream employee.

"I have a special assignment for you today, Cam. And it's not just because you're the only one here." Ben smiled. "I need you to go search Chester's room at the Willis house and talk to the housekeeper if she's there."

Sheriff Bradley and Detective Nichols had filled everyone in on the Chester Willis case after Rick left the office the previous day.

"Sure thing, boss. Do we need a search warrant for that? What am I looking for?"

"I'll give you the phone number so you can call the Willis house and get permission for the search, but I'm sure Leonard— Chester's father—won't have a problem with you coming by.

He's anxious to get to the bottom of this. Look for anything out of the ordinary. Someone besides Chester was with him in that room on the night of his death. Trust your instincts. If anything seems wrong or unusual to you, let me know."

Cam poured the water into the back of the coffee maker, added a filter and coffee and pressed the button. "The housekeeper probably cleaned that room already," she pointed out. "But I'll do a thorough search and talk to her if I can."

Ben found the phone number and gave it to Cam. By the time George, Rob, Wayne, and Dory straggled in, Cam Gomez was on her way to the Willis residence. Knowing how meticulous she was in her work, Ben expected her to be there most of the day.

BEN PICKED UP a Greek salad and a take-and-bake pizza on the way home, as Mae had requested. She had taken Matty and Cupcake back to Katie's after lunch and gone to visit Tammy, Patrick, and baby Ben, so Mae arrived at the house a few minutes after Ben put the pizza in the oven.

"It smells great in here," Mae said as she walked into the kitchen and put her purse on the counter. She gave Ben a lingering kiss, which he returned with enthusiasm. "Thanks for picking up dinner."

"You're welcome. You smell great too, by the way."

Mae widened her eyes. "It's from holding the baby and kissing his head. He smells so delicious."

"I missed out on so much with Matty," Ben said with regret. "He weighed thirty-five pounds by the time Katie decided to tell me about him, almost too big to hold."

Mae's pupils dilated, darkening her brown eyes to almost black. "I'm so sorry you missed that stage with him. I've been doing a lot of thinking about having a baby of our own. I know I told you I wasn't sure I wanted children, but I …" she paused, looking down and then back up at him, "I want to have a baby with you."

Ben smiled at her, tilting his head to one side. "Great! Should we start right now or have dinner first?"

She gave him a playful slap on the arm. "I'd like to get married first, if you don't mind. But I'm fine with getting pregnant on our honeymoon."

"Speaking of getting married, we really ought to set the date, you know." The oven timer dinged, and Ben pulled the pizza out, using the dishtowel as a hot pad. "What would you think about St. Patrick's Day?"

"Perfect." Mae put plates, forks, and napkins on the table and opened a bottle of Cabernet. "Could you grab some wineglasses and bring the pizza over? And after dinner we can practice for our honeymoon." She gave him a saucy wink. "St. Patrick's day isn't that far away."

Chapter Twelve

Dr. Lucy Ingram

O N THE MORNING of July 9th, Lucy was on the phone with Mrs. Cantrell's primary care physician, Dr. Adams—detailing her follow-up recommendations for the episode of chest pain that brought the bright-eyed elderly woman to the ER—when one of her residents tapped her on the shoulder.

Lucy turned to look at Dr. Bryce Alexander, a third-year resident, but continued speaking on the phone, "Excuse me, Dr. Adams. I'm needed for another emergency. I wanted you to know that we're keeping Mrs. Cantrell overnight. She's scheduled to have a cardiac stress test in the morning and I'll have the hospitalist take a look at her later this evening. If you want to visit her in the hospital and talk further with me, I'll be here." She ended the call and turned to Dr. Alexander and her nurse, Channing Soldan, both of whom were gesturing for her to cut the phone call short.

"What is it?" Lucy asked, exasperated.

"The EMT in Emergency Bay 2 has a Mr. Leonard Willis in his ambulance. He's *in extremis*," Dr. Alexander said.

Lucy knew Dr. Alexander wouldn't use the phrase lightly. It meant "on the point of death."

She ran toward Ambulance Bay 2, her white coat streaming behind her.

Zack Randall, the EMT who had brought Chester Willis' body to the ER on July fourth, was standing outside on the cement delivery area by the ambulance.

"What's the patient's status?" Lucy asked him.

"We've got an IV started on Mr. Willis and initiated respiratory therapy, but he's not responding." Lucy was surprised to see Zack, with almost a decade of experience as an EMT, visibly shaken. "The man's got bad fluid retention."

"Is his congestive heart failure the fluid redistribution type?"

"Yes it is," Zack told her and Lucy shook her head, knowing that type of CHF was particularly difficult to treat. She stepped into the ambulance. As she asked the EMT in the vehicle more questions, she gave Mr. Willis a rapid examination. The patient was already slipping into a coma.

"Let's get him in the ER now," Lucy said and glanced back at Zack, who was talking with a young, blonde woman standing on the loading dock.

"Zack," she called. "Can you give us a hand here?" Zack walked rapidly toward them and the young woman came along with him. As the men were carefully loading the patient on to a gurney, Lucy spoke to her.

"Are you a family member?" she asked.

"No, I'm Brooke Piper, Mr. Willis' massage therapist," she said. "He couldn't stop coughing so I called 911. I drove my car behind the ambulance to be here with him."

"Well, since you aren't a family member, you'll have to wait outside the treatment room," Lucy told her. "You should get in touch with the family if you can. We need to get him stabilized." She turned away, walking beside the gurney, giving rapid instructions to Dr. Alexander and Nurse Soldan. "We need chest radiography, a 12-lead ECG, cardiac troponin testing, electrolytes, and a complete blood cell count. Let's go, people."

She could feel her adrenaline rise, and she chewed her bottom lip as she focused her attention on Mr. Willis. He looked bad. While Channing positioned the patient in the private ER cubicle toward the back of the department—an area reserved for cardiac patients—Lucy turned to Dr. Alexander. There was little more they could do until the initial test results came back. She was needed on other cases, but first she wanted to be sure the resident was capable of handling Mr. Willis' case in her absence.

"Beyond the tests we discussed, what do you think are the next steps?" she asked Dr. Alexander.

"Relieve his congestion, balance his hemodynamics, achieve euvolemia, and avoid myocardial and renal injury." He paused before adding, "And we need to decide whether the patient requires ventilatory support, either via endotracheal intubation or noninvasive ventilation."

"Correct," Lucy said. Since Dr. Alexander was a third year ER resident and there had been talk of adding him to the staff, Lucy felt confident she could give him responsibility for Mr. Willis for an hour or two. "While you get him stabilized and transferred upstairs to the ICU, I'm going to talk with Miss Piper who came in with Mr. Willis. I need as much information about the patient's presenting symptoms as possible."

As Lucy walked toward the area where Miss Piper was sitting, she was surprised to see Channing Soldan talking with her.

"Dr. Ingram, have you met my friend Brooke Piper?" Channing asked. "We were in nursing school together. She's two years behind me, hasn't finished yet."

"We met outside. I need to get some more information from you, Miss Piper," Lucy said. "Nurse Soldan, Dr. Alexander needs you."

After getting a list of Mr. Willis' current medications and finding out exactly what led her to call 911 for the patient, Lucy was paged to handle the victims of a domestic disturbance.

IT WAS NEARLY midnight when Dr. Alexander walked up to Lucy.

"Sorry, but I've got to go off shift," he said. "Mr. Willis is going downhill fast."

"Damn it," she said under her breath as she handed off the chart of another patient with a broken arm. "Sorry, John," she told the physician, "one of mine is in serious trouble. Can you take over?'

When the resident nodded, she turned back to Dr. Alexander. "Didn't you get Mr. Willis transferred up to ICU?"

"We couldn't get him stabilized enough to even move him," Dr. Alexander said. He sounded discouraged. "We've been working on him for two hours. I'm afraid we're going to lose this one."

They walked to the back of the ER, where a group of medical students and Lucy's first-year intern Dr. Thompson, as well as Nurse Soldan, were gathered around Mr. Willis. He was barely breathing.

"Okay, everybody but Nurse Soldan and Dr. Thompson needs to leave." As the medical students departed, Lucy said, "Dr. Thompson, please give me an update on Mr. Willis."

Emily Thompson was pale and swallowed several times before she began her presentation. "In the last hour, Mr. Willis has shown a further decrease in consciousness and complete physical withdrawal. His urine had become concentrated earlier, but currently he is not putting out any urine. His skin is cool. His serum electrolytes are low with both potassium and magnesium depletion. He's having periods of shallow breathing, and sometimes thirty seconds of no breathing at all. His breaths are wet and noisy." She glanced at Channing.

"We've repositioned him several times, and Dr. Alexander added medication to help decrease his secretions," Channing said, "but he's leaving us, Dr. Lucy."

"Is he in pain?" Lucy asked. At that moment Mr. Willis groaned, a horrible sound of extreme anguish. Dr. Thompson winced. "Up his morphine," Lucy said. The monitor measuring his heart started to beep.

"He's going into cardiac arrest," Lucy shouted. "Get the defibrillator on him now!"

The three women worked on Leonard Willis frantically, shocking his chest repeatedly, but twenty minutes later, Lucy stopped them. "It's no use. He's gone." They looked at each other in silence. "I'm pronouncing him dead at one-oh-five a.m. on July tenth." They were quiet for a while, and then Lucy said, "This is the part I hate about my job. We need to tell the family."

"Should I come with you?" Dr. Thompson said, and Lucy nodded.

Lucy and Channing, followed by a serious-looking Dr. Thompson, walked to the waiting area. Brooke Piper was still there, together with two other people, a blond man in a suit and tie and a thin woman with long brown hair.

"I'm Dr. Ingram," Lucy said. "This is Dr. Thompson and Nurse Soldan."

"I'm Rick Willis, Mr. Willis' son, and this is Meredith Flynn, my girlfriend. I assume you met Brooke earlier. Do you have an update for us on my father?"

Lucy took a deep breath. "Let's go down to the small conference room." She led the group into the room, and once they were seated, said, "Mr. Willis Senior passed away just moments ago. I am so very sorry for your loss." Rick's girlfriend Meredith put her arms around him. Brooke Piper started to cry, and Channing asked her if she wanted something to drink. She nodded, and Channing left the room.

"I knew he was sick, but I didn't think I'd lose him so soon." Rick Willis looked at Lucy. "I feel like the bottom just dropped out of my life."

"I'll go get you both some coffee," Dr. Thompson said.

Lucy reached for Rick's hand and sat beside him in silence as he stared at the floor.

"I just lost my brother a few days ago, and now my dad," he said quietly. He wiped tears off his face. "He was the last of my family." He swallowed and then asked, "What caused his death?"

"Your father died of a sudden cardiac arrest," Lucy replied. "I'm sure you were aware that he was in congestive heart failure and had been for some time. We did everything we could to save him. There's no need for an autopsy if you don't wish to have one."

Channing returned with a soft drink and gave it to Brooke, who took it with a murmur of thanks.

"No autopsy then," Rick Willis said. Dr. Thompson handed them their coffees. Seeing the creamy color of the coffee, Lucy nodded. Milk and sugar often helped mediate sudden drops in blood pressure that could lead a person to faint.

"Do you have any questions, Mr. Willis?"

"No, Doctor." He brushed his face with his hands and stood up.

"Do you have a funeral home you'd like us to call?" Channing asked.

He gave the nurse the name of the funeral home. Lucy handed Rick Willis her card. "Once the shock wears off, if you think of any questions you want to ask, please don't hesitate to contact me. That goes for you too, Brooke," she said, handing the massage therapist a second card.

"Thank you, Doctor," a subdued Rick Willis said. Channing was talking quietly with Brooke Piper. Lucy followed Rick and his girlfriend out of the room.

She sent a quick text off to Wayne. He was already working the Chester Willis murder and would need the information about Leonard Willis' passing away.

"Mr. Willis Sr. died this evening," the text read. "Natural

causes. Brooke Piper followed ambulance, son and girlfriend arrived later."

She stood leaning against the wall of the hospital corridor for a moment or two, hoping Wayne would call or message back. The tiles were cold against her shoulders. Feeling weighed down by a sudden heavy fatigue, Dr. Lucy Ingram walked slowly down the hall to resume her treatment of the domestic abuse victim. She felt very sad about losing Mr. Willis and even more troubled about his son Chester's murder.

Chapter Thirteen

———

Chief Detective Wayne Nichols

WAYNE COULD HEAR Sheriff Bradley and Deputy Gomez's voices when he arrived at the office on Tuesday. He walked down the hall and stuck his head in Ben's open office door.

"Come on in, Wayne," Ben said. "Cam found something at the Willis home that could break this case wide open. Go ahead, Cam, tell Detective Nichols what it was."

"Good Morning, Detective," Cam said.

"Good Morning, Cam. Before you tell me what you found, I need to tell you both that Mr. Willis Senior died of a cardiac arrest in the ER at about one a.m. this morning. Lucy sent me a text."

"Damn," Ben said. "Please tell me it was natural causes."

"It was."

"That poor family," Cam said. "When I went over to the house, Mr. Willis was devastated about losing his son. I bet that loss led directly to his death."

"Back to what you were saying before, Cam. Please tell Detective Nichols what you found."

"Sheriff Bradley sent me to take a look around the Willis residence day before yesterday. Unfortunately Mr. Willis' housekeeper had cleaned Chester's room the day after he died, so I didn't have much hope of finding anything. The trash pick-up service came early on the seventh, so there was basically nothing in the wastebaskets either, except for a couple of tissues. I sat and talked with Mr. Willis for a while until Miss Piper arrived and set up the table for his massage."

Wayne nodded. He stole a quick glance at Ben, who was watching Cam intently.

"When Mr. Willis and Brooke were occupied with his massage, I took one more look in Chester's room and his bathroom. On the floor in back of the toilet, there was one small rectangular pill. It was Xanax, ten milligrams."

"Aha!" Wayne said. "So now we know why Chester Willis was so out of it that he could be injected under his toenail. It makes perfect sense."

"Cam then checked with Chester's primary care doctor and his endocrinologist to see if either of them had written a prescription for Xanax," Ben explained. "Because Chester was deceased, they were willing to let her have the information. He didn't have a scrip for that drug," Ben said. "He did have one for Ambien, a common sleeping pill. And the medicine cabinet contained the painkiller that Dr. Ingram prescribed when Chester cut his leg with the chainsaw."

Ben paused, and Cam took up the thread. "After finding the tablet, the sheriff asked me to find out if Rick Willis or Brooke Piper had a Xanax prescription," she said. "I asked Brooke if she had a prescription for Xanax. She said no, but I wanted to double check that information with her doctor. Mr. Willis told me Rick's doctor's name and Brooke gave me the name of her physician, but," she paused and shook her head, "the doctors probably won't tell me. They'll claim physician-patient privilege."

"And now we have another death in the family." Ben's voice was gloomy. "I doubt very much if Rick Willis will be amenable to providing information or giving us permission to do a search of his residence. We'll need search warrants. We'll need to take a look at Brooke's place, too. As of today, they're both 'persons of interest' in Chester Willis' murder."

The three of them were quiet for a few minutes. Wayne heard the front door open. The phone rang and Dory's voice said, "Sheriff's office." Then they heard Rob say, "Where is everybody?"

"Now that the staff seems to be arriving, let's get everyone together for a meeting," Ben said. He stood up and Cam and Wayne followed him down the hall. George Phelps walked in and Ben asked them all to come into the conference room.

"Okay, people. Let's get an update on the Chester Willis case," Ben said. "Rob, I asked you to look into Leonard Willis' financial status and Chester's cellphone records. As it happens, Leonard Willis died late last night at the ER of a cardiac arrest."

"Any suspicions on that one?" Rob asked.

"No, it was natural causes," Wayne said.

"It turns out that Mr. Willis has a substantial estate, probably close to three million dollars," Rob said. "I couldn't find out anything specific on the will, but now that he's deceased, I'm sure we'll know soon. I did get the name of the family attorney; it's Shane Connor. I'll call and find out if there's going to be a funeral and a reading of the will."

"What about the cellphone records?" Wayne asked.

"Unfortunately, they aren't going to help much. Chester Willis had a brand new iPhone. He was probably just learning its features because I couldn't find any text messages that he sent. I did find a couple of calls he made. He called his brother before noon on July fourth. He also called the electric company and the gas company to turn off the power to the apartment he was vacating. He called a local storage company where he may be storing some of his things. He called his father several times. And there was one call to Meredith Flynn—she's Rick's girlfriend. That's it."

"What about social media?" Ben asked.

"I also checked Facebook, Twitter, and Linked In. He wasn't on any of those sites."

"He had a computer in his room at his dad's," Cam piped up. "Do we want to get his hard drive?"

"Yes," Ben said, "I want his emails, browser history, favorite sites, everything." Ben smiled. "We'll have to borrow our favorite nerd Mark Schneider from Captain Paula's outfit to take a look. I hate to keep asking her to loan him to us, but he's the best."

"Mark Schneider's dating Emma Peters from our lab," Dory said with a knowing look. "He's coming by here on Friday to pick her up. If we can get the hard drive from Chester's computer before then, you might not have to make the call. I'll have Emma ask him to do his magic while he's here."

Wayne hid his smile from the good-looking black woman. Dory was an irrepressible gossip, but that quality did make her an excellent investigator.

"How the hell do you know that?" Ben looked annoyed.

"As an investigator, I'm naturally required to cultivate my sources," Dory said with a self-satisfied twitch to her lips. She cast a sidelong glance at Wayne. There were a number of smiles around the room and an outright giggle from Cam.

"All right, people." Ben shook his head. "Here're the assignments. Rob, I want you and Cam to go to the Willis residence and get Chester's hard drive. I suggest you call the housekeeper to let you in."

"Getting into the house now is a bit of a legal stretch, Ben," Wayne pointed out. "We never got a warrant to search that house. When Cam was there earlier, Mr. Willis let her in, but now he's dead."

"Damn it," Ben said through clenched teeth. "Okay, let's hold off on the computer for the time being. Wayne, I need you to get a search warrant for both Brooke Piper's and Mr. Rick Willis' residences as well as permission to bring in Chester Willis' computer. Take the request directly to Judge Cochran, please. Rob, take a look at Rick's financials, will you? George, you need to be here in case anyone calls in with a complaint." The redheaded deputy nodded.

"On it," Wayne said, getting up to follow the others out of the room.

"And I'm going to ask my fiancée for a little help," the sheriff said.

Wayne paused in the doorway, giving his boss an inquiring glance.

"Mae probably knows the people involved, or knows someone who does," Ben said in answer to the detective's unspoken question. "I'm going to ask her to see what she can learn about Brooke Piper and Meredith Flynn—on a personal level. And Rick Willis, of course."

Wayne approved. The more information, the better. And Mae December was very connected in Rosedale. "Good idea," he told the sheriff with a smile. "She'll probably find out even more than we need to know."

WAYNE LABORIOUSLY TYPED up the request for the search warrants. He hated paperwork, although spellcheck did make it a little easier. He explained the probable justification for needing the warrants to find evidence in Chester Willis' murder. He identified Brooke Piper and Rick Willis as "persons of interest."

Of the three markers for murder: means, motive, and opportunity, both Brooke and Rick had two of the three. Rick had the means—access to insulin and syringes. Having two siblings with diabetes, he was sure Rick Willis would have learned to give shots. And Lucy said that Brooke was in nursing school. She would have known how to give shots too. Both had opportunity; they were in the house earlier the evening Chester died and could have slipped back to give him the fatal injection.

The case hinged on motive. He wished they had Mr. Willis' Last Will and Testament. He wondered if Rick's share of the estate increased because of Chester's death, and whether the new will would mean Brooke would now receive money in addition to Mrs. Willis' jewelry. Knowing that piece of information could be critical to finding Chester Willis' killer.

With the paperwork for the search warrants complete, Wayne placed the copies in a manila folder and said goodbye to Dory, who was sitting in the front office. She had already talked to Emma in the lab in case they were able to get the computer that day. Now she was stuck at the desk answering the phone, her least favorite job. Wayne told her that he was going to drop off the search warrant requests at the judge's home.

Wayne stopped by Judge Cordelia Cochran's home again early the next morning. Judge Cordelia was a handsome woman in her mid-sixties who was the primary judge for Rose County and a force to be reckoned with. She was also the sheriff's aunt. When he rang the bell, she answered, already dressed for work in beige slacks and a bright yellow blouse.

"Hello, Detective," she said with a smile. "Come on in. I have the coffee on."

"Did you have a chance to look at the warrant requests yet?"

"I did and I have them here." She placed the warrants on the shining surface of her kitchen countertop. "I have a question before I sign, however. I understand from the supporting documentation that Chester Willis has been declared a homicide by Dr. Estes and that he was killed with an insulin overdose."

"Yes, ma'am," Wayne said, feeling somewhat uneasy. Judge

Cochran was sharp, and she could rip his requests for the warrant to shreds if she chose to do so.

"I'll sign the warrants. The one for Chester Willis' computer is not a problem, but I will expect a copy of Chester Willis' toxicology report to be faxed to me today." She looked meaningfully at Wayne. "It was not included with the supporting documentation."

"Of course, Judge," he said. He would call Dory and get it done immediately. "One of our new deputies in the office found a Xanax tablet on the floor of Chester Willis' bathroom. We don't know whether the victim had a prescription for that medication. We're chasing down whether either of our chief suspects had a scrip for the drug."

"You might have included that fact in your documentation," the judge said. Then she signed the warrants with a flourish and handed them to him, saying, "I doubt the searches will turn up anything. You should have subpoenaed Mr. Willis and Miss Piper's prescription records in addition."

Wayne felt like an idiot. Judge Cochran was right.

"Do you have time for coffee?" she asked. Sometimes Wayne wondered if the divorced woman was flirting with him. He had been more interested in her in the past, before his relationship with Lucy deepened.

"I wish I did," Wayne told her. "Got to get going. The sheriff will probably be requesting the subpoena later."

He exited her house into the steamy morning, loosening his collar and tie. He was starting to get a bad feeling about this case. They could end up with two prime suspects and no hard evidence to arrest either of them. He started the patrol car, but before pulling out of the driveway, he quickly texted Dory and asked her to fax the toxicology report to Judge Cochran. She called him back immediately.

"No problem getting Judge Cochran to sign the warrants?" she asked.

"No. You can send someone over to get Chester's computer

now. Where's Ben? I need to talk to him. We should have requested a subpoena for Brooke Piper's and Rick Willis' prescription records."

"He and Rob just talked with Brooke Piper, who came in early this morning. She didn't have much to tell them, apparently. I can ask him to request the subpoenas for you."

Chapter Fourteen

——

Dr. Lucy Ingram

L UCY GOT UP late on July 11th. Wednesday was her day off from the hospital. She had been working a lot of shifts lately and was looking forward to a lazy day with no schedule. She showered and dressed without consulting her mental to-do list. Checking her cellphone, she saw no messages. She clicked on the calendar. It had been a week since Chester Willis died, four days since Dr. Estes declared the crime a murder, and only one day since Mr. Willis Sr. passed away. While she was gathering up her laundry and tossing a load into the washing machine, Wayne called.

"Good morning."

"Same to you," he said. "Are you working today?"

"No, I have a whole delicious day to lounge about. Any chance you could drop by?"

"No. Working a murder, remember? In fact I was going to ask for your help on something. It involves hospital records."

"I suppose that requires me physically going to the hospital?"

"It does."

"Fine," she said in a defeated tone. "When do you want to meet?"

"As soon as possible."

"Doctor's lounge, top floor. See you in twenty minutes." She clicked the phone off.

LUCY DROVE TO the hospital in a funk. If she had to live her life over again, she would work less and have more time to play, she thought. She heard an ambulance siren in the distance and her lips quirked. *They're playing my song.*

Wayne was standing just outside the doctor's lounge, holding a cup of coffee in each hand. He held one out to her in mute apology.

"Not as good as flowers or candy," she said with a smile. "But it'll have to do."

They walked into the room. There were three physicians standing together and talking quietly. It was the power elite of the hospital: the CEO, the chief medical officer, and the CFO. She carefully steered Wayne away from them to the farthest corner of the room.

"What's up?" she asked in a low voice.

"We found a Xanax tablet on the floor of the Willis residence, in Chester's bathroom. There wasn't a bottle, just a single tablet, so we don't know whose prescription it was. We think whoever killed Chester must have drugged him with Xanax and then injected him with insulin. I don't know if you can do this ethically or not, but I want to know if either Brooke Piper or Rick Willis have a scrip for Xanax. I know a lot of doctors working in the community use the hospital or clinic pharmacies."

"Don't want much, do you?" Lucy looked down at the floor. "I can't just prowl through the pharmacy records in the hospital without a subpoena, Wayne. Plus there's the whole street availability of the drug."

"Figured," Wayne said, sounding discouraged. "Just thought it was worth a try."

Lucy gave her boyfriend an irritated stare. "Why the hell didn't you just ask me whether I could do this? Why drag me down here?"

"Sorry," Wayne said. "I had something else I wanted to share with you." Glancing at the power brokers still conferring quietly, he said, "Can we go down to the Meditation Garden?"

The hospital had recently completed work on a lovely garden that anyone from the hospital or its patients could use to spend a few minutes alone in quiet. It contained a labyrinth—a spiral path with plantings that would eventually grow tall enough to shield the garden from street noise. There were benches to sit on and a small reflecting pool.

Lucy and Wayne took the elevator down to the first floor and entered the garden. It was hot, and the roses were wilted. They walked to a bench and took a seat, sipping their coffees.

"My foster mother, Joci, passed away last night," he said. Lucy turned her gaze on him, compassion wiping away all traces of irritation. Wayne's foster mother had been ill from lung cancer acquired after decades in prison. Wayne had gotten her released and then learned that she was actually his aunt, his father's sister. After her release, Joci had been living with a cousin in Michigan's Upper Peninsula. Wayne called her nearly every day.

"I'm so sorry, Wayne."

"Her cousin called me last night. She slipped into a coma yesterday and died quietly. I talked to her a couple of days ago. I had some good news for her finally—about Kurt, my little brother."

"What was it?" Lucy asked.

"I found his remains."

Wayne's young foster-brother Kurt had been murdered decades earlier. Although Wayne purchased a cemetery plot and a headstone for him, the police had taken possession of the body shortly after the murder and until recently, Wayne had not located them. His foster-mother had asked Wayne to give Kurt a proper burial. Until he located the remains he had been unable to grant her last request.

"I can't believe it. After all this time." Lucy put her hand on his arm. "Where were they?"

"The Escanaba police initially moved Kurt's remains to the morgue. You remember that they suspected Joci had killed him but ultimately realized she hadn't. Although she gave them Kurt's name, after she went to prison nobody was around to claim the body." Wayne cleared his throat. Lucy knew he was still struggling with his guilt about not keeping in touch with his foster-mother for so long.

"So what happened to him?"

"When the Escanaba police finished their investigation and marked Kurt's file as 'murder by person or persons unknown,' they waited a decent interval for someone to claim him. When nobody did, he was buried in a cemetery plot for unclaimed bodies owned by the city. I feared he would be in an unmarked grave, but when I called, they had his name and plot number. All I had to do was pay to have his remains disinterred and moved to the Potawatomi Cemetery." Wayne exhaled deeply, probably relieved to have this task accomplished.

"Were you able to tell Joci this before she died?" Lucy's brows drew together.

"Yes, it was the last thing we talked about, except for me thanking her for taking care of me when I was a kid." Wayne rubbed his face.

"I remember you telling me she wanted him buried so that he would never be forgotten. Finding Kurt and burying him— that was a kind thing you did, Wayne."

"Not kind," he said, shaking his head. "I didn't do it to be kind. Only because it was right, because I owed it to him," his face tightened, "and to her."

"I remember the inscription you put on his gravestone,

'His was the valor of the lion.' I thought it was beautiful." Lucy kissed Wayne gently on the cheek.

They sat there in the heat of the July day, holding hands, the only sound the water falling in the fountains. After a while, Wayne stood up and began to walk the labyrinth. Lucy watched him, knowing the spiritual track could help a person ponder life's greatest mysteries. Wayne was trying to put his foster-mother's life and death behind him.

One of these days, Lucy thought, I'm going to have to tell him about my mother and the day she died.

Chapter Fifteen

—

Mae December

MAE WAS TALKING to her best friend Tammy on the phone at ten in the morning. *Listening* might be a better word. The baby and Patrick were both sleeping, and Tammy had treated Mae to a detailed description of her hemorrhoids, cracking nipples, and stitches in areas that hurt Mae to think about.

"But according to my mom this is all normal," Tammy concluded. "Just wish it didn't hurt so much. What's up with you?"

"Ben has a murder case and he asked me to help. He wants me to look into four people who all live in Rosedale. The weird thing is that I don't know any of them, so I'm not sure I can really help."

Tammy was quiet for a minute. "Sorry, thought I heard the baby on the monitor. Are these people single, by any chance?"

"Yes," Mae said, looking at her notes on the kitchen counter. "Rick Willis—his brother Chester was the murder victim." She stopped, hearing Tammy's quick inhale. "So you knew him?"

"I knew him. He was a 'Local Love' client and so was his brother Rick." Tammy ran a dating service in Rosedale. "Chester was such a sweet guy … I can't believe anyone would kill him! That's terrible."

"What's the brother like?"

"Oh, Mae, Benny's crying. I've got to go. Tell you what … I'm going to try to get out of the house this afternoon for a few hours. Could you meet me? We could go into my office and look at the files I've got on Rick and Chester."

"Sure," Mae agreed with alacrity. "What time?"

"I'll call you after the baby goes back down for a nap. 'Bye."

HAVING COMPLETED HER kennel chores and a little work on her current painting—a scene of three horses in a stone-walled pasture—Mae was running errands in Rosedale when Tammy called back several hours later.

"Okay," she said breathlessly. "Benny's been fed, changed, and is sleeping. Patrick and I both got showers and I'm dying to get out of the house. I'll meet you downstairs."

"Be there in five minutes."

Tammy, Patrick, and their baby lived on the top floor of a historic building in the heart of Rosedale. Tammy's mother, Grace Rodgers, owned the building and her business, Birdy's Salon, was on the street level. The other ground-floor tenants were Tammy's dating service, Local Love, a coffee shop, an antique dealer, and an estate jewelry store. Tammy originally fixed up one corner of the top floor as a studio apartment. When Patrick moved in, they expanded the space to include the baby's room, another bath and a study where Patrick could write. He was almost finished with his MFA in creative writing and needed a quiet place to work. They'd used about half of the available square footage so far and planned to enlarge the kitchen and living room next year.

Mae parked in the alley behind the building and got out of her Explorer.

"Hi, Mae," Patrick called down from the balcony. "Tammy's in her office already. How are you?"

She looked up with a smile. He was leaning over the railing between two flower boxes overflowing with orange and purple annuals and lime-green foliage.

"I'm fine. How's the new daddy?"

"Great. Tired, but great. If you and Tammy want to go anywhere else this afternoon, go ahead. I'll hold down the fort."

Mae waved at him, walked around the corner, and opened the heavy oak door into her best friend's business. It was like entering a very classy valentine. The walls were painted the palest possible pink. Tammy's antique desk had once graced a mansion in New Orleans Garden District and was covered with pictures of happy couples in silver frames. A dove gray divan with throw pillows in creamy silk had been placed in front of the corner window's sheer draperies.

"I'm back here." Tammy's voice issued from behind a fretwork screen. "I found the files on Rick and Chester." She emerged and set the files on a small table near the door. "Hi."

Tammy had dark circles under her eyes and a slight curve to her belly, but other than that she looked great in a short, sleeveless green dress with a high waist and brown, low-heeled sandals.

"Look at you." Mae gave her a hug. "I can't believe you just had a baby."

Tammy hugged Mae back, then stepped back and looked down at her chest. "I can believe it." She laughed. "My boobs are out of control. I'm not used to having all this cleavage."

"Enjoy it while it lasts, I guess. I didn't have a chance to ask you about the other two people. Do you know Brooke Piper or Meredith Flynn?"

Tammy tilted her head. "Not Brooke. But I introduced Rick to Meredith almost a year ago. Let me see if I can find her file. Sit down." She waved at the slipper chairs with pale aqua upholstery that sat opposite her desk. "I'll be right back."

Mae picked up the Willis brothers' files and took a seat. Chester's file was on top and she flipped it open. A photo of a smiling dark-haired man looked back. She heard her friend rustling around, followed by the clunk of a metal drawer sliding shut; then Tammy reappeared and sat in the chair next to Mae.

"He was cute, wasn't he?" she said, looking at Chester's picture. "He was a little old for you, but I did consider introducing the two of you before Ben came along." She gave a shiver. "Just think, Mae. What if I had and you two hit it off? You'd be grieving for him now, instead of being engaged to Ben. It gives me chills."

"Did you fix Chester up with anyone? Was he in a relationship when he was killed … do you know?"

"I introduced him to several women. In fact," she put another file on top of Chester's and flipped it open to reveal a brunette woman with dark eyes and a half-smile. "I introduced Meredith to him first. They just met for coffee as I recall. Chester called me afterward and told me he thought she was more his brother's type. He said something else about Meredith too, something about her past, but I can't remember what it was."

Mae set all three files on Tammy's desk and got her notes out of her purse. "Turns out he was right. Ben said Meredith is Rick's girlfriend now."

Tammy nodded. "Yeah, Chester was too nice to say so, but I think Meredith was looking for a rich husband. Rick's a stockbroker and drives a nice car, wears expensive clothes. Chester was sort of a loveable screw-up, but a lot more fun than Rick." She sighed. "Let's get outta here. You can borrow those files and summarize them for Ben. Just tell him to be quiet about where you got the information, please. All my information is confidential, but since this is a legal case, I feel okay about sharing this."

"I'll be sure to protect your confidentiality, don't worry." Mae stood up and put her notes and the files inside her oversized shoulder bag. "I'll text him and let him know I've got information about everyone but Brooke Piper. And then I think we need ice cream."

Chapter Sixteen

———

Sheriff Ben Bradley

B EN WAS PONDERING their next move on Chester's murder case when Dory stuck her head in his office doorway. As usual, his former office manager and current investigator was dressed in the height of fashion. Her black and ivory short-sleeved dress and black stilettos were accessorized by black and gold bracelets and dangly pearl earrings. Ben beckoned her in and gave Dory an inquiring glance.

"I just got off the phone with Rick Willis," she said, raising her eyebrows. "*Not* happy. Says a necklace is missing from his mother's jewelry box. He accused Brooke Piper of taking it."

"What was he doing digging through his mother's jewelry, I wonder?" Ben frowned. "What'd you tell him?"

"I told him I'd talk to you and we'd look into it." Dory's smile flashed brightly in her coffee-colored complexion. "Can I investigate this one, boss? I'm something of a jewelry expert, you know."

"Could I stop you from investigating anything you had a mind to?" It was a rhetorical question and they both knew it. Eudora Clarkson had been the power behind the throne of the Rose County Sheriff's Office since Ben was in diapers. A complacent expression stole over her face as she shook her head. "What's your plan then, Investigator Clarkson?"

"Wayne has a search warrant for the young lady's apartment," Dory replied. "I have a complete description of the missing necklace. Seems Rick knows a little something about jewelry himself. Anyway, I thought Cam and I could go search her place and keep an eye out for the necklace."

"That's fine," Ben said. "Just be sure to get the warrant from Wayne before you go."

"Oh, that reminds me," Dory said. "Wayne needs two subpoenas—prescription records for Brooke Piper and Rick Willis."

Ben nodded. She turned on her heel. "Wait," he said. Dory looked back over her shoulder, pausing in the doorway. "How's the search going for my new office manager?"

"I've narrowed it down to two candidates," Dory said. "They're both coming in tomorrow for interviews. I hope to have a new person on the job early next week."

"Great. You can go." She disappeared around the corner and Ben sat at his desk for a few more minutes, head down and his mind fixed on the case. *I don't see Brooke as a thief, but she's certainly had the run of the Willis place with plenty of opportunities to help herself to jewelry. Did Rick's animosity toward Brooke run deep enough to try and frame her for theft or even murder?*

He wondered if Rick was looking to give his girlfriend a little present out of his mom's jewelry collection before the will was even read. *I need to talk to that attorney.* He stood up, grabbed his phone and hurried out of his office, calling for Detective Fuller.

"What's up, Sheriff?" Rob appeared in the entryway in slacks and a collared shirt with no tie. Rob Fuller had passed his detective's exam in January and Ben was finally accustomed to seeing him in street clothes instead of the deputy's uniform.

"I need some information from that attorney—Connor, I think it was."

Rob adjusted his silver-framed glasses and said, "Leonard Willis' attorney? Shane Conner. Should I call him, or do you want to pay him a visit?"

"Let's go to his office. You can call on the way over. I'll drive my truck. Has Wayne come in yet?"

"Not as far as I know. I'll get the number for Shane Connor."

Ben turned to Deputy George Phelps, who sat at Dory's desk with a look like he knew what was coming. "Have you seen Detective Nichols this morning?"

"Dory and Cam left with Emma to go track him down, Sheriff. Miss Dory stuck me on phones again." His expression was gloomy.

"I know, George. We'll have a new office manager soon. Let me know if there's anything urgent. We'll be back in a few hours."

"Yes, sir," was the doleful reply.

With Rob Fuller on his heels, Ben walked out to his truck in the merciless heat of a July morning in Tennessee. Although he was already sweating as he climbed into the driver seat, it was even worse inside, since the one spot of shade in the parking lot had already been occupied by Dory's red T-bird when Ben got to the office this morning. He started the truck and put all four windows down until the AC kicked in.

Rob slid into the passenger seat and handed Ben a slip of paper. "Here's the address of Shane Connor's office. I confirmed that he was in today and had time to see you. Turn left out of the parking lot," he told his boss. "About a ten minute drive."

A bad feeling began to ferment in Ben's stomach. "What firm's he with?"

Rob bit his lip before replying, "Babcock, Woolsey and Tremaine."

"Shit. I was afraid you were gonna say that. I know where their offices are, but I sure hope my opponent isn't there today."

WHEN THEY ARRIVED at the law firm of Babcock, Woolsey and Tremaine, they were greeted by a diminutive, grandmotherly woman at the front desk.

"Good morning, Sheriff," she said. "I'm Lorene."

"Nice to meet you, Lorene. This is Detective Rob Fuller," Ben said.

"Good morning, Detective," she rose to her feet, gesturing down the beige-carpeted hallway to her right. "I'll show you to Mr. Connor's office. I'm sure Mr. Tremaine will be sorry to have missed you, Sheriff Bradley," she said with a flash of a wink, "but he's in court in Nashville today." She tapped on the last door on the left, then opened it for them. "Go on in."

"Thank you, Lorene." She gave Ben a little grin before going back to her desk.

A tall, thin man with gray hair and a youthful face stood up and walked around his desk to greet them. He wore a white shirt with the sleeves rolled up, a loosened yellow tie and gray trousers. "Shane Conner, good to meet you, Sheriff." He held out his hand to Ben.

"Ben Bradley. This is Detective Fuller. Thanks for taking the time to see us." Shane Conner had a firm, dry handshake.

"Not a problem. Please have a seat. Lorene says you're here about the Leonard Willis estate." There was a twinkle in his dark brown eyes. "Why anyone thinks it's a man's world, I'll never know," he went on. "We all just work for Lorene around here."

Ben smiled, leaning back a little in his chair. "We also work for a benevolent dictator. It's my investigator and former office manager, Dory Clarkson. I don't know how much you're comfortable sharing with us about the estate, but we'd be grateful for any information you can give. I believe the will has a direct bearing on Chester's Willis' case. Did you know he was murdered?"

"Yes. It's so sad. Chester was one of my favorite people. So was Leonard." Shane Conner grew pensive. "However, I can't tell you much until the will is read to the heirs."

"I understand," Ben said. "I could compel you to talk, but it would take time and a judge. We need to focus on catching Chester's killer." He looked closely at Shane Connor, who was looking down at the papers on his desk. "How about this ... I ask you a question and you nod or shake your head? That way you've said nothing."

"That works," Shane said.

"All right. First off, did Mr. Willis change his will after Chester's death?"

The attorney nodded.

"Did the change result in Rick Willis receiving more money?"

Again, the attorney nodded.

"Okay, other than small bequests, were there others who inherited besides Rick?"

Shane Connor nodded.

"Last question, did Brooke Piper inherit anything?"

"Um hum," the attorney said.

"Did she inherit any money?"

"Sheriff, I'm really uncomfortable telling you any more than I already have. I'm sorry. I know this is a criminal investigation, but I would prefer to give you the will in its entirety once I speak with the family. I will say to you, and in court if necessary, that Mr. Willis was *compos mentis* when he made his final dispositions."

"I understand. One last thing: when you do read the will, could you do me a favor? Could you please pay special attention to the facial expressions of Rick Willis and Brooke Piper? I'd like to know if they were surprised or pleased or perhaps disappointed."

"Certainly," the attorney said. "Now, if you don't mind, I have another appointment."

AFTER BIDDING FAREWELL to Lorene, Ben and Rob Fuller left the attorney's office. Once seated behind the wheel of his truck, Ben turned to the young detective.

"I never got a report on what Mark Schneider found on Chester's computer. Do you know what turned up?"

"Yes, Dory and I both talked to Mark after he finished his analysis. Just let me check my notes here." Rob paused while he tapped on his tablet. "Okay, here it is. Mark said Chester had a lot of family pictures on his computer. He had recently subscribed to ancestry dot com. He had all his finances on his computer, as well as a link to his bank account. There were three computer games on the system—Assassin's Creed, Valiant Hearts, and Age of Dragons. That was about it, except for one email I found interesting. Chester sent Meredith Flynn an email that said, 'You promised me you would tell Rick. I'm uncomfortable knowing something that you haven't shared with my brother.' "

"Interesting, very interesting. You were going to look into the older brother Rick's financials, right? What did you find on him?" Ben asked.

"Rick Willis has been living way above his income level. He depends on a big end-of-year bonus to make him whole for his expenditures. He wasn't going to get one this year because some major investors followed his lead and lost enough money that they pulled their investments out of the company Rick works for, Arden Capital Group."

"So Rick had motive in spades. He knew his father's life was coming to an end and not having to share his father's estate with Chester would have pulled him out of a big hole. What's your take on Brooke Piper as the killer?"

Rob scanned the notes he'd taken during the meeting with the attorney. "I don't see her motive being strong enough, but if Brooke inherited a large portion of the estate, I wouldn't be surprised if Rick contests the will."

Ben kept his eyes on the blacktop in front of his truck, shimmering in the heat haze of a Tennessee summer day. Without looking at Rob, he nodded and said, "Seems like Shane Connor went out of his way to let us know Leonard was of sound mind. Of course Rick will allege that there was undue influence from Miss Piper."

"It always comes down to money, doesn't it?" Rob's quiet voice was barely audible above the blast of the air-conditioner's fan.

Chapter Seventeen

———

Chief Detective Wayne Nichols

W AYNE CRANKED UP the minimal air conditioning in the patrol car while he waited for Emma Peters, their lab tech, to join him. He had already given the search warrant for Brooke Piper's apartment to Deputy Cam Gomez. The other warrant for Rick Willis' residence lay on the seat beside him. The air conditioning in the vehicle was becoming less effective each day, and although it was just after 11:00 a.m., the heat index for the day was close to 98 degrees. He ran his finger around the collar of his uniform shirt, loosening it slightly. Emma got in the passenger seat, holding her gloves and collecting gear.

Rick Willis had reported a necklace stolen from his mother's jewelry box, and Ben had assigned Cam Gomez and Dory to check Brooke Piper's place for the missing necklace. It was the perfect opportunity to do a search of her residence. While Dory was looking for the necklace, Cam could search the rest of the apartment. He would catch up with both of them later.

Wayne drove to the outskirts of Rosedale, where a lot of new construction was taking place. Rick Willis lived in a brand-new condo complex with all the amenities. It stood out like a sore thumb in the small antebellum town of Rosedale, standing three stories tall and built in a C-shape that wrapped around an Olympic-sized pool. They parked the car and walked into the large glass entry. Even with all of that exposed glass, the inside temperature was delightfully cool. Wayne sighed, thinking he was going to have to talk to Ben about getting a new patrol car. The repair shop had already said the air conditioning was one of several things wrong with the car, and that it wasn't worth trying to fix again. Funds were tight. Especially now, only months before the election, Ben was unwilling to spend any extra money.

They walked over to the bank of elevators and glided smoothly to the third floor.

"Rick Willis is our prime suspect, right?" Emma asked, with an excited lift of her mouth. She was in her late twenties with a lush figure and dark curls cut short.

"Why do you say that?" Wayne asked.

"I know we have warrants for both Rick Willis and Brooke Piper's residences, but as a woman, Brooke's less likely to commit homicide."

"Percentage-wise, that's true, but the killing of Chester Willis was done by injection. That's a low-violence type of crime. We think the victim was probably sleepy from taking Xanax, like the tablet that Cam found in Mr. Willis Senior's place."

"I've read that women are far more likely to use poison, or other non-bloody means to kill," Emma said.

"Unfortunately, nothing so far narrows this case down to either a man or a woman," Wayne told her.

Emma nodded and rang the doorbell of number 310. It was the last door off the long silent hall on the top floor. The hall was carpeted in royal blue, with a gold stripe on either side. They waited quietly until they heard the click of the lock. Rick

Willis, in a white terrycloth bathrobe, rubbing his wet hair with a towel, stood in the doorway.

"Good morning Mr. Willis. Sorry to disturb you. This is Emma Peters, from our lab. We have a warrant to search your apartment."

"It's a condominium," Rick said coldly. "And mine is the penthouse." He stood aside for them to enter. "I presume this is in relation to my brother's death."

"It is." Wayne handed him the warrant. *The penthouse? What a jerk.*

Rick glanced at it and handed it back. "I just need to get some clothes on." He turned and stalked down the hall.

"Go ahead. We'll begin with the public spaces and wait to search your private quarters until you're dressed." Wayne strove for a polite tone, but he could feel the coldness in his gut that invariably arose in the presence of a homicide suspect. He didn't like this arrogant snot one little bit.

Rick's residence occupied the whole south end of the building and had a fine view of downtown Rosedale to the west and yellow cornfields to the east. The large open space was flooded with light. The living room ceiling was at least twelve feet high and beamed. The kitchen was placed slightly to the left of the open concept room and had state-of-the-art stainless steel appliances and sleek gray cabinets. Beyond the kitchen was a smaller den with bookcases that flanked a marble fireplace surround.

"Doesn't have much furniture, does he?" Emma said quietly. The living room had only a large sectional and a massive television. There wasn't even a coffee table. No art hung on the walls. "Looks like he spent all his money on the condo."

"His brother's death would probably have provided him with a bigger share of the estate," Wayne murmured.

They could hear voices from the corridor off the living room. A long-legged brunette woman in high heels and a navy suit clicked down the hall.

"Good morning," she said in a sulky tone of voice. Then, as if remembering her manners, she stuck out a hand. "I'm Meredith Flynn, Rick's girlfriend."

Wayne shook hands with Meredith. "I'm Chief Detective Wayne Nichols and this is Emma Peters from our lab. Are you on your way to work?"

"Yes, I have a meeting to get to. Rick needs to go in to his office soon as well. He was working from here this morning and I just, um, stopped by."

Wayne glanced at Emma, whose mouth was curved in a little grin. "We're here to search Mr. Willis' condo. The two of you are free to leave. We'll lock the door behind us," he said.

Meredith nodded with a little frown. She turned and went back down the hall. A few minutes later, the couple emerged together.

"I expect you to leave this place as you found it." Rick gave Wayne a challenging glare.

Wayne didn't respond, just turned his back on Rick and went to join Emma in the kitchen. The front door closed behind the couple with a click.

Wayne and Emma finished their search of the kitchen and living room spaces. Except for two wine glasses in the sink, none of the dishes, glassware or pans looked as if they had ever been used. The refrigerator held only orange juice, yogurt, and several bottles of wine. There were a few microwaveable frozen meals in the freezer. There wasn't a single personal thing in the place, and nothing that would help in their investigation.

"Bag the wine glasses, please," Wayne said. Emma hurried to do so. There was a lipstick print on one of them. "We might get DNA for Meredith from the lip print and Rick's from the other glass. Both sets of prints will be on them too."

They proceeded down the hall to the bedroom area. There was an empty guest room with no furniture whatsoever and an enormous master bedroom, master closet, and bath. The master bedroom was as large as the living room. The closet itself was as big as the guest room and furnished with custom walnut cabinetry.

"Wow." Emma's eyes were wide. "Just look at this closet." She paused a moment, looking at the beautiful fitted cabinetry. "I'll go through the pockets of the hanging clothes and then I'll look for the hamper," she said.

"Good idea," Wayne told her. "If we get really lucky we'll find a syringe or drugs in a pocket."

Emma searched for some time until she slid aside a walnut door panel and located a laundry hamper. There were only two T-shirts, two pieces of white underwear, and two pairs of dark socks inside.

They moved on to the bathroom and its medicine cabinet. Emma opened the mirrored door to reveal a bottle of men's cologne, deodorant, toothpaste and two toothbrushes. There were several bottles of ibuprofen, calcium, and assorted vitamins, but only one prescription bottle.

"Xanax, ten milligrams." Emma plucked the bottle from the shelf. She was wearing gloves.

"Who was the prescription written for?" Wayne asked. Emma turned the bottle around.

"Meredith Flynn." She looked up at him. "This is coming with us."

The tops of the bedside tables were virtually empty, except for a copy of *Bonfire of the Vanities* by Tom Wolfe and a copy of *Freedom* by Suarez. Wayne turned the book over to read the back cover. Rick Willis obviously liked thrillers, a sure sign of a risk-taker.

In the top drawer of the nightstand, there was a packet of condoms. Emma gave Wayne an oblique glance; then she checked the wastebasket. Other than some crumpled tissues, it was empty.

"All right, we're done. Let's go."

They walked into the silent hallway and left with their finds. The door shut and locked behind them.

Investigator Dory Clarkson and Deputy Cam Gomez arrived back at the sheriff's office around one o'clock and joined Wayne in his office. Emma Peters had returned to the lab and was busy processing their finds.

"So what did you two discover on your visit to Miss Piper's?"

"First off, I called Brooke to tell her we were coming. She said it was an inconvenient time but she was willing to skip her first class and wait for us," Dory said.

"What was her place like?" Wayne asked.

"She lives in a two-story apartment building that backs up to a scrubby wooded area. The complex was run down and there was a pickup truck at the end of a row of cars. It didn't look drivable. A dumpster was filled to overflowing." Cam was reading from her notes. "I called and told them to skip this week's pick-up date," she added. "Do you want George and me to go through it?"

"Yes. Good idea, Deputy."

Cam checked her notes once more. "When Brooke came to the door I apologized for the inconvenience. She said it was the day student nurses were going to learn how to do prostate exams, but that she would reschedule."

"I said I could see why she would want to skip *that*." Dory, eyes wide, nodded emphatically. "Cam asked her if they started right off practicing on men and she said no, they had a plastic training model to practice on. A plastic guy's butt. Sure wish I didn't have that image in my head. I need brain bleach."

"Okay, can we get back to what you found?" Wayne was acutely uncomfortable with the drift of the conversation. Prostate exams were not something he wanted to think about at all, much less those performed by young women. "Cam, please describe the interior of the apartment."

"Okay. First off, it didn't have air conditioning. There was a square fan on the floor. The living room had an old couch, two chairs, and a small TV. There was a coffee table stacked with books and periodicals. Other than reading material, the space was clean and well organized. The kitchen was minimal—just one bank of cabinets with a sink, stove, and a small refrigerator."

"While Cam was checking out the room, I asked Brooke if she had a jewelry box," Dory said. "She said she did and that it was on top of her dresser. When I lifted up the lid, I noticed a folded piece of paper. It turned out to be a recent insurance valuation for the jewelry. Most of the pieces were described as costume jewelry of minimal value, but there were two pieces that were expensive. One was an old diamond ring which Brooke said was her grandmother's engagement ring. The other piece, valued at fifteen hundred dollars, matched the description of the necklace Rick Willis reported stolen."

"Well, well." Wayne nodded in approval. "Good work, Dory."

"I asked Brooke where it came from and she said it was a gift from one of her clients. She said as a massage therapist she had a policy that tips were not expected but appreciated."

"Did you ask who gave it to her?"

"I did. She said Mr. Willis had. She looked sort of defensive at that point. I asked her if she had any proof that it was a gift and she got huffy and said she wasn't a thief. I said it had been reported stolen and we would be taking it with us. Rick Willis will have to tell us if the necklace is the one he reported stolen."

Cam waited until Dory was finished speaking, then said, "I wanted to bring Brooke back with us to the office, but she said she couldn't afford to miss any more classes. I didn't want to insist and put her in a position where she lawyered up. I hope that's okay." Cam gave Wayne an uncertain look.

"It's fine. Ben and I need to talk before we interview her anyway."

Dory grinned. "I felt pretty good about my part of the mission, since I recovered the stolen property," she said.

"Did you find anything else, Cam?" Wayne asked.

"One other thing." Cam paused and raised her eyebrows. "In Brooke's bathroom I found a package of needles, point-five millimeter by twenty-seven gauge. And on her desk, I found a second notice from the university. She hasn't paid her tuition for this semester yet."

"Great work, both of you."

"The little gal might be a petty thief, but I can't see her killing anyone," Dory told him, lips pursed and head tilted to one side.

"Anyone can kill, given a sufficiently strong motivation," Wayne said, thinking out loud. "It was an interesting set of contrasts today. Rick Willis has a penthouse condo, but he can't afford furniture. And Brooke Piper is struggling to pay her bills. She may well survive on tips from her private clients, and she just lost a good one."

"Rick Willis is a stockbroker," Cam protested. "He can't be short of money."

"Depends on how much risk he takes in the market," Wayne pointed out. "A lot of people have lost big recently."

"Do we have any background on Meredith Flynn?" Cam asked.

"Not much," Wayne told her, "but that woman looked expensive. Emma said she was wearing Jimmy Choos, whatever that means."

"What the heck are Jimmy Choos?" Cam asked Dory, their resident fashion-plate.

"Shoes. They cost about a thousand dollars a pair. I wish investigators made enough money to own Jimmy Choos," Dory said, wistfully.

Once the women had vacated his office, Wayne thought through what they had found. It really wasn't much, although the bottle of Xanax prescribed for Meredith Flynn and a packet of syringes found in Brooke's apartment gave them something to use to put the women off balance in subsequent interrogations. And both prime suspects seemed to have money problems. However, unless they found some actual evidence, fingerprints, or DNA, it was looking like a toss-up as to whether they could prove Rick was the perp. Despite telling Emma that anyone could kill, Wayne doubted Brooke Piper's guilt. *And what role, if any, did Meredith Flynn play in this tragedy*?

Chapter Eighteen

—

Dr. Lucy Ingram

L ucy's cellphone rang. She was in the attendings computer room catching up on her patient notes. The screen on her phone read "Wayne Nichols." It was her boyfriend.

"Hello there," Lucy said.

"Hello yourself. I'm sure you're busy and I won't keep you long. I'm still trying to find out which of our suspects had prescriptions for Xanax. We now know that Rick's girlfriend Meredith Flynn had one. We found the bottle in Rick's medicine cabinet when we searched his condo. I got the name of Rick Willis' doctor and called him, but even with this being a murder investigation, he claimed doctor/patient privilege. So no luck on Rick."

"Wayne, you know the constraints I'm operating under. I didn't write Mr. Willis Senior a prescription for that drug. Finding out whether he had a scrip from someone else is a stretch."

Wayne made an irritated sound. "Used to be there was no

problem with law enforcement getting prescription records, and we could search Tennessee's database right from the office. Now we can only look for controlled substances to curb the flow of prescription drugs. And right now the whole damn database is down for firewall installation."

Lucy paused, then said, "Well, the good news is that Xanax is a controlled substance, so I can look for hospital patient prescriptions for my patients and employees. Chester Willis was my patient, so I'll double-check his records. And of course Mr. Willis was a congestive heart patient, and as such was in and out of the hospital quite a bit. I'll check informally with his cardiologist. Could be I'll turn up something, but you'll have to wait until the database is back on line to check Rick Willis."

"Whatever you can find will be a help. I have another favor to ask. We're sending Dory to talk with the ambulance drivers who brought Chester Willis in on the night he died. Could you go with her and check their documentation for what happened?"

"No problem. Dory can come over around five if that works for her. Do you want to stop by my house later?"

"I sure do, babe. See you around ten o'clock."

As THE HOT summer night was finally beginning to cool down, Lucy saw Wayne's truck pull into the driveway. The moon was a fingernail clipping in the dark sky. Her place was just far enough away from Nashville that the haze of city lights didn't blot out the stars. Lucy flipped on the porch light. She had decided on this method of giving Wayne permission to come inside, as she was often held up late at the hospital and so far had not offered Wayne a key to her place. Nor had he asked for one.

Lucy watched Wayne walk up to the door. The cicadas buzzed shrilly and a breeze rattled the leaves. They had had so little rain lately that the trees were parched. She opened the door. "Come on in."

They sat in her living room with glasses of wine. Silence reigned for several minutes as both of them let the high stress of their jobs drain away into the dark summer night.

"My conversation with Mr. Willis' cardiologist paid off. He checked his records, but Mr. Willis didn't have a scrip for Xanax."

"Thanks for doing that," Wayne said. He inhaled deeply. She could tell he was enjoying the scent of her skin, fresh from the shower. She was wearing a long sleep T-shirt and her legs were bare. She thought about whether she would invite him to stay over.

"Did you and Dory get to talk to the ambulance guys?" Wayne asked.

"We did. Zack Randall was on duty the evening of July fourth with Kevin Ryan. Zack's African American and so I thought it would be best to let Dory do most of the talking. She seemed to have a good rapport with him, and those ambulance guys are always sort of defensive around physicians. They're just waiting for us to criticize their work, especially when the death occurs in the ambulance."

"Were there any anomalies on the record?" Wayne asked.

"Chester coded in the vehicle and Kevin had to resuscitate him. He shocked him with a defibrillator several times before he gave up. The whole thing was textbook. Perfect documentation, plus those guys had no motive to want Chester dead."

"Did they inject him with anything in the vehicle?"

"No, there wasn't time. He went pretty quickly."

"That gets them off the hook, not that I ever thought they were suspects, but Ben promised Mr. Willis before he died that we would speak to everyone who took care of Chester that evening."

"I'm not worried, Wayne," Lucy said. "I'm sure you'll get this solved. I wish all detectives were as thorough and conscientious as you are."

Wayne tipped his head to one side, looking carefully at her.

"That's an interesting comment, Lucy. Have you been involved in a murder investigation before?"

"I've treated some prisoners who were brought to the ER. One was a murderer, and I talked with him for a while. He'd been shanked in prison. The injury had gotten badly infected. That's the reason they brought him in. It was interesting treating a patient who was handcuffed to the bed. But the reason I said that," she paused for a moment and inhaled sharply, "was that my mother was murdered."

There was a long silence as Wayne reached for her hand. "God, that's rough. How old were you?"

"I was ten."

"Did they get the guy?"

"No. The case is still unsolved." Her voice was flat. Her mother's death was decades ago, but she still struggled with the memory of that horrible day. She had been the one who found her mother dying on the bathroom floor.

"I'm so sorry," Wayne said. His voice was so quiet she could barely hear him.

"So many times I've thought that if I'd known first aid, I might've been able to save her." She paused. "I'm sorry I didn't tell you this before, Wayne." She tried to smile but couldn't pull it off. "You and I broke up once, you'll recall, because you wouldn't tell me anything about your past. I felt guilty then and I feel guilty now, because I've done the same thing."

"Sharing this old stuff is hard for both of us," Wayne said and bent his head to kiss her. She melted into his solid embrace. After a moment he pulled away and asked her if she wanted to talk about it some more.

"No. Let's just go to bed. It's been a long day."

"Another time then." Wayne smiled at her.

While he checked his phone for messages and went out to his truck to lock it up, Lucy thought about their relationship. They had been a couple, on and off, for more than two years. His commitment to his job, to finding justice for victims, moved her profoundly. She was proud of how he had managed to get his foster mother out of prison, to right the old wrong of her unjust sentence. His passion for victims matched her passion for her patients.

Wayne was getting older—probably had only a decade and a half to live before the beatings his body had taken over the years ended his life. But then you never knew. People often lived far beyond expectations. Her fortieth birthday was coming up. She was no longer young, although she knew she was still attractive. They had fallen into an exclusive arrangement without ever discussing it. For some time now Lucy had wanted to ask Wayne where he thought they were headed.

Lucy had not planned to tell Wayne about her mother. The words had just slipped out, making her realize how comfortable she was with him. There were only two other people in the world—beyond the law enforcement personnel who investigated the crime—that remembered how her mother died: her sister and the killer. The investigating detective had long since assigned her mother's death to cold cases. The last time she talked to him, he urged her to get past her mother's death. It had been almost thirty years.

Some months ago Lucy realized she had fallen in love with Wayne. Did she want marriage? If she and Wayne were married, could she let go of the past? She took a deep breath. She wanted to tell him more about her mother's death, but not tonight. Tonight she only wanted to sleep with his strong arms wrapped around her. Soon, though, she would offer him a key.

Chapter Nineteen

—

Sheriff Ben Bradley

Bᴇɴ ʜᴀᴅ ᴀsᴋᴇᴅ Mae to write a report summarizing everything she had found out about Rick and Chester Willis and Meredith Flynn. She was careful not to list Tammy as her source, mindful of her need for confidentiality. She wasn't getting very far, though. Her efforts to write were being hampered by Matthew Bradley and Cupcake, his new basset hound. Katie, Matthew's mom, had dropped them off earlier that morning. Matt and his puppy were going to stay with Mae and Ben for the next three days—Thursday through Saturday.

Even though Tatie, a female corgi and the youngest of Mae's dogs, was just over a year old, it was exciting to have a puppy in the house again. Exciting, noisy, and messy. Mae sighed and saved the document she was working on as Matthew's voice grew louder. She put her computer into sleep mode and stood up just as Ben's son raced into her kitchen.

"Where's Cupcake?" Mae asked him.

"She's outside. Can you come help me?" Matthew's thick golden-brown hair was sticking to his forehead in sweaty clumps. His full cheeks were flushed and he was breathing hard.

"Of course." Mae smiled, grabbed her cellphone off the counter and took his sweaty little hand. "Is she standing on her ears again?"

Matty nodded, pulling Mae toward the back door, which stood half open. "Both of them! She can't walk. She's stuck. See her over by the shed?"

Cupcake was indeed stuck. Tatie and Mae's two older dogs—Titan, a male corgi, and Tallulah, her black pug—encircled the pup, whose front feet were planted firmly on her extra-long ears. Mae shook her head, snapped a quick photo with her phone before putting it in the pocket of her shorts, and then picked up the distressed baby basset.

"Mommy says she needs a barrette." Matthew looked up at her earnestly. "This happens all the time."

Mae cradled Cupcake to her chest and laughed. "Your mom's right. But maybe I can find something softer than a barrette to hold her ears up until she grows into them. Did she go potty before she got stuck, Matty?"

"Yep. She did both things and I gave her one of the little marshmallows like you told me. I ate the other ones, so I need some more for my pocket."

Mae attempted to give him a stern look as they walked back toward the house with the other three dogs trailing after them. "Are the marshmallows for you or Cupcake?"

"We're sharing them." He appeared unfazed by her sternness. "When's my daddy coming home?"

Mae closed the back door and ushered her dogs into the laundry room. "Get in your beds. Stay," she told them. "He'll be here in an hour or so. Let's put Cupcake in her crate for a nap and you can go to your room for some rest time, okay?"

The five-year-old gave her a horrified look. "I'm not tired. And she isn't either. Why do we have to rest?"

Because I'm tired. And I need to work on my report. "You

don't have to sleep, Matty. You can look at a book or work on a puzzle or just lie down and rest your eyes. But puppies are like babies and they need naps." After Matthew kissed his pet on her head, she put Cupcake in her crate and latched the door. "Shall I come up and read to you?"

Half an hour later, after reading two and a half stories to Matty—whose eyes had drifted shut by the middle of his third selection—Mae was back at her desk in the kitchen. The house was quiet in the drowsy heat of the afternoon. She finished her report, a summary of what she'd learned from Tammy's files and the Internet, and sent it to Ben's personal email, along with the super-cute picture of Cupcake. Mae stashed Tammy's files in a drawer. *I'll take those back to her in a day or so. And go have a little lie-down my own self.* Ben was bringing dinner home, and she didn't have any kennel chores to do since Ray, her teenaged employee, had taken care of that already. With any luck at all, she might have time for a nap and a shower before her fiancé returned.

Chapter Twenty

———

Sheriff Ben Bradley

Ben was having a frustrating day at work. As far as he could tell, they were nowhere with Chester's murder, and everyone he wanted to bring in for questioning was at the Willis funeral. Shane Connor, the attorney for Leonard Willis' estate, had filled him in a little bit, but he couldn't give Ben any specifics until after the reading of the will, scheduled for tomorrow. Wayne was attending the double funeral for Chester and Leonard Willis with Lucy, so that was enough of a sheriff's office presence.

I don't need to be at the funeral, but I'm certainly not accomplishing anything here.

His cellphone pinged, the sound indicating an email on his personal account. He logged in on his desktop computer, smiling when he saw the picture of Cupcake standing on her ears. There was an attachment, which Ben downloaded and read with interest. He didn't know where Mae got the information. She'd listed no sources, but she'd come up with quite a dossier on Meredith Flynn and the Willis brothers. He printed out the report and read it carefully.

BACKGROUND REPORT ON CHESTER & RICK WILLIS &
MEREDITH FLYNN
MAE DECEMBER, SHERIFF'S OFFICE CONSULTANT
JULY 12, 2014

Richard Allen Willis: known as Rick, 43 years old, single, works as a broker for Arden Capital Group. Has been employed there for the last 12 years. Has a reputation as a good, though aggressive, broker. His clients tend to be younger investors who are looking for portfolio growth vs. management. He's never been married or in a long-term relationship, other than with his current girlfriend, Meredith Flynn. Image is very important to Rick. He leases a new BMW every two years, wears custom-made suits and belongs to the Rosedale City Club, an exclusive men's group composed of the self-proclaimed movers and shakers in and around Rosedale.

Rick is the oldest of Leonard and Corinne Willis' three children. His sister Jillian was a college freshman when she died from diabetes complications. She was visiting Rick, who lived in Chicago at the time, when she passed away unexpectedly. Rick was not close to his brother Chester and was somewhat embarrassed by Chester's lack of ambition.

Chester James Willis: 41 years old when he died, the family's middle child. Well liked but still trying to "find himself," much to his brother's chagrin. A communications major who didn't finish college, Chester job-hopped through his twenties and thirties. He was briefly married to Gail Carmichael, who divorced him after two years. The couple had no children and the divorce was uncontested. In his mid-thirties, Chester moved back to Rosedale and got a job managing a small marketing firm. Leonard, his father, was the company's primary investor. MidSouth Marketing was sold last year. Chester was living off his share of the profits and had moved back into Leonard's house to take care of his father. At the time of his death, Chester was unemployed and did not have a significant other.

Meredith Flynn Carnton: 39 years old and single, no children. Meredith is the only child of Marjory and Eli Carnton of Houston, Texas. By all accounts she enjoyed a privileged upbringing as a child of wealth, attended private schools, and was presented at the debutante ball in her home town in the spring of her 19th year after a semester in France. She planned to attend Baylor University in the fall, but Eli Carnton, under FBI investigation for a variety of financial misdeeds and facing indictment, fled the country. His assets were seized and his wife and daughter were left penniless. In the two decades since her father's disappearance, Meredith put herself through college, legally changed her last name to Flynn (her mother's maiden name and Meredith's middle name), and distanced herself as much as possible from the scandal. She has had several long-term relationships but never married. She is a fundraising consultant who specializes in uniting philanthropic individuals and foundations with cancer treatment and research facilities. Her mother Marjory died of pancreatic cancer when Meredith was 26. She and Rick Willis have been dating for a year. Before she began her relationship with Rick, Meredith went on one date with Chester.

Ben put the report down. He had asked Mae to research Brooke Piper as well, but she must have had no luck on that front yet. He stood up, stretched, and walked out to Dory's desk.

"What's up, boss?" his investigator asked. "Have you got something for me to do? I'm bored to tears."

Ben could see why. The office was completely quiet this afternoon. "Wayne's attending the Willis funeral, but where's everybody else?" he asked. "Wasn't the new office manager supposed to be here today?"

Dory raised her eyes briefly to the ceiling, as if seeking heavenly guidance. "Rob's at the dentist. George and Cam went out on a domestic disturbance call, and Sophie Coffin starts work tomorrow."

"Our new office manager's name is Sophie Coffin? Surprised the funeral home didn't hire her first."

"Glad you got that little joke out of your system before she starts." Dory shook her head. "And I do mean *little.* Anyway, did you need something?"

"I do. I need you and Mae to team up on a little project for me. I know you talked to Brooke Piper and found that necklace in her apartment, but I'd like you and Mae to look into her background … dig a little deeper. I'm going to take off early since it's so quiet around here. I'll talk to Mae about it tonight."

"We do work well together," Dory said. "I'm sure that between us we can come up with some dirt. I don't know about Mae, but I can start tomorrow … as soon as I show Sophie around and she gets settled."

Ben smiled. "Thanks, Dory. I'll ask her to call you about it. Can you stick around until the deputies get back?"

"Sure thing, go ahead. I'll call you if things get too exciting for me here at action central."

Ben locked his office door and walked out into the parking lot. He had just installed a remote start on his truck, which enabled him to start it and let the AC run for a few minutes before he climbed inside. So far, he was very happy with his purchase. Especially on July afternoons. He made a quick stop to pick up barbecue, then drove a little ways out of town to the old farmhouse on Little Chapel Road.

When he walked into the kitchen, Ben burst out laughing. He put the food down on the counter and looked at Mae. "What have you done to that poor little dog?" he asked, pointing at Cupcake, who was sporting a pink ponytail holder. On her ears.

"Hi, Daddy." Matthew was lying on the kitchen floor beside his puppy. "We didn't want her to step on her ears anymore, so Miss Mae tied them together with one of her ponytail holders. It's just until she grows into her ears."

"She looks ridiculous," Ben whispered in Mae's ear. He gave his fiancée a quick kiss. "Are you sure it's not uncomfortable?"

Mae raised her eyebrows and gave him a little grin. "I'm sure it's more comfortable than standing on her own ears all the time."

"She likes it, Daddy. Don't worry," his five year-old reassured him. "Girls like pink stuff, you know."

Chapter Twenty-One

—

Chief Detective Wayne Nichols

WAYNE WAS SUPPOSED to meet Lucy in front of St. Mary's Catholic Church at noon for the Willis funeral. Rick Willis had decided on a double funeral for his father and brother. The service would be held in the church and then the long, somber parade of funeral vehicles and attendees would drive to the cemetery. The heat had continued unabated, and Wayne was sweating profusely in his dark suit and tie. People walked quickly by as they entered the cool, dim sanctuary. He wasn't a believer in the urge of the killer to be present at the funeral—an idea that had been prevalent in law enforcement for years—but he still observed everyone with care.

The music was beginning and Wayne recognized the old hymn, "How Great Thou Art." He hadn't seen Lucy and wondered if she'd gotten held up at the hospital. He walked into the blessedly cool entryway, took a program from the hand of an elderly gentleman, but didn't go into the nave. Lucy had told him she planned to say a few words during the part of the ceremony after the Mass when the priest asked people if they wished to speak about the deceased. When the priest began the opening prayer, Wayne heard her quick steps and smiled as Lucy took his arm. They walked together into the back of the church and sat down in a pew.

After greeting the assembly, the priest said, "It is through the funeral rite that we commend the dead, Leonard and Chester Willis, to God's merciful love and plead for His forgiveness of their sins." Wayne was surprised to feel a slight lift in the normal despondency with which he greeted church services. Now that he had fulfilled his foster mother's last request by having found and buried his brother's remains, perhaps he was beginning to forgive himself for what he considered his old sins against her. Lucy squeezed his hand.

The priest continued, "The Church confidently proclaims that Jesus Christ, son of God, by his death and resurrection has broken the chains of sin and death." This was followed by a reading from the scripture and a responsorial psalm. The homily was short and consisted of some details about the lives of Leonard and Chester Willis. Then, at the injunction of the priest, people turned to their neighbors and hugged or squeezed hands. It was the part of the Mass that Wayne found most moving.

The priest then intoned the Lord's Prayer, together with the congregation. He offered communion and most people came forward. As people resumed their seats, the organist played, "A Mighty Fortress is Our God." After another prayer, the priest said, "Would those of the Willis family and friends who wish to say a few words about the deceased now come forward?"

Lucy rose, walked quickly to the altar and stood at the podium. "Good afternoon," she greeted the congregation. "I'm Lucy Ingram. It was my privilege to care for Chester Willis at Rosedale General Hospital only a few days before his untimely death. He was upbeat and spoke of his love for his father. He planned to be with him until the end. Tragically his life was cut short," she raised her face and looked directly at Wayne when she said, "by someone intent upon evil." There was a small shocked silence in the church. The sheriff's office had only recently released the information that Chester Willis had met with foul play. "I ask you to remember the members of the sheriff's staff who are investigating the case in your prayers." She paused. "I also cared for Mr. Leonard Willis on the night he died, and I deeply regret that I could not save him. He fought bravely to the end. They were both good men. It was my honor to serve as their physician."

Lucy stepped down, returning to her seat as Brooke Piper came forward. She had obviously been crying and her comments were brief and often disrupted by her tears. "Mr. Willis was my favorite client," she said. "He was a kind and loving man, and I will keep him in my heart." She started to turn away, but then said, "I liked Chester, too. He was very good to his father."

Rick Willis then stepped up to the podium, and Wayne focused on the man as if his gaze could cut like a scalpel through the prevarications and rationalizations of the last remaining member of the Willis family.

"I'm Mr. Leonard Willis' oldest son," Rick said, proudly. "I'm pleased to see so many of his friends here today. He was a good provider, a kind husband, and a loving father. By his hard work, he gave his children a sound foundation in education and ambition. I hope to follow in his footsteps when I marry and have my own family." Rick glanced quickly at Meredith. She was seated in the front of the church, so Wayne could not see her face, but her shoulders rose as she sat up a little straighter. "Although we weren't close in adulthood, my brother was able to make my father laugh toward the end of his life. For that I appreciated him. Our sister, Jillian, passed away before my mother. I pray they're standing together and welcoming my father and Chester into Heaven."

Wayne turned to Lucy, eyes wide at Rick's paltry reminiscence about his brother. "Didn't have much to say about poor Chester, did he?" she whispered. Wayne shook his head.

When no one else volunteered to speak, the organist played "Amazing Grace." The priest gave a final blessing and asked for a moment of silent prayer. After that, the people in the front pews started down the aisle to the back of the church. Rick and Meredith were standing in the entryway shaking hands and accepting condolences.

"Detective, Dr. Ingram," Rick said, acknowledging them as they exited the church. "Thank you for coming." His voice was tight, as if he resented their presence.

Lucy was shaking hands with Meredith when Wayne leaned in close to Rick and said in his quietest and most threatening voice, "I'm going to nail Chester's killer, and if you're the one who took his life, I'll see to it that you aren't free to enjoy any of your father's money."

Rick turned away, but not before Wayne saw his cheeks flush red with anger.

Chapter Twenty-Two

Dr. Lucy Ingram

A FTER THE FUNERAL, Lucy begged off going with Wayne to the cemetery. The hospital had called to say there had been a car accident involving multiple victims. The driver of the vehicle that caused the accident came across the dividing line and crashed right into oncoming traffic. She could tell from the stress in Dr. Alexander's voice when he called that he was over his head.

When Lucy entered the emergency department, her nurse, Channing Soldan, quickly told her about the auto accident victims. The driver had to be extracted from the vehicle by the Jaws of Life and his left foot was in tatters. It would have to be partially amputated.

Several hours later, having admitted three of the casualties to the hospital and stabilized two others, Lucy had time for a short break. She went up to the top floor to write her notes. Sitting down in front of her computer in a partly partitioned carrel in the attending's lounge, Lucy took a deep breath, telling herself it was over, for now. She had done the best job possible for her patients, but this one had lawsuit written all over it.

It was always easiest to write detailed notes when the situation was fresh in her mind. A page and a half later, she sat back in her chair to double-check her wording. Over the years, she had learned to print off her notes and read them again, prior to doing a final edit. At that point she did final changes and entered her notes into the electronic medical record. Her documentation had to be especially comprehensive this time, since the driver was unconscious and could not give his permission for the amputation. His wife had done so.

She was halfway through her notes when Lucy recalled the mention of Jillian Willis at the funeral. Jillian was the younger sister in the Willis family who had died some years earlier. Something was nagging at her, both about the sister's death and the family's decisions regarding cremation. The Catholic Church was in general opposed to cremation, yet Chester's body had been cremated. She recalled the crucial timing that saved Chester's body from cremation just long enough for Dr. Estes to discover the tiny injection site. Mr. Willis' body had not been cremated. A bad feeling came over her. Had Jillian been cremated? And if so, why?

She entered Jillian Willis' name into the hospital database, crossing her fingers that the case was in the records at Rosedale General. She got lucky, although the record was brief. "Jillian Willis, age 20, DOD August 18, 2001. Cause of death: Complications of Diabetes. Body transported by ambulance from Mercy Hospital and Medical Center, Chicago, IL to Rosedale General for decisions by family. Family authorized funeral home pick-up. Body transferred morning of August 20, 2001." The signature was that of Dr. Estes.

Wondering if she had time to call the Rosedale Funeral Parlor to find out if Jillian had been cremated or to ask Dr. Estes if he remembered the case, Lucy suddenly found herself completely exhausted. She sat back in her chair, too tired to finalize her notes. Lucy could enter her case documentation remotely and would do so, once she was home and had a cup of coffee.

THE FOLLOWING DAY was, as ER shifts go, fairly unremarkable, and Lucy was able to talk with Dr. Estes about Jillian Willis. Although almost thirteen years had passed since Jillian's death, Dr. Estes was able to take a quick look at the record and remember seeing her body when it arrived at the hospital. She had already been dead more than thirty-six hours by then, and his cursory inspection revealed no indications of violence. He knew the pathologist at Mercy in Chicago and trusted him. The family had refused an autopsy. It was totally routine and he had signed the paperwork to transfer her to the funeral home.

Dr. Estes agreed to come upstairs to discuss the matter. They met at Lucy's computer station. When he looked up after reading the record from Lucy's computer screen, Dr. Estes appeared very tired. "I hope to God you aren't going to tell me you want to exhume the body to see if this one was killed too," he said in frustration. "It's too late to see tiny needle marks, you know."

"No. It's probably nothing. I'm just getting paranoid about the Willis family," she said. "I'll call the funeral parlor though, just to see what was done."

"I certainly hope she *was* cremated, Dr. Ingram." Dr. Estes' tone was exasperated. "I have enough to do without chasing down murderers in Rosedale. That's supposed to be the job of the sheriff's office, and it seems to me you've been doing their job lately. And you're not making my job any easier." He stood up and stalked out of the room, looking a little like a tall gray heron.

A phone call to the funeral home confirmed that Jillian had been cremated. No one who still worked at the funeral home had been employed there in 2001. It was a dead end. If Rick Willis killed his sister and then his brother, the crime would be considered especially heinous. Murdering both siblings to increase his share of the estate would most certainly get him death by lethal injection. A stray thought entered Lucy's brain and she dialed Wayne.

"Wayne? I found out Jillian Willis was cremated. We aren't going to find anything more there. I'm probably way out in left field here, but if Rick Willis killed his sister and then his brother to increase his share of the estate, it crossed my mind that Brooke Piper might very well be in danger. Is she still considered a suspect?"

There was a fairly long pause. "Are you there?" Lucy asked.

"Yes." His voice was tense. "She's still a suspect. I'd like to have her take a lie detector test. Once that's done, if she passes, I'll talk to Ben about having George tail her. I have a feeling we're pretty close to making an arrest. Once we have Rick in lock-up, she'll be safe."

"Dr. Estes accused me of doing the job of the sheriff's office," she said, trying to keep her voice amused and light.

"He might be right," Wayne said dourly. "I should have caught this one." He was quiet. "Should I stop by around dinnertime tonight?"

"Yes, please do. I have a little something for you."

"Sounds intriguing. I'll bring pizza."

On the way home, Lucy stopped at the hardware store. "I need another one of these," she said, handing her house key to the older gentleman at the counter.

AFTER FINISHING OFF the pizza from their favorite place, Lucy and Wayne settled on the couch. Lucy brought the bottle of wine in from the kitchen, setting it on the coffee table.

"Were you going to give me something?" Wayne asked, with a hint of a smile.

"Yes. I'll go get it." She left the room and returned. "Hold out your hand," she said and grinned at Wayne.

He looked puzzled, but did so and Lucy dropped the key into his warm open palm.

"What's this?"

"I think we've reached the stage where it's appropriate that you have my house key," she said, grinning.

"Thank you." Wayne voice was serious. "What stage do you think we've reached, by the way?"

"The not-quite-but-almost living together stage," she answered and his eyes widened. A little crooked grin flashed across his face.

Chapter Twenty-Three

—

Sheriff Ben Bradley

B EN USHERED THE Willis' family attorney into his office.
"Thanks for coming in, Shane," he said, noting that
the man was more casually dressed today than he had been
when they met before. He was wearing khakis and a light-blue
collared shirt with the sleeves rolled.

"Not a problem, Sheriff. I'm taking a day off to run some
errands—dental appointment, things like that."

Ben gestured to the chair in front of his desk. "Please, call
me Ben. And have a seat. How did the reading go?" Shane
Connor sat down and Ben pulled his office door shut and went
to his own chair. He pulled out a legal pad and pen from his
top drawer and looked at Shane expectantly. "Any reactions
that surprised you?"

The attorney squinted, looking up for a moment. He seemed
to be considering his answer. "Well, let me tell you about
the bequests first, okay?" Ben nodded and Shane continued,
"The house and contents went to Rick, with the exception of
Corinne Willis' jewelry." He raised his eyebrows, giving Ben a

meaningful look. "All the jewelry went to Brooke Piper. There were some small bequests—ten thousand to the housekeeper, some amounts to various charities and such. The remainder was split fifty/fifty between Brooke and Rick."

Ten thousand is a small bequest? Ben thought as he wrote down what Shane had told him so far. "What was the total value of Leonard Willis' estate?"

"Just over three million." Shane shook his head. "I'd say half of that constitutes quite a motive."

"It does if you're aware of it," Ben answered thoughtfully. "What changes did Leonard make to his will after Chester's death?"

"In the original will, the house and its contents would have gone to Chester, except for the cars and some of the artwork. That went to Rick." He smiled. "Chester never cared much about the trappings of wealth, not like Rick. But Leonard wanted Chester to have a nice home, and Rick had his condo already. As I said, the jewelry went to Brooke." He paused. "In that version, Leonard's major assets would have been divided three ways between Chester and Rick, with Brooke receiving just the jewelry.

In the will he wrote after Chester's death, the division was half and half between Rick and Brooke, after Rick got the house and contents other than jewelry."

"So both Brooke and Rick gained a substantial amount because of Chester's death. Who was there for the reading, besides Brooke and Rick?"

"Meredith Flynn and the housekeeper, Marina Hernandez. Four people."

Now they were getting to the body language of the people in the room. Ben put his pen down and focused on Shane. "How would you characterize Rick's reaction to the news that Brooke Piper was getting so much of the estate?"

"He was angry. Meredith kept squeezing his hand. He started to say something—sounded like 'gold digger'—and she actually bent one of Rick's fingers back a little bit. It was kind of funny. She never said a word, and her face was expressionless." He paused. "No, I almost forgot; she frowned after I read that the jewelry went to Brooke."

"Rick had probably promised her some of the jewelry," Ben mused. "What about Brooke?"

"That girl sat as far from Rick as possible and didn't look at him once as far as I could tell. She seemed pleased with what she heard. Not thrilled, just ... pleased. She gave one little nod when I told her about the jewelry, like she had been hoping for or expecting that."

"You're very observant. Did you notice anything else?"

"Marina was quiet, but she was so busy watching the other three that she didn't hear her bequest. Mr. Connor had to repeat it."

"Watching them?" Ben asked.

"Like a hawk."

WAYNE WALKED INTO Ben's office about an hour after Shane Connor left. "Boss, we need to compare notes," he said.

Ben looked up from Mae's report, which he was rereading. "You're right. Want to get out of here and get some lunch?"

"If we can go in your truck," Wayne said. "It's a furnace out there."

Ben grabbed his keys and the legal pad with his notes from his meeting with Shane Connor. He paused, looking at his chief detective. "Did you read Mae's report that I forwarded to you?"

Wayne Nichols nodded his graying head. "I did, but you may as well bring it. I've got a lot of info about Rick and Brooke, but your fiancée came up with some interesting stuff." His hazel eyes twinkled. "I believe she and Dory were working on getting more information on Brooke today." He lowered his voice. "What do you think of our new office manager?"

Ben gave him a look. "C'mon. I think we can discuss that

over lunch. And I want to show you my remote start." He aimed his key fob out the window toward his truck and hit the button for the automatic start, giving Wayne a smile. "The AC's already crankin.'"

They walked out past Dory's old desk, now occupied by the redoubtable Sophie Coffin. She had short, iron-gray hair permed into submission and glasses on a chain around her neck. Her glance was steely. "We're going to a lunch meeting, Mrs. Coffin. Is there anything you need?" Ben asked.

"No, Sheriff, I'll call Ms. Clarkson if I have any questions." The phone rang and she answered it, so the two men made their escape.

The interior of Ben's truck was blessedly cool after the steamy parking lot. "You okay with Sonic? The car hop will bring the food out and we can just eat in the car."

Wayne nodded, his face already damp with sweat from the short walk. "Sounds good. Any regrets about the regime change?"

Ben buckled his seatbelt and put the big truck in gear. He laughed. "You mean trading Dory for Sophie Coffin?"

"I didn't know she had a first name," Wayne said, his tone dry. "She introduced herself to me as Mrs. Coffin."

"Well, we need to give her a chance, Wayne. And Dory was ready for a new challenge, so we were getting someone else in that seat no matter what."

"I'll give her a chance," the big man muttered, "but she's scary."

Chapter Twenty-Four

—

Mae December

AFTER MAE SPOKE to Dory the previous night about teaming up to dig into Brooke Piper's background, she had gone to bed frustrated. So far, she had nothing on Brooke and no way that she could think of to find out anything. This morning she had woken up with an idea and called her neighbor Lucy Ingram.

"Hi, Mae," Lucy cleared her throat. "How are you?"

"I'm fine. Hope I'm not calling too early."

"No, I'm awake. Just sleepy. What can I do for you?"

"Well, I'm helping Ben on the Chester Willis case. Dory and I are looking into Brooke Piper's background—we're supposed to meet up in a few hours, but I don't have any connections in the medical community—"

Lucy laughed. "Yes, you do. And you called the right one. I don't know Brooke personally, but we have a mutual friend. A nurse I work with was in nursing school with her. If you and Dory want to come to the hospital, I'll get you some time with her."

"Thank you, Lucy. That would be great!"

"Just give me a couple hours, and text me when you're coming. Mornings are usually quiet in the ER, but you never know. It's Friday the thirteenth."

Mae sent Dory a quick text, then made a phone call to Ray Fenton, her one and only employee. She had hired him as a favor to Dory, who had taken the teen under her wing. Dory met Ray during a murder investigation last winter that Mae had also been involved in. The young man had lost his job after reporting his suspicions of animal cruelty and neglect to the sheriff's office. Mae's work was hampered by a broken wrist at the time, and Ray had been a big help. She had kept him on after her wrist healed, even though she didn't always have a lot of work for him. He was small for his age, and quiet, but great with the dogs. He was also great with kids, specifically Matthew, which was the reason for today's call.

"Hi, Miss Mae," he answered on the second ring. Fortunately his voice had finished changing. Now that he was sixteen, it had settled into a lower register and no longer squeaked.

"Hello, Ray. I know you're not scheduled to work today, but I was wondering if you might be available for a few hours of babysitting. Matthew and his new puppy, Cupcake, are here, and I need to get out and take care of some things. I'll pay your normal hourly rate plus a bonus."

"You don't have to pay me extra. I like Matthew; he's real good for me."

"Well, he and Cupcake can be a handful, so I need to do it for my own conscience's sake," Mae said with a laugh. "Can you be here in an hour?"

He assured her that he could.

DORY HAD AGREED to meet Mae at BonCup, a new coffee shop close to the hospital. She waved from a corner booth when Mae walked in, and Mae hurried over to embrace one of her mother's closest friends.

"You look great, Miss Dory." It was true. Dory looked stylish as ever in a teal green, sleeveless dress and black sandals; her gold jewelry glowed against her smooth, coffee colored complexion.

"You too, child, you too. How's your mama?"

"Mama's fine. She's after me about picking out my wedding dress, but I've been busy. Tammy had her baby, I've been helping Ben with this case, Matthew got a new puppy and he's been with us a lot …" she trailed off. "Anyway, I want to lose a few more pounds before I go dress shopping."

Dory shook her head. "Honey, trust me, you don't need to lose another pound. Some of the good stuff's gonna start to go away too. Speaking of which, I ordered you the BonCup du jour. It's a vanilla latte with a chocolate-chunk espresso muffin. And fruit. I'm having the same thing."

After the two women caught up over their coffee and treats, Mae climbed into Dory's red T-bird, rather than drive two cars to the hospital. Mae texted Lucy that they would be arriving soon. Lucy replied "okay," and five minutes later Dory pulled into a parking spot near the ER door. There they found Lucy, who greeted them with a smile.

"Channing's going on break soon. She'll meet you in the cafeteria in about ten minutes. You can't miss her—her hair's got aqua streaks today."

"Thank you kindly for setting this up, Dr. Ingram," Dory said.

"You're welcome. And as I've asked you before, please call me Lucy."

Dory nodded. "All right, Lucy. You keepin' that man of yours in line?"

"I'm trying, Dory, I'm trying. I better get back to work. See you." She was gone in a flash of her white coat, and Mae and Dory wound around through the maze of hallways and elevators until they reached the cafeteria. Shortly after they found an empty table, a young woman wearing aqua scrubs came in and glanced their way. Her hair was short and blonde with bold aqua streaks.

"Are you Channing?" Mae asked as the woman approached.

"Yes, Channing Soldan. You must be Mae and Dory. I'm just going to grab a coke and a salad and then we can talk. Do you want anything to eat or drink?"

After they reassured Channing that they were stuffed and not at all thirsty, she was gone, returning quickly with her salad, coke can, and glass of ice. She tore open the dressing packet and poured it over her salad. "So Dr. Ingram said you had questions about Brooke Piper?" Channing looked at Mae before spearing a cherry tomato with her fork. "She's not in any trouble, I hope."

Twenty minutes later, they were back in Dory's car with a lot more information about Brooke Piper. Dory started the T-bird, put the windows down and fanned herself. "Do you want to type all that up for Ben, or shall I do it?" she asked.

Mae reached for her seatbelt, but it was too hot to hold. She gathered her hair in her hand, lifting it off her neck. "After you take me back to my car, you could follow me to the house and we could do it together, if you want." She knew Dory would love to see Ray and Matthew. And Cupcake would be the icing on the … well, on the cupcake.

Dory's bright smile flashed. "I'd love to come over, and we can email a report to Ben later, but maybe you should call right now and give him the highlights?"

Mae nodded and pulled her phone out of her purse.

"And I wouldn't say no to a cold glass of anything you've got handy," Dory added.

"Hi, babe. What'd you learn?" Ben answered his phone on the first ring.

"Brooke's friend told us that she has a juvenile record for boosting a car with a boyfriend named Tyler in Johnson City, where she grew up. Brooke says she was innocent. Anyway, she was under eighteen and he wasn't, so she got probation and the record was sealed, or maybe expunged. Sounds like her boyfriend went to jail. Then as soon as she finished high school, Brooke's parents kicked her out and she's been on her own ever since."

There was a short silence from Ben. "Did the friend know anything about Brooke's relationship with Leonard, or about his will?"

"She said Brooke told her about the necklace. Leonard was her most generous client, apparently. Hang on," Mae felt a tap on her hand. "What, Dory?"

"Tell him what she said about Chester."

"Right. Brooke was hoping that Chester was going to ask her out. Sounds like she thought he was cute."

"Thanks, Mae. Tell Dory thanks too; that could be very helpful information."

"You're welcome, sweetie," Mae said. Out of the corner of her eye she caught Dory making a face. "I mean, you're welcome, *Sheriff.*"

Ben laughed. "Oh, by all means, let's keep things professional. I expect a full report ASAP, Miss December. Sheriff Bradley, over and out."

Chapter Twenty-Five

Dr. Lucy Ingram

Tʜᴇ ᴘʜᴏɴᴇ ʀᴀɴɢ at 5:30 Saturday morning and Lucy came out of a deep sleep to reach for it, but it was Wayne's cell ringing, not hers. She lay quietly, listening to him speak to the person on the other end.

"Right, okay. I'll meet you in about an hour at the Donut Den."

"Who was that?" Lucy asked when he finished the call.

"It was Ben. He's really frustrated with the Willis case and wants to review it point by point. We've decided to bring Brooke Piper in this morning for a lie detector test, and he wants to go over the questions I'm going to ask her. Go back to sleep if you can. Sorry about disturbing you."

"No problem. I thought it was the hospital calling. Do you want some coffee?"

"Yes, can you make a pot while I take a shower?" Wayne asked.

"Sure can," she said and walked to the kitchen.

After he showered, they sat at her kitchen table with coffee mugs. Something about the early morning light made Lucy feel nostalgic, remembering her childhood years when her mother was alive and well. Sharing her feelings with Wayne a few days earlier had given her some relief. It had been solely her burden to bear for so many years. Her sister had long since retreated into the haze of her numerous addictions. It frightened Lucy that her sister might die from what she was taking, just like her mother had.

"Wayne, do you remember the other night when I mentioned my mother's murder?"

"Of course," he said, looking at her intently.

"If you have a little time, I wanted to tell you more about it. Not that I want you to take this on. I don't. Don't worry that this is going to be another Chester Willis investigation. I just want to get it off my chest. Can you stay for a little longer?"

"I'm listening," he said, his voice deep and his posture attentive.

"I'm used to presenting patient cases in the medical world. Do you mind if I tell you about it in that way? If I think about my mom as a patient, it seems to help keep my emotions in check." Wayne nodded. Lucy took a deep breath and began.

"My mother, Mrs. Rachel Sherman, was a Caucasian female. She was forty-three years old at the time of her death. Her chief complaint was prescription pain medication overuse. The patient's problems with addiction began shortly after her second marriage to Dr. Richard Sherman." Wayne stiffened in his chair at the mention of Richard Sherman, and she gave him an enquiring glance.

"So Dr. Sherman's your stepfather?" Lucy nodded and Wayne frowned, looking down at the kitchen table. "I remember hearing about the Sherman case. If he wasn't your dad, why did you and your sister live with him after your mother's death?" Wayne's hazel eyes were piercing when he looked back up, and Lucy met them unflinchingly.

"My dad died when I was little. I barely remember him. We

had no one else to live with after Mom died but it was … pretty bad."

"I'm sorry I interrupted you," Wayne said quietly.

Lucy cleared her throat and continued, "Rachel's medical and surgical history was unremarkable up to that time. She had two uncomplicated pregnancies, resulting in normal vaginal deliveries. She had been seen in the emergency department of Memphis General on five occasions in the months leading up to her death—all with symptoms of overdose. On those occasions, the patient admitted to using OxyContin, Vicodin, and Percocet. She told the physicians she had recently increased the dosage she was taking. She also told them she had used pain killers for over three years and as a result had experienced increased urgency for more drugs. She reported needing the drugs to 'feel normal.' On the day she died, she was found unconscious on the floor of the bathroom by her ten-year-old daughter, Lucy Ingram." She stopped, looking at Wayne in mute appeal.

"I'm so sorry, Lucy." He patted her hand. They were both quiet for a few moments before Wayne said, "I'm confused. Tell me why you believe it was murder. I assume her death was classified as accidental overdose or suicide."

Lucy took a deep breath, trying to focus on the facts she knew. "You're right. Her death was listed as an overdose. However, an overdose is normally caused by a patient either taking too much of a medication or injecting too much of the drug into his or her body. In her case, she wasn't taking the drugs herself; she was being injected by her husband, Dr. Sherman."

Lucy's jaw was tight as she looked down at the table. She took a sip of her coffee. It had grown cold and the bitter smell nauseated her. "Her cause of death was listed as a lethal dose of the painkiller Demerol, given by injection."

Wayne seemed to be deep in thought. Lucy could tell he was caught up in the story.

"But Demerol wasn't among the drugs she admitted to taking, was it?" he asked.

"No, it wasn't."

"And was her husband indicted?"

"There was no indictment at the time, but I got the case reopened fifteen years ago and her body was exhumed. They did indict him then, but he was acquitted. His lawyers maintained she'd been taking the Demerol voluntarily, and it was present in her hair. The length of the hair strands indicated that the drug had been taken for several months at least. I've never been convinced that she took the drug voluntarily."

Wayne frowned. "Clearly Dr. Sherman had the means to kill her. As a doctor he had access to both drugs and syringes. He also had opportunity, since they were living together. What do you think Sherman's motive was?"

"There were rumors that Dr. Sherman was having an affair with a nurse from the OR and didn't want to divorce my mom for the other woman because it would be so expensive. Shortly before she died, Mother told one of her friends that she feared for her life."

"That piece of crap belongs in prison." Wayne's low, fierce voice was almost a growl. "But he's been acquitted. They can't try him again—it'd be double jeopardy. He got away with it." He shook his head and stood up. "Is he still in practice?"

"No," Lucy said with satisfaction. "He lost his license shortly after the trial. They apparently found quite a few problems with prescriptions he'd written. At least he's unable to practice medicine in Tennessee anymore. I guess that's something."

Wayne put his hand under her chin and tilted her face up. He kissed her mouth with more tenderness than usual. She clung to him for a minute, feeling his strength.

"I have to go, Lucy. Ben's waiting for me, I'm so sorry."

"It's okay. I know you need to go meet Ben. I keep thinking I should be over this, but I loved my mother very much, and I know in my heart that he killed her. I was so young, but I knew even then. Thank you for believing me."

"Of course I believe you," Wayne said. "Both the police and the legal system failed you. My gut tells me that there might have been a cover-up of some of the evidence, possibly by one of Dr. Sherman's colleagues. You know how doctors stick together. I can't tell you how sorry I am about this." He shook his head, grabbed his phone and keys from her kitchen counter, and walked out of the house.

Lucy watched Wayne back out of the driveway. She stood staring at her front yard for a while, thinking about her motives in dating Wayne. By choosing a detective as a boyfriend, was she still trying to prove to the world that her mother was murdered? The similarities of the Chester Willis case to her mother's struck her. Both people were killed by injection. In both instances, she had to try to convince the police that a murder had even occurred.

At least I convinced Wayne about Chester and my mother, she thought, and felt a little better.

Chapter Twenty-Six

—

Chief Detective Wayne Nichols

FEELING TROUBLED ABOUT Lucy's mother's murder and the escape of Dr. Sherman from justice, Wayne thought again about the similarities of Lucy's life to his own. Wayne's little brother had been killed decades ago. He knew his foster mother's husband had done it. Yet he had failed to nail the bastard, just as Lucy had failed to convict Dr. Sherman. As a result of her mother's killing, Lucy had become a physician who was vigilant about watching for murderous cover-ups. Wayne had a similar motive for becoming a detective—a hatred for murder and a determination to get the perpetrators. Both of them were driven by demons from their pasts.

There was one big difference, though: the gun that would convict Aarne Outinen of Wayne's brother's murder was in a box on a shelf in his closet. Despite years of thinking about it, Wayne had never figured out how to give the evidence to the police without self-incrimination. *Before my life is over, I swear I'll find a way.*

Looking through the windshield of his truck from the

parking lot at Donut Den, Wayne could see Ben at their usual table with coffee. He was drumming his fingers, obviously impatient to get started. When he saw Wayne walking up, he stopped drumming, stood and came to the door. Holding it open, he said, "Thought you were going to be here a half hour ago. What the hell, Wayne? It's been a week already since Dr. Estes declared Chester Willis' death a murder. I'm surprised you don't feel a little more urgency about this." He ran his fingers through his hair. The sheriff was on edge.

"Sorry, man."

"Well, you're here now anyway. Let's sit down and get started." Ben still sounded disgruntled, but Wayne did not explain what had kept him. Lucy's story was confidential.

After they were seated and Ben gulped down the rest of what was probably his third cup of coffee, he said, "I don't think I mentioned that Rob and I interviewed Brooke Piper the day before yesterday."

"Did you get anything?"

"Not much. She told me the same story she gave us at the Willis house the day we told Mr. Willis that Chester had been killed. She was there July fourth for dinner. She admitted to having money troubles, but not insurmountable ones. She owes the university money and is a month behind in her rent. Her credit cards will be canceled soon if she doesn't pay. She owes one back payment on her car. Sounded to me like the situation a lot of young people get themselves into. I asked her if she was willing to take a lie detector test. She said she was and we set it up."

"Should be interesting," Wayne said, distractedly.

"So, George is bringing Brooke Piper in this morning for the lie detector test. I'd like to get her off the radar if she didn't do it, so we can concentrate on Rick Willis. What do you think we should ask her?"

Wayne took a deep breath, tearing his mind away from his personal demons and Lucy's tragic story. "I think the key is exactly what Brooke knew about the will before Chester died. The girl's got money troubles, but she only had a motive to kill Chester if she knew she was going to get a share of the estate and that her share would increase if Chester was out of the picture. Otherwise his death didn't benefit Brooke."

"Of course," Ben said. "That's exactly right. If she knew, she's right in the center of the frame. If she didn't know her share would increase—then despite the nursing training that would have enabled her to give Chester the insulin—she's out." Ben tapped his fingers on the scarred old table.

"Let's go to the office and meet with the technician who's going to administer the lie detector test."

"Didn't Rob get certified to give lie detector tests?" Wayne asked.

"He did, but I didn't want some defense attorney to be able to say we were biased either for or against Brooke Piper. Mae learned that Brooke got into trouble for auto theft when she was seventeen with a boy named Tyler in Johnson City. I put Rob to work on finding out what he could."

"So the records would be sealed, then, right?"

Ben nodded. "Brooke was a juvenile, but this Tyler guy was over eighteen and did time for it, so Rob should be able to track down some details. If he gets here in time, I'll send him into the room with you and the polygraph examiner. His name's Jim Warwick, on loan to us from Captain Paula in Nashville."

DRIVING INTO THE sheriff's office parking lot behind Ben's truck, Wayne saw George escorting Brooke inside. She was wearing white jeans and a short-sleeved blue shirt. George was wearing his uniform, and although it was only 8:30 in the morning, he actually looked awake.

"Good morning, Ms. Coffin," Ben said to the new office manager as Wayne followed his boss through the door.

"It's Missus," she said, giving him a frosty glance.

"Sorry, Mrs. Coffin. Where did you put Mr. Warwick?"

"He's in the conference room setting up. George is putting Miss Piper in a cell."

"In a cell? Good Lord." Ben closed his eyes briefly before walking to the end of the hall. "George," he called. "Get out here."

George Phelps ambled into the reception area a few moments later and gave them all a smile. No one smiled back.

"Why the hell would you put Brooke Piper in a cell, George? You wear me out sometimes …" Ben trailed off, shaking his head in frustration.

"She's a suspect, isn't she? Where was I supposed to put her?"

Ben sighed. "Just bring her back out here. Mrs. Coffin, would you get Miss Piper some coffee or whatever she would like to drink and keep an eye on her until we're ready to begin?"

"Certainly, Sheriff." Mrs. Coffin gave a little sniff.

"And George, you will apologize to Miss Piper."

"Yes, sir," he said gloomily.

Wayne and Ben were looking through the one-way glass when the polygraph examiner started talking with Brooke. They could hear the questions and her responses clearly through the microphone in the window. Brooke could not see any of them.

"Good morning, Miss Piper," he said. "I'm Mr. Warwick. I've already gone over all your demographic data with Deputy Gomez, so we won't need to confirm all that. At this time I'm going to tell you about the test you're going to take and then we're going to find out what kind of responder you are. Okay with you?" he asked.

"Of course." Brooke nodded, her blonde braid sliding up and down her shoulder.

"A polygraph, popularly referred to as a lie detector, is an instrument that measures and records several physiological indices such as blood pressure, pulse, respiration, and skin conductivity while the subject is asked and answers a series of questions. I understand you've freely and voluntarily agreed to this test. Is that correct?"

"That's right." Her voice was soft.

"Very good. The first part of this test is going to tell me whether you're generally a truthful person." He smiled at Brooke. "I'm going to list several dates on or around your birthdate and ask you which one is yours. What I want you to say is 'no' to all of them, even your actual birthday. I'll look at your responses on the screen and be able to tell which date it is. Ready?"

She nodded again.

"October seventeenth? October thirtieth? December first? November third? January tenth?"

Brooke replied with a quick "no" each time.

"Okay. You're a good responder and the indicator tells me that November third is your birthday, correct?"

"Yes, that's correct."

"Good. I have one other test to check your general truthfulness. It's pretty low tech." He smiled at her, trying to put her at ease. "It's a deck of cards." He pulled out a deck from his briefcase. "We're trying to identify the Queen of Spades. I'm going to show you some cards one by one with their faces turned away from me. I'll ask you if any one of them is the Queen of Spades. Again, I want you to reply 'no' every time."

One by one the examiner held the cards up for Brooke to see. "Is this the Queen of Spades?" he asked after each card, and she replied in the negative. Afterward he said, "Very good. It was the third card, right?" He turned them over and the third card was the queen. "I can tell by this test that you're a very honest person, Miss Piper. Now, Detective Wayne Nichols is going to join us and ask you some questions. I want you to answer his questions fully and completely. Will you do that?"

"Yes," Brooke said. She looked scared, and her voice was almost a whisper.

Wayne entered the room and greeted both Brooke and

Mr. Warwick. He nodded briefly to Ben outside the window and began. "Miss Piper, as you know, we're trying to learn everything we can to solve Chester Willis' murder." He and Ben had discussed doing the interview in a supportive manner, up to a point. "In order to do that, I need you to tell me whether you had any foreknowledge that Mr. Leonard Willis was planning to leave you money in his estate."

"I thought he was leaving me something," Brooke said, shaking her head. "But I really had no idea I would inherit so much. Mr. Willis had already given me a piece of jewelry as a gift, and a tip for each massage, but that was all. I was shocked when I found out how much I would get."

"Would it be accurate to say you're struggling financially?" Wayne asked.

"Yes, it would. Massage therapy doesn't pay all that well in a little town, and I'm trying to go to school also."

"So you needed the money," Wayne gave her a searching look.

Brooke's cheeks flushed. "It's a godsend," she said. "I'm so grateful to Mr. Willis."

The door opened. Rob walked in and took a seat.

"This is Detective Fuller, Miss Piper. He has some questions for you as well." Wayne leaned back in his chair.

"Have you ever stolen anything, Miss Piper?" Rob Fuller got right to the point.

Brooke gave him a challenging stare. "No, why?"

The polygraph technician threw Wayne a quick glance. *Interesting*, Wayne thought.

Rob Fuller tilted his head. "So it really was Tyler Franklin who stole the car, then?"

Red flooded upward from her neckline, blotching her face. "How do you know about that? Those charges were expunged. And like I told everyone at the time, it was Tyler, not me! He said the car belonged to a friend."

Rob smiled at Brooke. With his short, light brown hair,

glasses and smooth cheeks, Rob Fuller looked more like a college freshman than a detective who was almost thirty. He appeared to be harmless, but Wayne knew better.

"Was Leonard Willis aware of your criminal record, Brooke?" Rob spoke quietly.

"I don't know." She sounded like a sulky teenager.

Wayne took over. "Going back in your mind to the night of July fourth, you were invited to have dinner with Mr. Willis and his sons, right?" She nodded. "What time did you leave the Willis household that night?"

"Around ten o'clock."

"At any time that evening, did you give Chester Willis an insulin injection?" He deliberately kept his voice light, like her answer was of no particular importance.

"Give Chester an insulin shot?" Brooke sounded confused. "Of course not. I'm not finished with my nurses training. Mr. Willis told me Chester was a diabetic, but all I know is to give people orange juice if they say they're diabetic and ask for help."

"Did you know that Chester died of an insulin overdose?" Wayne asked, his eyes on Brooke's face.

"I heard that later. It's so sad. Chester was a nice guy."

"Going back to the reading of the will, you said you were surprised by the inheritance?" Wayne paused, looking at her directly.

"I still can't quite believe it."

"Did you discuss the inheritance with anyone who could attest to your reaction about the gift?"

"Well, I called a friend of mine right after Mr. Willis' attorney read his will. I told her I had no idea, that I was stunned …" Brooke's voice trailed off.

"But that was after the fact, you see, Brooke," Wayne's voice was soft. "What we need to know is if you had any inkling *ahead of time* that if Chester died you would get more." Wayne's voice changed at the end of his statement. His body posture was now quietly threatening.

"Are you saying that Chester was murdered for money?" Wayne nodded.

"That's really terrible." Brooke was breathing loudly.

"So, I'm going to ask you again if you knew what Mr. Willis Senior was going to give you before the reading of the will or that if Chester died, you would get more."

"I already told you I thought Mr. Willis might leave me something." Brooke paused and cleared her throat. "I overheard something Meredith said to Rick that made me wonder, but I didn't know anything for a fact. When I was in the lawyer's office that day, I felt so alone and vulnerable. I didn't even know why I was there. I was just hoping that Mr. Willis would have said something about the necklace he gave me because I knew Rick Willis thought I stole it. And I didn't."

She paused and then continued, "I told Mr. Connor's secretary, Lorene, I hated even going inside the lawyer's office. I asked her if I had to be there. I told her about the necklace and I asked if Mr. Connor could just call me later and let me know if I was going to get it back."

"Brooke, did you kill Chester Willis?" Rob asked, his voice very soft. "Was it an accident? If you gave Chester too much insulin by accident, you need to tell us."

"I never gave Chester a shot," Brooke said. "And I wouldn't kill anyone."

Wayne exhaled slowly. He prided himself on being able to read people. He didn't even need the lie detector test. The woman was innocent.

"I think we're done here. C'mon Rob." The two men stood and left the room.

After completing some post-test paperwork and reclaiming her necklace, Brooke Piper left the office. Wayne walked back in to see Jim Warwick. "I take it she passed?" he said.

"In all my years of administering this test, I've seldom come across a more consistent subject than Brooke Piper. Other than the one anomaly—her reaction when Detective Fuller asked her about her juvie record and which she explained later—there were no hesitations, nothing from her physiological responses that contradicted her statements. I'll be sending the sheriff my written report, but I think you need to do some more detective work to get your killer. Brooke Piper didn't give Chester Willis that injection."

"Afraid you're right," Wayne said, grimly. He took a deep breath, lowered his shoulders and walked out to join Ben. They had work to do.

Chapter Twenty-Seven

Sheriff Ben Bradley

Ben TRIED TO smile at his new office manager. He wasn't sure if he'd quite managed to look sincere. "Mrs. Coffin, I need you to call Rick Willis and tell him to come in for a meeting. Do you have his number?"

The woman looked up at him with no trace of a smile. "Of course, Sheriff. Ms. Clarkson gave me all the pertinent information for the case when I came on board. When would you like Mr. Willis to be here?"

She sure is efficient. No trace of a personality, though. "At his earliest convenience please." Ben tried another smile he hoped was more friendly, trying to win her over.

She turned away, looking down at an open folder on her desk and picking up the phone. Ben wandered back to his office feeling dissatisfied and missing Dory's sass, especially since the investigation had no clear direction. He sat down at his desk and checked his emails. After a few minutes, he heard a throat-clearing noise and looked up. Sophie Coffin stood in his office doorway.

"Mr. Willis will be here at one thirty this afternoon," she announced. *Still no smile.*

"Thank you, Mrs. Coffin."

She gave a crisp nod, spun on her heel and was gone. Ben called Dory's cellphone and she answered on the third ring.

"Hello, boss, what's up?"

"Are you going to be gracing us with your presence today, Investigator Clarkson?"

Dory laughed. "Right after my hair appointment I will. Do you have an assignment for me?"

Ben sighed. A hair appointment was not much of an excuse for missing work. "Not really, but I want to pick your brain about a few things. Will you meet me for lunch somewhere in half an hour?"

There was a brief pause and Ben heard another woman's voice in the background. "I need forty minutes and then I'll meet you at the Rosedale Deli," Dory said. "Going under the dryer now. 'Bye."

Ben hung up, shaking his head at the continuing challenge that was Miss Dory Clarkson.

The office had been very quiet after Brooke and Jim Warwick left. Ben told Wayne that Rick Willis would be there at 1:30, and he wanted Rob Fuller and Wayne to do the interview while he observed. "You'll take the lead, right, Wayne?" The big detective had assured him that he would do just that.

Everyone else was working quietly at their desks, and Ben was happy to get out of the office. He hit the remote start button and let his truck run for a few minutes to cool off. He could see the sign at the Rosedale Bank and Trust from the office window—not yet noon and already 99 degrees. Ben climbed in his truck and made the short drive to the restaurant, where he was lucky enough to snag a parking spot in the shade.

When he walked in, Dory waved at him from a booth toward the back of the deli and Ben made his way between the crowded tables, smiling and greeting people he recognized along the way.

"Lookin' good, boss-man," his former office manager, now investigator, greeted him with a grin.

"You too, Dory." As usual, Dory Clarkson wore a stylish ensemble and looked much younger than her actual age, which Ben suspected was around seventy. Her freshly coiffed hair was a little shorter, and she seemed unaffected by the torrid heat and humidity of the July weather in Tennessee. Ben sat down and quickly scanned the menu. Dory ordered the special and sweet tea.

"I'll have the same," Ben told the waitress. As soon as she was gone, he gave Dory a serious look. "You and Mae work well together, don't you?"

"We sure do. She's good at getting people to talk—almost like they don't realize she's getting information out of them. And if they start to clam up, I change the subject a little, or tell them something about myself to get 'em going. Before they realize it, they've told us everything."

"I haven't said anything to her yet, but I'm thinking about offering her a paid position at the office," he said. Dory shook her head. "What, not a good idea?"

"It's not a bad idea, just bad timing from a political standpoint." She waggled her eyebrows.

The waitress set their plates in front of them, along with tall glasses of sweet iced tea. "Do y'all need anything else right now?" she asked.

"No, honey, we're fine," Dory said, and she left them alone once more.

"So you think I should wait until after the election, right?"

"Um-hum." Dory took a bite of her turkey avocado sandwich and a swig of tea. "I do. That Ramsey Tremaine would just go to town on you if your fiancée was on the payroll. What would Mae's job title be, anyway?"

"Community Liaison for Special Projects has a nice ring to it."

His investigator gave an approving nod. "It sure does. In

the meantime, you should probably put her in charge of your campaign. Of course that's an unpaid position ...." She winked.

"You're right as usual, Dory." Ben smiled. "I'll ask her to do that, but not until after we get this murder solved."

They discussed the case while finishing their food, then Ben paid the bill and went back to the office in his truck. Dory followed him with the top down on her red T-bird, wearing her movie star shades.

ONCE BACK AT the office, Ben took his position on the outside of the one-way glass of the interrogation room. Dory, Cam Gomez, and George Phelps all came in to observe as well. He looked over his shoulder at his staff. "I want all of you to pay close attention during this interview," he told them. "Rick Willis is our primary suspect now and we need to get something on him. Money was probably the motive for Chester's killing, but maybe there's something more. We'll go to the conference room as soon as our detectives finish questioning him. We'll all compare notes, and I'm going to want your impressions and ideas, okay?"

Serious nods from all of them followed, and Ben turned his gaze back to the interrogation room. Rob and Wayne were seated on one side of the table with their backs to the window. The door opened and Mrs. Coffin escorted Rick Willis inside. Rob Fuller reached over and flipped the switch for the speaker, enabling them all to hear what was said.

"Thank you for coming in, Mr. Willis," Rob began, speaking in his quiet, pleasant voice. "Is it all right if we call you Rick?"

"That's fine."

"All right then, Rick. We're trying to get a feel for what your brother was like as a person, so we have some questions about your childhood memories of him." At a glare from Rick, Rob Fuller stopped talking.

"What possible relevance could my childhood memories of

Chester have to with his murder?" Rick asked, frowning and shaking his head.

"The character of a murder victim can hold clues—clues that can lead us to his killer." Wayne Nichols' baritone rumbled through the speaker. "And character is formed in childhood."

Rick turned his scowl on Wayne. "You want to know about Chester's character? I'll tell you all about him. He was a tattletale, always trying to make himself look good by making me look bad. My dad never saw through Chester; he was the favorite, but I knew what a manipulative little sneak he was!"

The two detectives exchanged a glance. "So you felt like your dad was unfair to you and favored Chester?" Wayne asked in the deceptively mild tone Ben had heard him use to good effect many times before.

Rick began to turn a mottled red under his tan. "I don't *feel* that he was unfair, I *know* he was. Chester always got what he wanted without working for it." He paused, taking a deep breath through his nose.

"It's interesting to me that everyone we talked to liked Chester but you, his own brother. It seems to me you didn't particularly care for him," Wayne mused. "Even when you spoke at the funeral you could barely muster up a good word about him. We're thinking he was killed for his share of the estate, but maybe there was something else. Was there another reason you killed him, Rick?"

Rick Willis recoiled, leaning back in his chair as though he'd been slapped. "Chester died before my dad," he said. "So how could he have been killed for the estate? And I may not have always liked him, but he was family. I don't care for your insinuations, and I'm calling my lawyer."

"That's certainly your prerogative, Rick." Rob said, smoothly. "But we're just having a conversation here. No one's accusing you of anything. If you bring your lawyer into this, it doesn't look good."

Rick stood up abruptly. "I don't care how it looks. If we're done here, I'm going. If you want to ask me anything else I'm calling my lawyer."

"Could you excuse us for a minute, please?" Wayne asked. Rick gave a short nod and Wayne and Rob stood and left the room. Rob closed the door behind them, looking over his shoulder at the one-way window as he did so. Ben got up and walked around to meet them outside the door.

"What was your reaction?"

"It's not a crime to dislike your brother," Ben told his chief detective. "We may need to let him go and keep digging. I certainly don't have enough to hold him right now. What do you think?"

"I'm pretty sure he's our killer," Wayne answered slowly. "What about you, Rob?"

"I don't see it. We've got nothing but circumstantial evidence," the younger detective replied. "I've got a little brother who's annoying as hell, but I certainly wouldn't kill him over it. The money seems like a strong motive, but we need more than that."

Ben's mind was made up. "Tell him we're through for today please, Detective Fuller. We'll need to bring him back again, and I'm sure he'll lawyer up then. Let's hope we can find some solid evidence in the meantime. After Rick leaves, both of you need to come to the conference room so we can all put our heads together on this."

Chapter Twenty-Eight

—

Mae December

Mae's conversation with Matthew's mother Katie earlier in the day had been difficult enough. Explaining the upshot of their talk to Ben was proving to be even more of a challenge. Ben had come home early, in a bad mood, saying they were nowhere on the investigation. He had hoped to get there in time to see Matthew before Katie picked him up, but Ben had missed his son by fifteen minutes. Cupcake, however, was still in residence at the old farm house on Little Chapel Road.

"So explain this to me again, Mae. We all agreed that Cupcake would go back and forth with Matty, between our house and Katie's, right?"

She was beginning to lose patience, and Ben had apparently arrived home without any. "I know that's what we agreed to. The situation has changed and Cupcake will be here fulltime."

"Because Katie's new boyfriend has allergies, we now have four dogs?"

Mae glared at her fiancé. "In case you've forgotten, we had

four dogs until Thoreau died. I think if your five-year-old son can be a good sport about this then you can too. This isn't working out the way any of us wanted, but we'll be fine if you can get over yourself!"

Ben took a deep breath and a step back. "I think it's working out exactly the way Katie wanted it. You just got played, Mae." He ran his hand through his brown, curly hair, making it stand on end. His blue eyes were so fiery they almost gave off sparks. "Of course I can be a good sport about this for you and Matty, but *four* dogs?" He looked questioningly at Mae and she gave a little nod. "Oh, for dog's sake, all right."

Mae started to laugh and Ben gave her a surprised look. "What?"

"You just said 'for dog's sake' instead of 'for God's sake,' " she told him. "It was funny."

Ben bent down to pet Cupcake, who was curled up on the rug in front of the kitchen sink. Her ears were gathered up on top of her head by a soft, yellow hair ribbon, and she seemed oblivious of the controversy surrounding her living arrangements.

"For dog's sake, huh girl?" Mae heard him murmur. He straightened up and kissed Mae on the cheek. "I think you need to paint that on a sign for your kitchen wall, babe."

Ben went upstairs to shower and change out of his uniform. He was back in the kitchen in fifteen minutes, looking much more comfortable in shorts and a faded orange T-shirt. Mae pulled a bottle of un-oaked Chardonnay from the refrigerator and poured two glasses. She handed one to Ben and picked up her own, giving him a little smile.

"Cheers." He tapped his glass against hers with a rueful expression. "Can we start this evening over?"

The clock on Mae's stove read 5:03. "Of course," she said. "Here's to some time to ourselves—just us and four dogs."

MAE PREPARED A simple dinner of grilled salmon, rice pilaf,

and a green salad, which they ate on the screened porch. Ben did the dishes and then they went out to the barn together to check on her three current boarders. They worked in companionable silence, filling water dishes and ushering the dogs out into the fenced area for some exercise while they cleaned out the kennels.

They went back to the house, and Mae got Cupcake out of her crate and called her other three dogs, who were in their beds in the laundry room. "Tallulah, Titan, Tatie, c'mon!" The black female pug and older male corgi sauntered out behind Tatie, the young female corgi who had already raced to the kitchen door. In lieu of a tail, she wagged her entire rear end.

Mae opened the kitchen door and carried Cupcake out for a bathroom break. She was progressing really well on the potty training, and did everything right away. Mae gave her a treat and lavish praise. The sky had turned a deep pink with streaks of magenta, and the crescent moon was peeking over the roof of her house. Ben walked out to stand beside her.

"Beautiful night, isn't it?" He took a deep whiff. "Something smells great out here."

"I think it's the honeysuckle vine."

He put his nose next to her ear and sniffed again. "I think it's you." He kissed her neck and she shivered at the touch of his lips. "Yep, it's you. Listen, Mae, I was wondering if you'd like to be my campaign manager for the election. You wouldn't need to start until August. Do you think you'd have time for that?"

Mae suppressed a smile. She'd received a heads-up call from Dory before Ben got home and she'd been waiting for this question. "I think I'm available for that job, especially since the pay is so high," she teased.

"It's a volunteer position." Ben gave her a wink. "But the benefits are pretty spectacular." He put his arm around her, pulling her in close. They watched the moonrise while their four dogs played together.

Chapter Twenty-Nine

———

Chief Detective Wayne Nichols

EVERYONE HAD ALREADY left the sheriff's office for the day except Wayne and Deputy Cam. It was almost 6:00 in the evening and Cameron Gomez was occupied in switching the sheriff's office's phones over to the Mont Blanc PD. A much bigger police department, they answered night phones and did dispatch for the Rosedale Sheriff's Office from 6 p.m. until 6 a.m. All the members of the sheriff's staff kept their cellphones or pagers on overnight and could be summoned at any time to attend to disturbances in Rose County.

Wayne was sweltering in the heat and sighed irritably. Before he found himself too hot to concentrate, he had been looking through everyone's reports on the Chester Willis case, hoping something would strike him. The old air-conditioning in the building wasn't cutting it. Wayne walked out to the reception area to check the thermostat setting. Despite it being set on 70, the temperature in the room was 82. He raised his eyes from the reports in his hand. "Pardon me, Cam."

"Hello, Detective Nichols," she said, looking up. "I'm about ready to leave for the evening. Did you need anything before I go?" She picked up her car keys.

"I've been going through everyone's reports on the Willis case and happened to notice something on yours that we failed to follow up on," Wayne said.

"What was it?" Cam looked concerned. "Did I forget something?"

"No, but you spoke with Marina Hernandez, Leonard Willis' housekeeper, shortly after Chester's death, correct?"

"Yes, I did." Cam took the seat across from Wayne. "Sheriff Bradley sent me to the Willis residence on July eighth. Unfortunately Ms. Hernandez had already cleaned Chester's room several days earlier and there was nothing to find, except the single Xanax tablet somebody dropped in the bathroom. I picked it up using gloves but there were no fingerprints on the tablet. My guess is that it fell out of the bottle when the killer was getting a tablet to give to Chester Willis."

Wayne tapped the report. "I see you noted that here. Then on July thirteenth, Mr. Shane Connor, Mr. Willis' attorney, read his will and informed Ben that Marina Hernandez was present and that she received a bequest of ten thousand dollars from Mr. Willis' estate. Mr. Connor told the sheriff that Ms. Hernandez was watching the other people like a hawk. I think it would be worth our while to talk to her again."

Cam stood up again. "Did you want me to talk with her this evening?"

"I'd like you to call her now and set up a time to talk with her. I don't want her spooked or brought to the office. This conversation needs to be low key. See if you can meet with her at her home tonight, or if she would prefer, the Donut Den or her favorite place for breakfast."

"Okay." Cam took a small notepad and pen out of her purse. "What specifically do you want me to find out?"

"She was in the Willis household the day Chester was murdered. In fact, it says here on your report that she stayed to clean up the dishes in the kitchen after the meal. See if anything that happened that evening before she left the house struck her as unusual. For example, I would like to know if she overheard any conversations that seemed odd."

Cam looked up from her notepad and frowned. "I'll have to be tactful about that. I don't want to accuse her of eavesdropping."

"Somehow, I have a feeling you'll be able to manage that," Wayne said, drily. If anyone could ask sensitive questions without offending, it was Cam. "You're the most tactful officer I know."

"Thank you," Cam said and smiled, revealing the dimple in her right cheek.

AN HOUR LATER, Wayne was seated in front of the television in his apartment watching a baseball game when the phone rang. Deputy Cam's phone number came up on his phone.

"Detective, this is Deputy Gomez," she said. "I reached Ms. Hernandez. She said I could stop by her place around seven thirty this evening. I'm wondering if I should bring a bottle of wine or a dessert or something. What do you think?"

"Unless you know what she drinks, I'm thinking a dessert would be good. There's a Hispanic bakery on the traffic circle in town. It's called Tres Leches. I know they have flan and empanadas. Maybe ask Tio Torres what he recommends."

"Good idea. Papa Tio might even know Marina Hernandez. I'll stop by there before I drive over to her place. Should I call you with a verbal report tonight?"

"Of course. I'll be waiting for your call."

AT NINE O'CLOCK, Wayne was on his way out to meet with one of his confidential informants. He was picking up his keys and cellphone when it rang.

"Detective?" It was Deputy Gomez.

"Yes, Cam. What did you learn from Ms. Hernandez?"

"Not much, but Marina did remember one odd thing from that night. She apparently saw Meredith Flynn and Chester talking together in the hall outside his bedroom. This was after his father went to bed."

"She was sure it was Chester and not Rick that Meredith was talking to?"

"Absolutely. She said Meredith sounded frustrated with Chester. She caught something Meredith said that sounded like, 'That's mine to tell. Not yours.' Chester said something like, 'I told you before that I don't like knowing something about you that you haven't told Rick.' "

"Very interesting. Can you get that written up tonight? Send it to the office by email. I'll go over it with the sheriff in the morning. We may want to speak with you then."

"Right." Cam was gone.

As WAYNE DROVE out of Rosedale toward Bar None, the local hangout for the serious drinker, he reviewed the timeline for the night Chester Willis died. Mr. Willis had announced before dinner that he was making a change to his will and planned to leave Brooke the jewelry. With Rick and Chester knowing about the change and Brooke being unaware, it must have been an awkward and uncomfortable dinner for all of them.

If he and the sheriff were right in their suspicions that Chester was killed for his share of the estate, Mr. Willis' announcement had been the flash point, the trigger for the murder. *But if Rick was the killer, why would he not kill Brooke, instead of his brother?* It would have been the logical thing to do. Brooke was the newcomer, not a member of the family, and Rick had referred to her as a gold digger several times. He had also turned her in for stealing a piece of jewelry that Mr. Willis had given her. Rick clearly resented Brooke getting any of his father's money.

"This damn case," Wayne said aloud and hit his steering wheel with his open palm. He had never come across a case with such a dearth of actual evidence. They didn't have a murder weapon. Since the murder had been committed with a needle and not a gun, and they had never found the syringe, there was no blood spatter to analyze or bullet to track back to a weapon. Without that syringe, there were no fingerprints that would point to the killer. They had no DNA, no trace evidence, and the only indication of assault on Chester's body was the needle mark on his toe.

Obviously, Chester was killed by someone who could have entered his bedroom without arousing suspicions, and that would logically be his brother. Wayne suspected that whoever killed Chester had given him Xanax in addition to his usual sleeping tablet. Once Chester was sound asleep, the killer had returned and injected him with insulin. It was a premeditated, coldblooded killing, and Wayne was furious with himself that they weren't any closer to nailing the perp.

Now something new had come up. Deputy Cam's conversation with Marina Hernandez seemed to indicate that Meredith Flynn had some sort of issue with Chester. Could Chester have been killed because he was about to reveal a secret about her? If so, their whole theory of the crime was wrong. But no, that didn't add up either. If Meredith was that angry after their conversation, Chester would not have been comfortable with her being in his bedroom. Rick had to be the killer, and the crime had to have been committed for the money, but only a confession would solve this one. And without an admission of guilt, they might never nail the perpetrator. Neither he nor Ben could afford that kind of blot on their record, especially with Ben's election coming up.

Ever since Brooke passed the lie detector test, she was no longer in their crosshairs. They were down to Rick Willis, and if he killed his own brother, he certainly wouldn't have a qualm about killing Brooke. The way his father's will had been written, if Brooke was dead, Rick would get the whole estate. Wayne remembered Lucy mentioning that Brooke might be in danger. He had briefly considered putting George on a protective detail, but with a sudden sinking sensation realized he had never mentioned it to the sheriff. Nobody had been assigned to protect Brooke. Wayne flipped on the red light atop his truck and did a rapid U-turn, eliciting honks from several cars. He drove to Brooke's apartment and knocked on the door.

She opened the front door a crack. The chain was still on. "Detective Nichols?" she asked with raised eyebrows. Her expression was wary.

"Yes, I'm sorry to disturb you, Brooke. Just wanted to be sure you were okay. Are you planning to stay in for the rest of the evening?"

"Yes," Brooke said, looking uncertainly at him. She had a questioning note in her voice.

"Keep your door locked," Wayne said and walked back to his truck.

Continuing on his way to Bar None, Wayne shook his head. It had probably been a bonehead move and undoubtedly alerted Brooke to his unvoiced concerns, but they had a murderer on the loose. It didn't pay to take chances. He would talk to Ben in the morning about getting George to keep an eye on Brooke. At least she was all right for the night. He could relax until tomorrow. He took a deep breath and felt in his pocket for the key to Lucy's place. He planned on stopping by to see her after his meeting with his informant. If he beat her to the house, it would be his first time using the key. He smiled.

Chapter Thirty

———

Dr. Lucy Ingram

Lucy, who was normally quite unflappable despite the chaos of emergencies all around her, was startled to see Nurse Channing Soldan fly past the draped cubicles in the ER calling her name. Channing's hair was streaked bright orange, and she wore a black sleeveless top and drawstring pants.

"Dr. Lucy," Channing said, trying to catch her breath, "the ambulance is at the dock."

"Okay, slow down girl," Lucy said. "You aren't even on duty tonight." It was nearly eleven p.m. and Lucy had hoped to get off early. She was meeting Wayne at her place after her shift.

"I know, I know," Channing's words were tumbling over each other. "I was going to help my friend Brooke Piper tonight with her neurology homework, but when I got there she'd been assaulted. I need you to look at her. I had her neighbor call 911 and got the ambulance to bring her here. She's not fully conscious."

Lucy ran toward the ambulance dock without another moment's delay. A partially conscious young woman who had been assaulted was always nerve-racking. If the patient had been sexually assaulted, it could result in a rape charge, or if the patient died, it could turn into another murder. Both Lucy and Channing reached the ambulance just as Brooke Piper's semi-conscious body was being loaded onto a gurney.

Lucy leaned down closer to the young woman's face and said, "Brooke, this is Dr. Ingram, can you hear me?" She hoped Brooke would remember meeting with her when Mr. Willis died.

Brooke started to say something, but it was impossible to hear her soft voice as the EMTs, medical students, and interns arrived and she was taken into the unit. They moved her carefully off the gurney and onto a bed in a draped cubicle in the ER. More time passed as IVs were inserted and her vital signs were checked. Brooke's blood pressure was 220 over 140. Her respirations were rapid. She didn't have a temperature. Lucy shone a light into her eyes; her pupils were pinpoints.

"Cut off her shirt," Lucy said and a nurse stepped up close to the body and cut her T-shirt right down the middle of the front. "Pull off her yoga pants," she said. Once Brooke was naked except for a bra and panties, Lucy checked her over carefully. There were no recent bruises on her body. Looking carefully at Brooke's throat, she could see that her hyoid bone was intact, and she was breathing normally. She had not been strangled. In fact, Lucy didn't see any sign that Brooke had been assaulted, and she started going through her mental checklist of odd diseases or drug reactions.

She picked up Brooke's small, clean hands, examining them one by one. As you would expect for a massage therapist, her nails were trimmed short and filed smooth. She wore no rings or bracelets, and there was no sign that she'd been in a fight. Lucy then checked quickly and was relieved to find no signs of recent sexual activity or assault.

"Let's roll her onto her side," Lucy said. "I want to look at the back of her head." Once she got a good look at Brooke's head, it was obvious what had happened. Brooke had been pushed into something hard and rounded, or hit with something of that shape. "Can I have it quiet in here please?" Lucy asked and again leaned down to hear what her patient was saying.

"The ring," Brooke whispered and then again, louder, "the ring."

"The ring?" Lucy repeated, looking at Channing. "Is that what she's saying?"

"I think so. That's all she's said the whole time."

"Okay, it looks like we have her stabilized for the moment. We'll need to get a CT scan of her skull and brain. Please take her upstairs for the CT, will you, Grant?" Lucy asked a young medical student.

"Yes, doctor," he said and with some help moved Brooke onto a rolling gurney and took her out of the ER. Brooke was still saying, "The ring" in an insistent tone of voice. The words didn't sound like a cry for help; rather it was as if Brooke was trying to tell anyone listening something important, something they needed to know.

"Channing, let's get some coffee. I want you to tell me what happened from the moment you arrived at Brooke's," Lucy said.

The two women walked to the back of the ER, took their coffees to a small conference room and sat down.

"First off, why were you there?"

"I've been tutoring Brooke in neuro and cardio over the last few weeks. She's coming up to final exams. I usually meet with her on Wednesday evenings, but this week she asked me to come over tonight instead. I was running late and I texted Brooke saying I couldn't get there until almost ten o'clock. I didn't get a return text and stared to worry. She always texts me back right away."

"Go on," Lucy said. She focused all her attention on Channing's rendition of the events of the night.

"Right. I arrived at nine forty-five and rang the bell. Brooke has this nosy neighbor in the next door apartment, and I saw her curtains twitch when I pushed the doorbell. Her name is Mrs. Brighton and when Brooke didn't open the door, I knocked on the neighbor's door. I told her I was Brooke's tutor and needed to see her. I said I was worried about her. Anyway, it turned out the woman had a key and we went back to Brooke's apartment."

"So where did you find Brooke?"

"We found her lying on the floor in her kitchen. Mrs. Brighton started to cry and ask a bunch of questions until I told her I was a nurse. I sat down on the floor and tried to lift Brooke's upper body into a sitting position. That was when I noticed a little smear of blood on the floor under her head. I told Mrs. Brighton to call 911 and watch for the paramedics. I said I'd wait with Brooke."

"Well, this was definitely assault, Channing. You were right. Even if Brooke fell and cracked her head, she wouldn't have hit her head that hard. Try to think carefully. The sheriff's office personnel are going to ask you if you saw anyone driving out of Brooke's complex as you were driving in. Did you see anyone lurking around the apartment?"

"A couple of cars went past me, but it was dark and they weren't driving particularly fast or anything. And I didn't see anyone hanging around … but I just realized something. When Mrs. Brighton used her key, she said that the door to Brooke's apartment wasn't locked. It was closed and latched but not locked. Brooke has been locking it every night lately, ever since she found out that Chester was murdered. She's been scared. Sometimes she calls me just to talk her down. She never would've left her door unlocked."

"I'm going to call Detective Nichols and ask him to come by here. I know he'll want to talk to you. Hang out here for a while. Okay, Channing?"

The young nurse, unusually pale, nodded.

Lucy walked out into the hall and called Wayne's cell. "Hi, it's me. Brooke Piper was assaulted tonight. She's here in the ER. My nurse Channing Soldan found her."

"Damn it," Wayne said. "This is my fault. I was worried about Brooke. I actually went over there earlier this evening. She told me she was going to be home the rest of the night. I told her to keep her door locked."

"Well, she let somebody in, because she's been hit on the back of the head and is only partially conscious. She keeps saying 'the ring.' That's all, just those two words."

"It must have been Rick Willis. He was the one who accused Brooke of taking his mother's jewelry. I'll be able to get the bastard now," Wayne said. "Keep Channing there."

Lucy walked back down the corridor where Channing was waiting. She glanced at her watch. She was definitely not going to get out of the ER early.

Chapter Thirty-One

Chief Detective Wayne Nichols

WAYNE HAD BEEN sitting in the bar with his confidential informant Jacko when Lucy's call came in. He said he had to run.

"Oh, man," Jacko said, shaking his head. "I've got a hot tip for you and I need money."

"Okay, but make it snappy. What did you want to tell me?" Wayne forced himself to take a deep breath and slow down. His nerves were on fire; he wanted Rick Willis in his custody tonight if possible.

"Would you be interested in having a little chat with a jewelry fence?" Jacko asked, his expression sly.

"Sorry, man, not right now. Hot on the trail of a killer who just attacked a young woman."

Jacko's mouth turned down at the corners. "How about a twenty, man? You'll need this jewelry guy's name at some point."

"Yeah, okay," Wayne said and pulled a twenty from his

wallet. "But I'm not your daddy, and I'm not an easy touch because you ran out of drinking money."

"Right." Jacko handed Wayne a folded piece of paper. The detective didn't wait another minute. He practically ran out of Bar None and with tires squealing, headed for Rick Willis' condo. He placed a call to Rick but got no answer. Wayne left a message asking him, in as polite a manner as he could manage, to come into the sheriff's office. Twenty minutes later, he was parked in front of the large condo complex where Rick Willis lived. He went up to the penthouse level on the top floor and knocked on the door. Nobody answered. He knocked again, harder this time, and a middle-aged woman from the apartment down the hall opened her door.

"Are you looking for Rick?" she asked.

"I am," Wayne said. "Do you know where he might be?"

"He plays tennis at an indoor club in Nashville in the evenings sometimes. He might be there or out with his girlfriend."

"Do you know the name of the tennis club, by chance?"

"Yes, it's Court One in Nashville. And his girlfriend's name is Meredith Flynn. She doesn't live here. Nice to see some young people have morals and don't live together before they get married." She raised her eyebrows.

"Thank you," Wayne said and hurried down the three flights of stairs. *Morals? Rick Willis?* Wayne checked his phone for Meredith Flynn's address. Her apartment was only a few minutes away from the Willis family home. He parked at her complex, got out of his truck, and knocked on her door. After waiting a few minutes, he knocked again but got no answer. Wayne went back to his truck and called the tennis club in Nashville, but the front desk was obviously not manned this late. Discouraged, he wondered if he should wait for Rick or Meredith to get home or go to the hospital. He called Ben.

"Hey man, what's up?" Ben asked.

"Brooke Piper was assaulted at her apartment tonight. She's in the hospital, partially conscious and saying only two words.

She keeps saying 'the ring.' According to Lucy, she says it over and over again. Anyway, it's got to be Rick Willis. I figured you would want him picked up. I just went by his condo and Meredith's apartment too. Nobody home."

"Damn straight I want him picked up. This might just be the break we needed on this case. We can get him for the assault, and that'll open the door to getting a confession for the murder. Hang on a minute." Wayne heard Ben talking with Mae at the other end of the line. He heard Ben say, "Yes, you're right, honey. Sorry." Then he came back on.

"Mae says I sounded happy that Brooke was assaulted. I'm not, of course." Wayne heard a short sigh from his boss. "But whatever Brooke tells us could help solve this murder. I'll call George and get him on stakeout at Rick Willis' condo, and I'll ask Cam to wait at Meredith's apartment complex in case Rick shows up there. What're you going to do now?"

"I'm headed to the hospital. Lucy's nurse found Brooke and called 911. I want to talk to her. Are you okay with sending Emma and Hadley to do forensics at Brooke's apartment tonight?"

"Yes, I'll send them over there and call you if someone spots Rick Willis."

"Sounds good," Wayne said. He pulled out of the parking lot of Meredith's apartment complex and headed for the hospital.

WAYNE FOUND LUCY and Channing in the hospital cafeteria. Wayne hadn't met Channing before and got a kick out of her streaky orange and blonde hair and black outfit. It would be a good look for Halloween, he thought, but it wasn't quite right for mid-July.

"Channing, can you go over the whole thing again for me?" Wayne asked.

"Of course," Channing said and recited the events of the evening.

"During the time when you and Brooke's neighbor, Mrs.

Brighton, were in Brooke's apartment, did you notice anything other than the smear of blood on the floor? Anything that was out of the ordinary? Anything out of place?"

"Only that the door to her apartment wasn't locked. That's very unusual." Channing's face was a study in concern.

"So it wasn't a stranger. Brooke must have let her attacker in. I'd guess whoever assaulted Brooke left via the front door and just pulled it shut after them. With luck we'll get fingerprints. Our techs are going over there now. And there's a neighbor … you said she was nosy, right?"

"Yes, Brooke likes her but says she's always all up in her business. Wants to know everything that's going on in Brooke's life."

"Those of us in law enforcement just love nosy middle-aged ladies with too much time on their hands. Thanks, Channing," Detective Nichols said. "You can take off now."

Lucy said goodbye to Channing.

"So where's Brooke now?" Wayne asked her.

"She's up in neuro ICU. We can go up if you want," Lucy said.

He nodded, and they rode the elevator to the top floor. Neuro ICU was very quiet. Feeling that even their footsteps were too loud, he followed Lucy to Brooke's room. She was sleeping, and just as Lucy bent down to ask her a question, the attending came in.

"Uh-uh," he said, shaking his head. "No disturbing her until tomorrow. The MRI shows brain injury. Sorry, Dr. Ingram."

"I hope she can answer some questions in the morning," Wayne said. He and Lucy left Brooke's room.

"I'm off duty now." Lucy put her hand on his arm. "Want to drive out to the house?"

"Sure, I'll meet you there," he said, "but this was going to be my first night to use the key—"

"Fine, then. I'll stop at the liquor store for some wine. You'll definitely beat me home."

They walked to the parking lot together, and Wayne made

sure she was safe in her car. He got in his truck and headed for Little Chapel Road. The crescent moon had laid a gloss on the fields, and his tires thrummed loudly on the road in the quiet of the night.

"Home," he said quietly. "Did Lucy mean she was going to *her* home, I wonder, or *ours*?"

He smiled to himself in the darkness.

Chapter Thirty-Two

—

Chief Detective Wayne Nichols

WAYNE RECEIVED A call from Ben at Lucy's just after midnight at the end of a long day. George had called the sheriff after spotting Rick Willis pulling into the parking lot of his condo complex. When Rick got out of the car, he appeared inebriated, walking slowly and humming under his breath. George had followed Rick up to the penthouse floor. He'd kept his distance and was now waiting just outside Rick's door.

"Sorry, Lucy," Wayne said "George just spotted Rick Willis at the condo complex. I'm going to go pick him up. This assault on Brooke is going to give us the ammunition we need to force a confession out of him for his brother's murder. He won't get away this time."

Lucy gave him a tired smile. Wayne kissed her goodbye in a thorough fashion and went out to his truck. On the way to the condo, he felt his spirits rise, as they always did when he was closing in on a perpetrator. It was all coming together.

Wayne parked his car and took the elevator to the top floor.

George was sitting on the floor with his back against the wall, checking his phone for messages.

"Stand up," Wayne growled. "What the hell, George? If Rick Willis tried to run, you couldn't get up quickly enough to stop him, not with your build."

"He didn't come out," George said defensively.

"Only because you were lucky. In the future, when you're watching a suspect, try being alert!" Wayne shook his head.

"Yes, sir," George got to his feet and shoved his phone in his pocket.

Wayne knocked loudly on the door. "Sheriff's office. Open up."

A bleary eyed Rick Willis, reeking of alcohol, opened the door. His neighbor lady opened her door to see what was going on. Wayne glanced at her briefly.

"Rick Willis, you're under arrest for assault. You have the right to remain silent, but anything you say can and will be used against you in a court of law. You have the right to an attorney. If you cannot afford one, one will be provided for you. Do you understand these rights?"

"I do." Rick blinked owlishly at them, swaying where he stood. The woman down the hall gasped and slammed her door.

"Put the cuffs on him, George," Wayne said.

The men escorted the cuffed and loudly protesting Rick Willis down the hall and into the elevator.

"Want to know why I was celebrating?" Rick looked at George and hiccupped loudly. The deputy stifled a laugh, then looked at Wayne with raised eyebrows.

"Yes, we'd like to know." Wayne said. "Why were you?"

"I got en-en-gaged today." Rick smiled, then hiccupped again. "I was celebrating with my friend. You know what?" A cunning look stole over his face. "He's a lawyer ... his name's Ramsey. I'm calling him now."

"Oh no, you're not." Wayne took Rick's phone from his back

pocket, and he and George escorted him out to the parking lot. "You can't call an attorney until you're in custody. You have to wait until you've been processed." He smirked at Rick. "Plus, it's pretty hard to make a call while you're cuffed, dumbass."

The inebriated man struggled, but when George pushed Rick's head down to put him in the back of the patrol car, he subsided. The deputy slammed the car door and they watched their suspect lean his head back. Within seconds, his mouth dropped open and he passed out.

"Well, shit." Wayne glared in irritation at the unconscious man. "We're not getting anything out of him tonight. May as well just put him in a cell and book him tomorrow when he wakes up."

"I'll take him in." Deputy Phelps' ginger brows drew together. "I just hope he doesn't throw up back there. Really don't want to clean that up tonight."

Wayne bit his lip to keep from laughing at the deputy's expression of disgust. "Do you need help getting him into a cell? I can follow you, if you want."

George said he could handle it, got in the car and drove off. Wayne called Ben, who picked up on the first ring. "Have you got him?"

"Deputy Phelps is going to pour him into a cell. Mr. Willis is passed out in the patrol car right now, so there's no sense trying to question him tonight. I'll go question Brooke's neighbor in the morning and meet you at the office if that's all right."

"I'll call off Cam," Ben said. "Hadley and Emma are going to take whatever they found back to the lab tonight and start processing. I'll see you tomorrow."

WAYNE WOKE UP in Lucy's bed. The room was dim, just a little light coming in around the pulled curtains. He breathed in the fragrance of his girlfriend's hair, then gently disentangled himself from her warm, sleeping body. She murmured and rolled away as Wayne stood up. The bedside clock read 6:42.

He quietly gathered some clean clothes from his corner of the closet and left the room, closing the door behind him.

A misty rain dotted the bathroom window. He showered, the smell of her shampoo displacing his focus on the case with thoughts of Lucy. *I've really got it bad for her.* Wayne got out, dried off, and applied shaving cream. As he looked in the mirror, he saw how tired he appeared. His hazel eyes had dark circles under them and what remained of his hair seemed even grayer this morning. He was in good shape for a man his age, though—his belly flat and his shoulders still well-muscled. He finished shaving and wrapped the bath towel around his waist before going into the kitchen.

The big detective started a pot of coffee, and while it perked, ate an apple. Pouring himself a cup, he drank half of it while standing at the sink and staring out the window at the foggy morning. Mae and Ben lived across the street at the top of the hill, but he couldn't see their farmhouse. His view ended at Lucy's mailbox. Wayne finished his coffee. After he rinsed the cup, he dug through Lucy's kitchen drawers until he found a pencil and some sticky notes. "I didn't want to wake you. I'll call you later, goodbye," he wrote and then somewhat self-consciously added "Love, Wayne," before sticking the note to her refrigerator door.

Wayne drove to Brooke's apartment complex and parked, observing the yellow crime-scene tape across the doorway of her ground-floor unit at the end of the building. He knocked on the next door over. When an older woman in a housecoat opened it, he said, "Mrs. Brighton? I'm Detective Wayne Nichols. I wonder if I could ask you a few questions."

"Oh, Detective, please come in. Would you like coffee or tea?"

"Black coffee would be welcome," Wayne said.

Mrs. Brighton bustled around in the kitchen. A man in his fifties came out from the back of the apartment. "This is my husband, Harry," she said.

"Detective Wayne Nichols," Wayne said and held out his hand to shake with the man.

The three of them sat down at the oval, laminate-topped table. The scent of the coffee was strong and pleasant in the air. Mrs. Brighton looked positively thrilled to have a detective in her apartment.

"As you know, Mrs. Brighton, your neighbor, Brooke Piper, was assaulted last night. I'm aware that you have a key to her apartment, and I understand you went over there at the request of her friend, Channing."

"Yes, that's right," Mrs. Brighton said. "I saw that poor girl lying in a huge pool of blood on the kitchen floor." Her eyes widened. "I thought she was dead! I helped Miss Channing check her pulse and everything."

Wayne frowned slightly. Mrs. Brighton appeared to be one of those women who enjoyed being in the limelight. According to Channing, Mrs. Brighton had been terribly flustered by the small amount of blood and stepped back instantly once Channing told her she was a nurse.

"Thank you for that information," Wayne said and turned to Mrs. Brighton's husband. "Mr. Brighton, were you home at the time of the incident?"

"No, I was bowling … just got here when the ambulance was leaving. My Janice here had quite the evening. She was practically hyperventilating." He looked at his wife fondly, but slanted his eyes at Wayne. It was clear he enjoyed his wife's stories but knew they were embroidered.

"At either time, when you left home or returned, did you notice any people or cars that seemed out of place?"

"Yes, when I left I saw a dark sedan, shiny. It was parked in the middle of the row on the far side of the lot."

"What did you see in the way of unusual cars or activity, Mrs. Brighton?"

"I'd say there were three or four cars that didn't belong here." Janice's eyes sparkled with excitement. "I saw a red car, a green

SUV, and a big white van. I don't know if you know, Detective, but it's always white vans that kidnappers use. I think they were planning on kidnapping Brooke, but she put up a fight and they left."

Wayne sighed. "Thank you, Mrs. Brighton. Did you see or hear anyone besides Channing at Brooke's last night?"

"No." She frowned. "I think you should check out those cars though."

"Pretty hard to do unless you got their license numbers," Wayne said.

"Oh dear … well, it was so dark out. I couldn't possibly have gotten those. Thinking about this some more, maybe I did see somebody. I would be happy to work with a police artist to help develop a sketch."

She looked hopeful, but Wayne doubted she saw anyone. "Not at this time. If either of you think of anything else that could help, please call me," he said, handing them his card.

He walked out to his car, mulling over the Brightons' information. Mr. Brighton had seen a dark sedan parked at the complex. Rick Willis owned a dark blue BMW. Driving to the station, he thought about Rick's personality and what it was going to take to break him.

Chapter Thirty-Three

Mae December

M AE WOKE UP a few minutes after nine to a quiet house. She stretched luxuriously, rolling over onto Ben's empty side of the bed to look out the window. Seeing the wind-tossed leaves and dark gray clouds, she got out of bed quickly, anxious to let the dogs out and get them back inside before the storm. She pulled on running shorts and a tank top and hurried downstairs to find a note from Ben on her kitchen counter:

> Left early, sorry about all the commotion last night, took care of our four before I left. Good luck finding the dress today. Love, Ben

A flash of lightning illuminated the kitchen, followed almost immediately by the deep boom of thunder. Mae grabbed her hooded raincoat, stepped into rain boots, and pulled on her coat as she ran for the barn. The first drops of rain splatted down, becoming a downpour just as she opened the barn door. Stepping inside, she flipped on the light switch. Another bolt of lightning flashed and the lights went out with the rumbling of thunder. One of her boarders whined in the dark.

Mae moved to her left, feeling along the shelf for her flashlight. Something moved under her hand and she jumped back with a scream. The lights came back on and Mae saw the muscular, red-brown coils of an agitated copperhead snake. Gasping, she backed toward the door. The copperhead turned its head to track her, then slithered off the shelf in one smooth movement. Mae watched in horror as the snake headed straight for the kennels.

With no time to think, Mae ran to the shelf and grabbed the axe her father had put there for this very occasion. She rushed to the snake and chopped off its head right just before the five-footer reached Scarlett, the Cavalier King Charles spaniel in the first pen. The small ginger and white dog looked up at her with huge dark eyes. Shaking, Mae stepped away from the twitching body of the copperhead. She rinsed the axe in the utility sink and hung it back up. *How do I get rid of a giant, dead snake that's in two pieces?*

Fighting down nausea, Mae put on her leather work gloves and took the lid off the large garbage can. She pushed it over beside Lucy's pen and tried to pick up the severed snake head, but even with gloves on, she couldn't bring herself to touch it. Glancing around, she saw the oversized pooper scooper leaning against the wall and used it to get the snake into the trash. Mae tied the bag shut, shuddering with relief and the aftereffects of adrenaline.

"Everyone okay?" She scanned Scarlett and her other two boarders, shepherd mix Taco and bluetick hound Dixie. All three dogs looked fine, and she filled their bowls with food and fresh water as her heartbeat gradually slowed to normal. Once her kennel chores were complete, she hefted the garbage bag full of snake, switched off the lights, and closed the barn door behind her.

The rain poured down and Mae dumped the bag into the

large container next to her driveway, where it would be picked up tomorrow morning. She squelched back inside for coffee, a little cuddle time with Cupcake, a quick breakfast and a shower. After that, she was meeting her mother and sister in town for some *very* welcome girl time—wedding dress shopping and lunch.

The rain had slowed its downpour a little, and there were some breaks in the clouds by the time Mae drove into Rosedale. The blacktop steamed, and the greenery looked lush and refreshed. She pulled into the gravel parking lot of the vintage store that Tammy's nurse had told her about. Located two blocks off Main Street near the railroad tracks, the building itself looked like an old warehouse. A small printed sign taped near the door read "The Attic." Mae was a little underwhelmed, but seeing the vehicles belonging to her mother Suzanne and her sister July, she parked and went on in.

"You're going to love this place, Mae," her sister said, after greeting her with a quick hug. "You okay? You look a little pale."

"I had a run-in with a copperhead," Mae said with a shudder.

"No!" Her sister's head jerked back.

"It's all right; it was headed toward the dogs, but I chopped it in two with the ax."

July looked at her in admiration. "I don't think I could do that. You're one brave girl."

"Who's brave?" Mama hurried over and hugged her as well. Mae gave her the quick version of the story, leaving out the part about the dogs being in danger. She didn't want her mother to worry.

They fussed over her for a while longer, then got down to business.

Mae stood in the marble-tiled entryway, looking around in amazement at the brightly lit, large and luxurious space. For just a moment she was speechless.

"I found three beautiful dresses already," Suzanne said,

grabbing her youngest daughter by the hand and pulling her toward an upholstered pink dais in front of a three-way mirror. "They're laid out over here."

"How long have you been here, Mama?"

"Ten minutes, tops. Your sister just arrived. I already called Grace to see if she could watch the baby while Tammy ran over here. I think you're going to want her input as well." The slender, dark-haired grandmother of three paused for breath. "Well, what do you think? Do you want to try on any of these? Some of these gowns are couture."

Mae exchanged a meaningful glance with her sister, who smiled back. Although July was the spitting image of her mother, her managerial tendencies were underdeveloped in comparison. As their father often said, he had married a petite and lovely four-star general. Mae knew resistance would be futile as well as time-consuming. She picked up the first dress and looked around for the dressing room.

An angular blonde woman who looked to be in her mid-sixties materialized at Mae's elbow. "Dena, I didn't know you worked here," Suzanne exclaimed before hugging her. "Is that a Chanel jacket you're wearing? You look wonderful."

Dena smiled. "So do you, Suzanne, as always. And yes, it's vintage Chanel. This is my shop, so I'm here every day—but it's more play than work." She turned to Mae and gave her a quick, professional once over. "You have a lovely figure, dear, but that dress won't suit you as well as the ivory dress on the mannequin. Are you between a six and an eight in size?" Mae nodded. "I thought so. Go get undressed. There are heels in various sizes in the fitting rooms back there." She pointed to a doorway swathed in crimson silk. "We'll get this gown off the mannequin and bring it to you."

"I'll come with you," July said. "Can you believe this place?"

Mae laughed. "Not what I was picturing for a vintage store called The Attic, that's for sure." She pushed the silky drapes aside and entered the glamorous dressing room. A crystal chandelier hung overhead, the walls were a soft gray, and numerous ivory-upholstered sofas and divans were grouped around the room. The plush carpet was pale pink with a subtle floral pattern. Mae removed her sandals and took off everything except her panties. "Would you see if they have any heels in a nine and a half?" she asked her sister.

July went to a huge armoire with half-open doors that stood on the opposite wall. She selected strappy, golden sandals with a medium heel and brought them over. Mae slipped them on just as Dena and Suzanne bustled in, carrying the dress. Tammy followed them, pushing a stroller.

"My mom offered to watch him," her best friend said, "but I wanted to show him off. It's a short walk and the rain stopped, so we strolled over." Tammy turned to Dena with a smile. "Do you have a strapless bra for her?"

The boutique owner glanced at Mae, who was feeling a little shy in her almost-nude state. "Thirty-six D? There should be one in the bottom drawer of the dresser over there."

Tammy parked the stroller next to July, who bent down to coo over baby Bennett. She quickly obtained the bra and brought it to Mae. Just like the shoes, it was a perfect fit. Dena and Suzanne pulled the dress over Mae's head. Her mother stood back to look as Dena fastened the tiny buttons up the back. Tammy fanned out the train of the gown and Mae looked in the mirror.

"It's … perfect," Tammy whispered, standing beside Suzanne on Mae's left. Dena smiled and nodded, stepping away to give them a moment. July came over and stood on Mae's right. "I don't think she needs to try on anything else, do you?" her sister asked. Mama shook her head and wiped her eyes.

"Looks like there's no need for that trip to Atlanta after all." She gave a little sniffle. "Why don't you two girls help her out of the dress while I go pay Dena? Then we can get some lunch."

Chapter Thirty-Four

—

Sheriff Ben Bradley

B EN LEFT THE house early and drove into town under threatening skies with a light drizzle. When he got to the office, his deputies—George Phelps and Cam Gomez—were already there. Wayne would be in after he interviewed Brooke Piper's neighbor, but Ben hoped Rob Fuller, his other detective, would show up soon for Rick Willis' interrogation.

"Good morning, Sheriff." Sophie Coffin was at her desk early today, but there was no sign of Dory.

"Good morning, Mrs. Coffin." Ben smiled at her. He had decided on a course of extra courtesy with his newest employee, determined to win her over. So far, her dourness was unrelenting. She was, however, very professional.

"The deputies have gone to wake Rick Willis," she informed him. "I already made the coffee. Is there anything else you need me to do?"

"Please call Dory, if you would. I need her to do a careful search of Brooke's apartment. Tell her she can get the key from Hadley and Emma in the lab. And if Detective Fuller isn't here in five minutes, call him and tell him I said to get his rear in gear."

If Ben wasn't mistaken, a hint of a grin flashed across the office manager's stern face. "Right away, sir," was her only reply. Ben turned around at the commotion behind him and was greeted by the sight of a handcuffed Rick Willis being unwillingly escorted to the interrogation room. Unshaven, wearing wrinkled clothes, and clearly in a foul mood, he gave the sheriff a red-eyed glare as he passed by.

"Send the detectives in as soon as they arrive, Mrs. Coffin." Ben followed Rick and his deputies, then closed the door behind him. "You can take his cuffs off now, George," he said. "Have a seat, Mr. Willis. I know you were read your rights last night." His portly, redheaded deputy unlocked the cuffs and Rick sat down. "But apparently you were unable to be booked, is that right?"

"I guess not, but she just booked me," Rick tilted his head at Cam Gomez, who was standing near the door, "on assault charges." He rubbed his wrists, frowning. "I'd like my phone back and I'm going to call my lawyer now."

Ben smiled. "Thank you. You're both dismissed," he told his deputies. After the door closed behind them he looked across the table at his hung-over suspect. "I don't have your phone, so I can't give it back," he cheerfully and truthfully told Rick, knowing that Wayne had confiscated it last night, "but you're entitled to one phone call. My office manager will be happy to get your lawyer on the phone if you give me the number." He took a pen out of his pocket, poising it above the legal pad on the table.

"I don't know the number," Rick said, "but it's in my phone." He scowled at the sheriff. "His name's Ramsey Tremaine, and he's going to get me out of here in no time."

Great, Tremaine. That's all I need. "We'll just see about that, Mr. Willis," Ben said. "I'll be right back."

Rob Fuller walked in as Ben was leaving the room. "Keep an eye on him, Detective."

"Will do." He sat down, facing Rick, and Ben went back to Sophie Coffin's desk.

"Ms. Clarkson is on her way to the lab to get the key so she can search the apartment," she said. Her eyes were unreadable behind her glasses.

"Thank you. I need you to call Ramsey Tremaine's office for me. Tell him we have Rick Willis in custody on an assault charge."

Mrs. Coffin jerked her head back at the mention of Rick's attorney. "He got an acquittal for the drunk driver who put my nephew in a wheelchair. I cannot stand that despicable man." She huffed out a breath. "I'll find the number."

"I'm sorry, Mrs. Coffin, that's terrible." Ben looked at her with compassion. "Is he your sister's son or your brother's?"

"My sister's only child." She paused and removed her glasses. "He's been paralyzed for three years now, but he has a great attitude—thinks he'll walk again someday." She swiped at her nose with a tissue. "It doesn't look like my sister's ever going to get over it. She's very depressed and fearful, hardly leaves the house anymore."

"I'll ask Cam to get him on the phone, Mrs. Coffin, and you can run an errand while Mr. Tremaine is in the office."

His office manager mustered a smile and put her glasses back on. "You've just got to win the election, you know?" She stood and picked up her oversized black pocketbook. "And thank you, Sheriff Bradley. You may call me Sophie," she took her rain jacket off the wall hook and paused at the front door, looking over her shoulder, "if you want to."

Wayne was just coming in. He held the door open for Mrs. Coffin, who nodded at him, put her hood up and went out into the rain. "Where's she off to?" his chief detective asked.

"Running an errand for me. Rob's in there with our suspect. Do you have Willis' cellphone? He needs to call his lawyer."

Detective Nichols took a black cellphone out of his breast pocket. "Here it is. I didn't learn much from Brooke's neighbors—Mrs. Brighton's a bit of a drama queen—but her husband saw a dark-colored sedan he didn't recognize. Said it was parked in the lot when he left to go bowling. Willis drives a dark blue BMW sedan."

They walked back to the interrogation room and went in. The big detective handed Rick his phone and clapped him on the shoulder ... hard. "How're you feeling this morning?" he boomed. Rick winced and didn't answer, staring down with an angry expression. "Can I get you anything? Coffee? Hair of the dog?" Wayne went on in a loud voice, obviously enjoying the suspect's discomfort.

Rick Willis shook his head. He turned away in his chair and tapped on his phone. "Hi, yeah, it's me," he said quietly. "Listen, I got arrested last night ... no, not for drunk driving, for assault. I'm at the sheriff's office and I need you to come get me out." He paused, listening. "Okay, I won't say anything until you get here, thanks." He pressed the 'end' button on his screen and put the phone back in his pocket. "He'll be here in ten minutes." He gave Wayne a stony glare and sat back, wordlessly awaiting his lawyer.

LEAVING ROB AND Wayne to guard the suspect, Ben went to his office and stood looking out the window. True to his word, Ramsey Tremaine stepped out of a Lincoln Town Car ten minutes later. His vanity plate read "Lawyerd Up." Ben shook his head and walked to the front door. Ramsey strutted in, looking around and ignoring Ben. "Needs some sprucing up before I move in."

"C'mon, Tremaine. Your client's back here." Gesturing toward the interrogation room, Ben dispensed with the pleasantries. "Let's go."

Ramsey gave him a sidelong look. "Not for long he isn't," he murmured, and walked on by. Without waiting for the sheriff, he threw open the door. Giving his client a gracious nod, he went to stand behind him, putting both hands on his shoulders. "When did this alleged assault take place?"

"It's not *alleged*." Ben felt the heat building in his core. "A young woman is in the hospital because of him."

The lawyer's eyes were cold. "How unfortunate for her. I repeat, when did this incident happen?"

"Between eight and nine thirty last night," Wayne Nichols informed him in a low growl.

Rick Willis looked up at his lawyer with a smile. Mr. Tremaine continued to stare at Ben. "Has this young woman identified my client as her assailant? She's lying if she did."

Detective Fuller spoke up this time. "She hasn't identified anyone as her assailant, you prick. I stopped by the hospital to check on her this morning. She's still unconscious in neuro ICU with a head injury."

Atta boy! Ben stifled a smile. "So we need your client to account for his whereabouts during that time."

Rick started to speak, but his lawyer gave his shoulders a squeeze. "I'm sorry to break the news, but you need to keep looking for her assailant. Mr. Willis and I played tennis at seven thirty last night. We got a bite to eat and had a few drinks before I went home. I can personally vouch for his whereabouts until eleven o'clock."

Ben closed his eyes for a brief moment, then had an idea. "So he got drunk with you, a candidate for sheriff, and you just let him get in a car and drive home?" He stared into his opponent's eyes, but Tremaine never blinked.

"On the contrary, he was unimpaired when I left the bar. I don't know what happened after that. If you wanted to book him for a DUI, you clueless idiots should have breathalyzed him last night. And I'll testify under oath that he was with me during the time in question." He gave a triumphant smile to the assembled lawmen. "Drop the charges and we won't sue you for harassment."

Ben was outfoxed and he knew it. "Fine," he said. "You have a deal."

Chapter Thirty-Five

—

Sheriff Ben Bradley

B EN WAS DISCOURAGED when he got home that night, convinced that the case was going nowhere. "We had to let Rick Willis go, and the lab techs haven't been able to find anything helpful from Brooke's apartment." He gave Mae a half-hearted kiss. "Dory said the only thing missing from her apartment was a gold and diamond ring that belonged to Brooke's grandmother. It may have been nothing more than a simple robbery, since that ring has no connection to the Willis case. Until Brooke wakes up and tells us something about her attacker, we've got nothing. I hope your day was better than mine."

Mae distracted him with the account of her day's adventures—including the snake—and he went to bed in a slightly better mood.

THE NEXT DAY he called before lunch with good news: Brooke Piper was awake and undergoing medical tests. Lucy had called

Wayne to say that the doctors were "cautiously optimistic" about her condition.

"I'd like you to go with me later today," Ben said. "I'm going to visit her at the hospital and see if she can answer some questions. She's been traumatized, though, and I don't want to upset her. I think having you there might put her more at ease. Can you be available this afternoon? Lucy's going to let me know when it's a good time to go see Brooke."

"I'm flexible today," she assured him. "Just text me when you hear from Lucy."

Mae said goodbye and then placed a call to Petals, the florist shop in Rosedale. She ordered a bouquet to take to Brooke, saying she or the sheriff would pick it up in a few hours.

THE TEXT FROM Ben came in at 3:15. Brooke was ready for visitors. Mae sent him a quick text back, asking him to pick up the flowers and meet her at the front desk of the hospital. She took Cupcake, who was sporting a red ribbon around her ears today, out for a quick break. After the puppy did her business, Mae praised her lavishly and gave her a mini marshmallow before placing her back in her crate. Grabbing her keys and dropping her phone into her purse, she went out to her Explorer. Twenty minutes later, she parked in the visitor's lot and walked through Rose County General's main entrance.

Ben had his back to the door, but his tall, uniform-clad frame was unmistakable. Mae walked over and tapped him on the shoulder. "They did a great job on the flowers, didn't they?" he asked, after kissing her cheek. The bouquet he held was breathtaking—a combination of white daisies, yellow lilies, and cobalt-blue delphiniums in a tall cylindrical vase made of clear glass.

He gave them to Mae to carry, and they took the elevator up to Brooke's room. Channing Soldan, wearing pink scrubs with fuchsia streaks in her short, tousled blonde hair, was just leaving the room when Mae and Ben walked up.

"Hi, Mae." She gave Ben a look of obvious feminine admiration. "Who's your friend?"

Mae laughed. "Channing, this is my fiancé, Ben Bradley. Ben, Channing Soldan works with our neighbor Lucy, and she's Brooke's friend."

"You're the one who found her after the attack, right?" Ben shook Channing's hand. "Good to meet you. How is she today?"

Channing gave a little frown. "She's okay. Has an awful headache, of course. Nausea too. She's still pretty out of it, but I know she'll appreciate those gorgeous flowers. Nice to meet you, Sheriff, but I've got to get back to the ER." She hustled toward the elevator with a wave.

Ben opened the door for Mae, who walked in after a slight hesitation. She didn't want to intrude on the poor girl, but Brooke was the only one who could describe her attacker. She might hold the key to finding Chester's killer as well. Mae set the vase of flowers down on a cart near the bed.

"Hi, Brooke," Ben spoke quietly. "This is my fiancée, Mae. We brought you some flowers. How are you today?"

Her face was pale, and she turned her head slowly to look at Mae. She was small, barely making a bump under the sheets of her bed. "Thank you." Brooke cleared her throat. "Those are pretty." Her eyes drifted shut.

Mae pulled a chair close to the bed and sat down. She touched the girl's arm gently. "Brooke, do you know who did this to you?" Without opening her eyes, she gave a small shake of her head. Mae looked at Ben.

He walked to stand on the other side of the bed. "What's the last thing you remember? Did someone come to your door?"

Brooke's eyes opened again. "Channing sent me a text," she said, and her eyes filled with tears. "She was going to be late. That's all I know."

"You were talking about a ring when they brought you to the ER." Ben handed her a tissue from the box beside the bed. "Do you remember why?"

Brooke took the tissue and dabbed at her eyes. "That's what Channing told me," she said helplessly, "but I don't remember." She looked at Mae and the tears flowed faster. "I just wish my mom was here."

Mae clasped Brooke's cold little hand between her own and gave her a reassuring smile. "I'll do my best to get her here. Thank you for talking to us, Brooke. You rest now."

She held the girl's hand until she was sure that Brooke was sleeping, then Mae and Ben tiptoed out. Ben closed the door softly behind them.

Chapter Thirty-Six

———

Chief Detective Wayne Nichols

WAYNE WAS DRIVING back to the office after a late lunch when Ben called.

"What's up?" he asked his young boss.

"Mae and I are just leaving the hospital. We talked to Brooke, but she doesn't remember anything other than a text from her friend Channing saying she was going to be late. I spoke briefly with the neuro attending who said that sometimes it takes a few days or even weeks before the memory returns after a hard blow to the back of the head. What do you think our next step should be?"

"I was just about to call Dory. As our resident jewelry expert and the person who originally went through Brooke's jewelry box, I was wondering if she had any ideas about why Brooke would have been talking about a ring."

"When I talked to Lucy, she said Brooke's tone of voice wasn't particularly anxious, more like she was trying to tell Lucy something she needed her to know."

"Victims of assault often try to point to their attackers by repeating the same words," Wayne said quietly, almost to himself. Then he added, "Damn, I wish Tremaine hadn't been able to provide an alibi for that useless Rick Willis. I was sure he was our man. My CI, Jacko, gave me the name of a jewelry fence last night. I'll hunt him down too, on the off chance the assault on Brooke was a robbery gone wrong."

"Right. I'm going back to the office now. See you there." Ben was gone.

Wayne called Dory's cell.

"Detective Nichols, I presume," Dory teased.

"Do you have any ideas about this ring Brooke was talking about?"

"Goodness. Not even a 'hello' for your best buddy?"

Wayne sighed. He felt the need for Southern courtesies could have been dispensed with in the urgency of finding Brooke Piper's assailant, but he gave in, saying, "Good afternoon, Dory. How is your day going? What are you up to at the moment? I wonder, if you *possibly* have the time to talk, why do you think Brooke Piper was talking about a ring?"

"Why certainly, Detective. As you know, traditionally, rings are exchanged at a wedding. Doorbells also ring. Sometimes ears ring due to loud noises, like getting too many phone calls from irritating detectives. A ring is what a man gives a girl when he proposes. George said Rick Willis was drunkenly bragging about getting engaged when you brought him in night before last, wasn't he?"

"Right. I'll have a little chat with Rick Willis' intended, Meredith Flynn. Would you do something else for me, Dory? I need to know whether the Willis jewelry was released to Brooke or whether it's still being held by probate."

"Your wish is my command," Dory said. "I think Miss Lorene, Shane Connor's secretary, will know."

"Text me when you find out," Wayne said.

"And *thank you*, Miss Dory," Dory said, pertly. Wayne sighed.

"And thank you, Miss Dory," Wayne repeated the words and

hung up, irked. Then, remembering the $20 he gave Jacko the previous evening, he called his CI and told him to find out if an antique gold and diamond ring had been fenced recently. Then he called Ben again.

"Hey," Ben said. Wayne was relieved that Ben at least was willing to overlook the pleasantries.

"Dory reminded me that the evening Rick Willis spent getting hammered with Ramsey Tremaine, he had just gotten engaged to Meredith Flynn," Wayne said. "Any problem with me having Meredith stop down at the office? The Willis jewelry went to Brooke Piper. Perhaps Miss Flynn went over to see Brooke about Mrs. Willis' ring and things got out of hand."

"None at all," Ben said. "Go ahead and bring her in. If she assaulted Brooke, we need to consider her for the Willis killing too. I'll be there soon."

WAYNE WAS IN his office when Dory walked in, wearing a colorful printed skirt and stilettos. Her arms were laden with jangling bracelets.

"Find out anything?" Wayne asked.

"Yes, I did. I went over to Mr. Connor's office to chat up Miss Lorene. The purpose of probate is for the court to collect the decedent's property, pay any outstanding debts, and then distribute the remainder. Most dispositions are uncontested. Someone was planning to contest Leonard Willis' estate."

"Rick Willis, I assume?"

"You assume correctly. Mr. Disgruntled Heir wants a larger share of Daddy's property. He believes his dad may have been *improperly influenced* in leaving his late wife's jewelry and money to Brooke Piper. Shane O'Connor persuaded him not to contest … said he would testify to Leonard being of sound mind and acting of his own free will when he made his final dispositions. He also told Rick that *all* of the estate could be tied up for months if he contested it, which seems to have done the trick." Dory paused and gave Wayne a wink. "Guess the walls are thin in that law office. Anyway, Brooke's share of the estate and the jewelry were released on the sixteenth."

"To whom?" Wayne asked.

"To Shane Connor's office, but the name on the form was Brooke Piper." Dory eloquently raised a single eyebrow.

AT 4:30, AN expensive-looking sedan drove into the sheriff's parking lot, and Meredith Flynn emerged, dressed in a blue skirt with a slit up the side, high-heeled sandals, and a crisp, white blouse. Wayne had been waiting for her arrival, pacing the floor, for almost two hours.

"Ben," he called out. "Meredith Flynn is here."

"Excellent," Ben said as he walked out of his office to join Wayne in the waiting room.

"Wayne and I are going into the conference room, Sophie. Would you please escort Ms. Flynn to the room when she comes inside?" Ben asked his new office manager.

"Certainly, Sheriff," Sophie Coffin said.

Dory was walking out the office door. She paused. "Nice use of the word 'please,' Sheriff," She said, glancing at Wayne. "I'm glad *some* people remember their manners when talking to the staff."

Wayne raised both his hands in the air in an "I give up" gesture.

Several minutes later, when Sophie Coffin opened the conference room door, Ben rose to say, "Please come in, Ms. Flynn. Thank you for stopping by. I believe you know Detective Wayne Nichols? I'm Sheriff Ben Bradley," he held out his hand to shake hers. He pulled out a chair for her and asked her if she wanted water or a soda. She declined.

"How can I help you?" Meredith asked.

Butter wouldn't melt in her mouth, Wayne thought. Her composure was studied—a high-born lady graciously deigning to spend time with the lower-class minions of the law. He nodded at Ben. They had discussed congratulating her on the engagement as a way of opening the door to whatever role she might have played in Brooke's assault.

"Congratulations on your recent engagement," Ben said, smiling at her.

"Thank you, Sheriff. Yes, it was quite a surprise. No ring yet, as you observe." She held out her left hand. "We're still discussing the ring. Rick and I met for lunch at Watermark the day before yesterday. Afterward we strolled through the park downtown by the river. Rick seated me at a park bench, knelt, and proposed. In lieu of a ring, he gave me a cashier's check for the down payment on a home we will be purchasing."

She smiled at Ben, but to Wayne's eye it looked like a smirk. *Probably the money for the down payment came right out of the estate of Mr. Willis Sr.* Watching Meredith and her near-flirtatious behavior with the sheriff, he saw a woman he didn't trust for a moment.

"Goodness, a down payment on a house," Ben said. "That's a creative alternative to a ring. Where is the house located?"

"In the East End," Meredith said. "There's a development there called Five Points, do you know it?"

Wayne mentally rolled his eyes and decided to intervene.

"Miss Flynn, I'd like to return to the question of your engagement ring, if you don't mind?"

"Certainly, Detective." She turned her megawatt smile on Nichols and crossed her legs, giving him a brief glimpse of her upper thighs when the slit skirt fell open.

"I understand that the Willis family jewelry was recently released from probate. When you mentioned that you and Rick were still *discussing* the ring, I wondered if Rick had wanted to give you his mother's engagement ring." *Light and easy*, Wayne thought, *just a touch of emphasis on the end of the sentence.*

Meredith looked discomfited for the first time. "He wanted to, but as you know, Detective, the Willis jewelry went to Brooke Piper in Rick's father's bequests." Her voice held an edge of irritation, tightly controlled.

"Perhaps Miss Piper would be open to selling you the ring?" Wayne said, his eyes locked on Meredith's. "In fact, a car like yours was seen in the parking lot by Miss Piper's apartment on the night of the fifteenth. Did you pay her a visit to discuss a purchase arrangement?"

"I had a fundraiser to conduct for work. You can check with anyone. It was an upscale crowd of over one hundred guests. We were raising money for the children's wing of Rosedale General Hospital. I managed to get my boss to let me go for a long lunch hour. That was when Rick proposed. I have no idea why someone would say my car was near Brooke's place, except that all dark sedans look pretty much the same." She smiled, catlike.

"Miss Piper was assaulted that night in her apartment, just after nine o'clock," Ben said. "Someone knocked her down in her kitchen. She received a serious head injury."

"That's too bad," Meredith said. Wayne doubted that she was actually concerned.

"Let's stop dancing here, Miss Flynn. You're lying to us. You went over there to get that ring. And you were going to get it one way or another," Wayne felt anger rise in his gut, and his nostrils flared.

"No, you're wrong. I went directly home from the fundraiser. I had nothing to do with any attack on that sleazy Brooke Piper." Meredith's upper lip was beaded with sweat. She put her hands in her lap, clasping them tightly.

"Can anyone confirm that?" the sheriff asked gently. "We're trying to determine who assaulted Miss Piper and we'd like to dismiss you from our inquiries."

"Unfortunately, no. I went back to my townhouse to change clothes. A couple of the men at the fundraiser were smoking cigars." Meredith wrinkled her nose. "After that I planned to find Rick and join him. I didn't attack Brooke, Sheriff, you're wrong. However, since Brooke was unconscious, her memories are probably inaccurate anyway."

Wayne smiled to himself. They had never mentioned that Brooke was unconscious.

"Brooke Piper returned to consciousness just an hour ago," Wayne said. It was one of the things he found paradoxical about his job. In pursuit of the truth, he often lied. And when he was closing in on a suspect, he actually quite enjoyed it.

Meredith paled.

"Why don't you tell me what happened?" the sheriff asked, his voice low and almost kind. "I'm sure you didn't mean to hurt her."

"I didn't," Meredith was breathing hard. "I just went over there to make an offer to buy the ring. I admit I was furious when she said she wasn't going to sell it. We talked a while, but I could see she was dead set against it. She opened the refrigerator to get herself a coke. There must have been some water on the floor because she slipped and hit the back of her head against the counter. I made sure she was okay and then I left. If she says anything else, she's a liar."

"According to the doctors," Wayne said, "Brooke could not have hit her head hard enough from a fall to cause the head wound she received. And no one but her attacker would have known the location of the head injury."

"I didn't do it." Meredith sounded scared.

"Cut the crap, Meredith," Wayne said. "You admit to being there at the time of the assault. You had a strong motive in wanting the ring, and you are the only person—other than the doctors—who knew the injury was to the *back* of her head. Brooke is going to identify you as her attacker. Until that formality happens, we're going to keep you here in custody." A slow smile played over Wayne's features.

"You can't do that," Meredith said, practically whimpering. She stood up and reached for her purse. "If I have to stay here, I want a lawyer."

Ben's voice wasn't gentle when he spoke this time. "Sit down, Miss Flynn. I can arrest you right now if that's how you want to play it. You'll be cuffed, and I'll read you your rights and book you. This is a serious charge, and you'll definitely spend the night in jail before bond can be set."

Her face and neck were flushed. Her neck was corded with rage, but she sat down without saying another word.

The sheriff nodded. "Good." He turned to Wayne. "I've got this, Detective. I'm sure there are some things you could check on while I continue my conversation with Miss Flynn."

Wayne could take a hint. He got to his feet and left the room. He needed to have Lucy check on Brooke. God, he hoped Brooke remembered what happened and could identify Meredith as her attacker. Otherwise slippery Miss Meredith could still get off.

Knowing Meredith left Brooke bleeding on the floor in her kitchen made Wayne shift his focus to her as their new prime suspect in the Chester Willis killing, although they still had not dismissed Rick Willis. He briefly wondered if it had been a conspiracy between the two of them. It would make sense.

As he was climbing into his truck, Wayne wondered whether Brooke had actually picked up the Willis jewelry from the probate court. If she had, they were going to be looking for two rings—Brooke's grandmother's engagement ring and Mrs. Willis' ring. He turned the key in the ignition but left the truck in park while he called Lucy's cellphone.

Chapter Thirty-Seven

—

Chief Detective Wayne Nichols

WAYNE CALLED HIS girlfriend, and she answered her phone on the second ring.

"Hello big guy," she said.

"Lucy, are you at work?" he asked.

"Yes."

"We've detained Meredith Flynn for the assault on Brooke Piper. I told a small white lie during her interrogation, saying Brooke was conscious and would identify her as the attacker. When you get a break, could you go up to neuro and see whether Brooke remembers anything yet? We can't hold Meredith very long before Ramsey Tremaine or some other slime-bucket defense attorney finds his way to the jail and springs her."

"I can send Channing right now; she's about to go on break. Will that work?"

"It will. I'm going over to Meredith's townhouse right now to have a look around. Call or text me with anything that Brooke says, please."

"Of course. See you soon," Lucy said.

WAYNE DROVE TO Meredith's address, dialing Dory on the way.

"Hello, Miss Dory. How are you this fine evening? Everything going well?" Wayne said.

"All right, all right, just get to what you want." Dory sounded vexed.

"Must I want something?" Wayne said archly. "I only wanted to talk to my best gal pal."

"Oh, *right*." The frustration was apparent in her voice.

"Would you check with Lorene again to be sure that Brooke Piper really did pick up her inheritance? I want to know specifically about the ring."

"As you wish." Dory drawled the words out.

Wayne hung up. He had no time to dally. He didn't have time to get a search warrant either. He had to get inside Meredith's townhouse before some shyster lawyer released her. He walked to the front door of her unit and tried the door handle; it was locked. He tried the front window—also locked. He checked to see if there was a back door—there wasn't. He walked around the corner of the building. Meredith had the end unit and the two windows were both locked. The drapes were open, however, and Wayne peered inside. To his complete delight, Meredith had left the bedroom light on. He saw a neatly made bed, bedside tables, lamps, and a dresser.

Wayne had better than 20/20 vision, for which he thanked his Native American ancestors who were supposed to be able to bring down a duck with an arrow fifty feet in the air. Even at nearly sixty, he could see extremely well. He pulled out a little pinpoint flashlight and focused it through the window on the surfaces of the dresser and night tables. Something caught the light on the nightstand and Wayne saw a little silver dish. In the dish was a gold ring.

His phone rang. It was Dory.

"Why Investigator Clarkson," he said with exaggerated

politeness. "I so appreciate your call. What might you have discovered?"

"Knock it off, Nichols. I found out that Brooke Piper didn't take the Willis jewelry with her on the sixteenth. She picked up her check for the money she inherited but told Lorene she was going to get a safety deposit box at the bank for the jewelry before taking possession. The Willis jewelry, including the ring, is still at the lawyer's office."

"Excellent work. I have a bit of a problem, however. I think I've spotted Brooke's grandmother's ring on Meredith's nightstand at her apartment, but the unit is locked up tighter than a drum. I'm going to the manager's office to try to get them to let me in. There's no time for a warrant. I'm also going to need some backup. Send somebody over here now, will you? Once the sheriff's done talking with Meredith, do everything you can to stop her from leaving the office, okay?"

"You'll owe me, but I'll keep her there if I have to lock her in the ladies' room."

"I'll be eternally grateful," Wayne said and grinned, knowing whatever Dory wanted in return for this favor, he would happily do. He set off at a trot across a large mowed commons toward the manager's office. He was sweating; the evening was muggy and very hot. Just as he yanked open the door to the office, breathing hard, Lucy's face showed up on his phone screen.

"Hi, Lucy."

"Wayne, Brooke still isn't talking much, but she's remembering more. She told Channing that she was wearing her grandmother's ring before the attack. She's not wearing it now, but Channing said there's a slight mark where it was. The ring must have been a tight fit, because where it was stripped off her hand, there are still faint red marks."

The bitch pulled the ring off an injured, unconscious woman. In his view, stealing the belongings from the dead or wounded was the action of a person without a vestige of conscience, the deed of a coward. In war, those who stole from their dead or injured brothers-in-arms were subject to court martial.

"I think the ring is in Meredith's townhouse, and if so, I could nail her on a theft charge at a minimum. Problem is, I can't get inside her place. I'm afraid she'll leave the sheriff's office, come here and hide it before I can retrieve it. I'm trying to get the manager to let me in. Ben and I will need to get to the hospital as soon as we can after I'm done here."

"Can I help you?" the woman behind the desk asked as he opened the door to the Manager's Office. Wayne clicked off his phone, identified himself, and thought of telling her a tale of a Meredith Flynn lying ill or unconscious in her apartment. It would work, but could be used against him once the case came to trial. He realized that there was no need to lie. He had legal grounds to open the locked apartment, to prevent the imminent destruction of evidence in a police case.

"Your tenant, Meredith Flynn, has some stolen property in her place, and she'll be on her way here soon. She'll hide the evidence if I can't get it first. I need you to open her apartment. Now, please."

It took a bit more talking and a phone call to upper management, but finally the woman picked up a key and they started walking quickly back across the large mowed commons.

Wayne saw Meredith's car pulling into the complex. She was about two hundred feet away from her designated parking slot when Wayne began to run. A sheriff's office patrol car with its siren on was right behind her.

"Move!" he shouted to the manager, and she did. They reached the front door and opened it quickly, just as an unkempt and furious Meredith got out of her car.

"What do you think you're doing?" Meredith yelled, but Dory jumped from the passenger side of the patrol car and put her imposing body in Meredith's path.

Already in the apartment, Wayne heard Dory say, "You

forgot something in the ladies room," and Meredith asking "What are you talking about?"

"You forgot to FLUSH!" Dory said.

Wayne heard Meredith say, "Get the hell out of my way!" as he slipped a pen from his pocket, used it to pick up the ring, and slid the ring inside an evidence envelope.

Meredith could claim that Wayne had entered her apartment without permission and taken a piece of her jewelry, but no judge would buy it. The ring wasn't hers. It was stolen property, and the assistant manager was on board.

"I never liked that woman," the assistant manager told him. "She always acts like she's better than everyone else."

Leaving Dory and Cam, who had driven the patrol car, to deal with a furious, sputtering Meredith, Wayne slipped away and drove to the office. He left the ring with Hadley at the lab, hoping there might be a fingerprint or a bit of blood caught in the little pave diamonds surrounding the major stone.

"Talk about a challenge," Hadley Johns said. "Round, little, and metal. Not making it easy on me are you, Detective?"

"You're up to it," Wayne said, clapping Hadley on the shoulder. "Let me get a picture of the ring on my phone so I can confirm that its Brooke's before you start working on it." He quickly took three different shots, said goodbye to the tall, thin lab tech, and went back to the office to find Ben. It was time to get to the hospital.

Chapter Thirty-Eight

———

Dr. Lucy Ingram

LUCY WAS AT her computer when Channing Soldan swept back into the ER after her break. Her hair had pink highlights and she seemed excited. She wore pink scrubs and had multicolored laces in her shoes.

"I've got news, Dr. Lucy," she said. "Brooke's remembering the night of her attack. She told me she was wearing her grandmother's ring, but it's not on her hand now. Let me know when you have time to talk to her. I want to go with you."

"Not right now," Lucy said. "As a matter of fact, I need vitals on the patients in cubicles three and four. Once we get those two triaged and stabilized we might have time. I'll call Detective Nichols and let him know."

She gave Wayne a quick call to fill him in. Though in the middle of trying to search Meredith's apartment, he said he and Ben would come to the hospital as soon as they could.

HALF AN HOUR later, Lucy and Channing were in the elevator on their way up to neuro. Reaching Brooke's room, they saw her sitting up and eating. That was a good sign, as up to now she had been lying down whenever they saw her.

"Hello, Brooke," Lucy said. "It's Dr. Ingram. Remember me?"

"Yes, I know who you are." Brooke put down her spoonful of mashed potatoes and pushed the tray back.

"Good. I've called Detective Nichols. He and Sheriff Bradley will be over here soon to take your statement. Channing said you remembered the attack, right?"

"Yes, I did. Where's my grandmother's ring? I was wearing it at my apartment."

"It looks like someone took it off your finger. You weren't wearing it when you were admitted."

"Then I know who took it," Brooke said. She looked pale, but there was a determined set to her jaw.

"This certainly isn't official—you'll have to give the sheriff and the detective your statement—but can you tell us who it was?"

"Meredith Flynn," Brooke said. "She came over to my apartment offering me money to buy Mrs. Willis' ring. She and Rick had gotten engaged, and he wanted her to have it, as it was a family heirloom."

"Did you agree?" Channing asked. "How much did she offer you?"

"No way." Brooke shook her head, then winced. "Ouch, I shouldn't do that. She offered me five thousand dollars. I wasn't even tempted. I figured if Mr. Willis wanted to keep his wife's jewelry in the family, he would have left it to Rick. He wanted me to have it. So I told Meredith I wasn't interested in selling."

"You go, girl," Channing said, patting her friend on the shoulder.

"Tell me about the injury," Lucy said. "How did that happen?"

"When I told Meredith I wasn't interested, I was in the kitchen. I opened the refrigerator to get a Coke to keep me awake for studying with you, Channing. Then Meredith charged into the kitchen and grabbed me by the shoulders. She was shaking me, and then she pushed me, sort of threw me away from her. I remember falling back. I saw a crack in the ceiling, there was a sharp pain, and then nothing."

"Do you think you hit your head on the edge of the kitchen counter when you fell?" Lucy asked.

"I think so, but it all happened really fast. Meredith looked so angry; her eyes were just blazing. Her fingernails were like claws." Brooke looked down and cleared her throat. Telling the story was obviously hard for her.

"The funny thing about all of this is that the ring Meredith took off your finger wasn't even the Willis ring. It was your grandmother's, right?" Channing said.

"Yes. She must have thought it was Mrs. Willis' ring, though. What's going to happen now?"

"The sheriff and Detective Nichols will get Meredith for this, don't worry," Lucy said. "And they'll get your ring back, too. I'm not your attending physician, Brooke, but your memory seems intact to me. I'm sure the neuro people will do more screens and tests. You'll be here a few more days, no doubt, but you look to be making a good recovery."

As Lucy said these words, the door to Brooke's room opened and Wayne and Ben walked in.

"Ooh, can I stay while you get her statement?" Channing asked excitedly.

Lucy saw Wayne roll his eyes. Ben shook his head with a little smile. Lucy and Channing said goodbye to Brooke and were leaving the room when Wayne turned. Putting his hand on Lucy's arm, he quietly said that he wanted to talk to her later. He had something they needed to discuss.

In the elevator, Channing gave Lucy a slow, considered look. "Are you and Detective Nichols getting, like … more serious?"

"Stop it." Lucy gave the young nurse a stern stare, suppressing a smile of her own.

WAYNE CALLED LUCY toward the end of her shift.

"What's your night been like?" he asked.

"Pretty light, all things considered," she said, "But I'm too whipped to do anything but go home and sleep."

"I understand, but it looks like the case is finally breaking, so I have a little time right now."

"Did you get a good statement from Brooke?"

"Yes, perfect. We have an airtight case against Meredith Flynn for robbery and assault. Brooke ID'd her ring from the pictures I took. Tomorrow we're going to work on Meredith to find out what she knows about the Chester Willis killing. We need a confession on this one. The problem is there's just no damn evidence."

"Good luck. What'd you want to talk to me about?"

"I got a call day before yesterday from a guy who wants to buy my condo. He has a connection through the Nashville police post. He's a police artist and getting married to a Rosedale woman. She's got two kids she won't take out of the Rosedale schools, so he's going to commute. If I'm willing to sell, he'd like to get the ball rolling so they could be in the new place by the time school starts in the fall."

"So, you were thinking what?" Lucy asked.

"Well, you did say that we were at the *not-quite-but-almost living together stage*, did you not?"

"I did. I guess that's what I get for dating a detective who can remember my every utterance word for word." Lucy was amused.

Wayne was quiet.

"But we've got a lot more talking to do before taking such a big step," Lucy went on. "You might not want to live across the street from your boss …."

She heard Wayne laugh. "Now it sounds like you're looking for an excuse to get out of living together, but I think you might still be interested."

"I just might be," Lucy told him, grinned and hung up.

Chapter Thirty-Nine

—

Sheriff Ben Bradley

AFTER ARRESTING AND booking Meredith Flynn for assault and robbery, Ben drove home, went straight to bed, and quickly fell asleep. He woke up in the dark. Mae was sleeping peacefully beside him, her breathing deep and even. He glanced at the clock on the bedside table—not quite 6 o'clock yet—but he decided to get up and reread Mae's report on Meredith. Now that they knew she was capable of violence, they would be looking at her for Chester's murder. Meredith certainly had means and opportunity. *But for the life of me, I can't come up with a motive.*

Ben pulled on some shorts and went downstairs. After letting the dogs out and getting a cup of coffee, he gave all four of them food and made sure the water in their bowls was fresh. The sun was starting to shine on the backyard of the old farmhouse, illuminating the peaceful, open space ringed by thick woods.

Ben finished his coffee and rinsed his cup. Leaving it in the sink, he got out his laptop, put it on the kitchen table, and turned it on. Then he sat down to look through his emails for Mae's report. Something cold and wet nudged the back of his bare calf.

"Are you ready to go back outside, Cupcake?" He looked down at the puppy with a smile. She was standing on her ears, but her tail was wagging. Ben picked her up and cradled her to his chest with one hand as he went over to Mae's desk and rooted around in the top drawer. After finding something he thought would work, he took Cupcake outside. Setting her down, he gathered her ears on top of her head, securing them together with the soft, lavender hair tie.

"Go on, girl. Hurry up and do your business." The little basset scampered off while Ben watched her from the step. When Cupcake was finished, he praised and petted her. She followed him back into the kitchen, where he gave her a treat and then put her in her crate.

Resuming his seat at the kitchen table, Ben found Mae's report and read it carefully. Then he read the section on Meredith Flynn again.

After showering and getting dressed without disturbing his sleeping fiancée, he left Mae a note and drove to the office, deep in thought. Wayne's pickup, Cam's older Honda, and Sophie Coffin's Ford Fiesta were the only cars in the lot, so there was one shady spot left for him.

"Good morning, Sheriff Bradley." His office manager greeted him with a smile.

"How are you this morning, Sophie?"

"I'm fine," she answered. "Deputy Gomez and Detective Nichols are in the conference room. George Phelps is on his way, and so is Detective Fuller."

Ben tilted his head. "Is Dory bringing some food in, do you know?"

"She is." Sophie looked down briefly at the notepad on her desk. "She said lots of food—both healthy and unhealthy."

"Good." Ben nodded his approval. "I'm going back to my

office for a minute. Please send everyone to the conference room as they arrive, and buzz me when they're all assembled."

He poured himself a cup of coffee and took it with him to his office. Closing the door behind him, he sat down at his desk and took a sip. His new office manager made better coffee than Dory ever had. It was obviously fresh and very hot. He scalded his tongue and set the cup down with a curse. An idea had occurred to Ben during his drive to the office and he placed a call to Rick Willis.

He answered on the first ring with an angry, "What is it now?"

"I have one question." Ben dispensed with the preliminaries. In the last few days, they'd arrested Rick, released him, and then arrested his fiancée, so he probably had less than a minute before Rick hung up on him. "Did you know that Meredith's father disappeared during a Federal investigation into his company?"

"Of course," Rick replied tersely. "We've been dating for a year and we're engaged now. We have no secrets from each other."

I wonder if that's true. The buzzer sounded on Ben's desktop. It was time to go. "All right, thanks." He ended the call and took his coffee cup with him to the conference room. Ben wanted to confer with his staff, especially Wayne, before interrogating Meredith Flynn. And maybe eat something as well. It looked like it was going to be a long day.

The conference room door stood open and Ben paused at the threshold, taking a moment to survey his team. Investigator and former office manager Dory Clarkson wore a light green silk dress and was biting into a blueberry donut. According to Mae, Dory's new beau had told her she would be perfect if she put on a few pounds, so Miss Dory had given up on dieting.

Chubby and freckled, with short red hair, his senior deputy George Phelps was also enjoying a donut. Most of the chocolate sprinkles were making it into George's mouth, but the front of his uniform sported a few as well. His other deputy, the quietly lovely Cam Gomez, smiled at him from the foot of the table, nothing but a bottle of water in front of her.

The two detectives were engrossed in conversation with their backs to the door. Wayne Nichols' thinning gray hair and powerful shoulders presented a striking contrast to Rob Fuller's slight build and cropped golden-brown curls.

Ben walked in, took a seat, and greeted his staff, smiling at each one in turn. "You know, I may or may not be reelected in November," he said, "but I sure have assembled a great team, and I believe we're going to get Chester's killer soon, working together."

"I think you're right." Wayne frowned, the skin crinkling around his piercing hazel eyes. "We may already have the killer in custody, but we're a little short on evidence. Also, I'm not sure yet about her true motive."

"It's money," Rob Fuller said with finality, his silver-framed glasses glinting in the fluorescent light. "It almost always is."

Cam shook her head. "You don't think Meredith did it?" Ben asked. She parted her lips to speak, then paused. "Go ahead," he told her. "I really want everyone to speak up, even if it's just an intuition."

From the foot of the table, Dory gave a derisive snort. "What, just because Cam's a woman, you think its intuition? Watch it, boss. Your chauvinism's showing."

Good Lord, she's never going to let up on me. Ben sighed. "That's not what I meant and you know it." He turned to look at Cam.

"I think she probably did kill Chester, but she and Rick weren't even engaged then. She couldn't have known that she'd get more money with Chester out of the picture."

"That's right," Wayne said. "Unless they were in on it together, but I don't know." His brows drew together. "I think something else must have set her off."

George raised his hand to get the floor. "Or she knew he

was about to propose. Our niece just got engaged and I swear, it's not like it used to be." He raised his eyebrows as he looked around the table. "She'd already agreed and they'd talked about all of it ahead of time. In my day, the man didn't propose knowing he was going to get a yes."

Ben scratched his chin thoughtfully. "You know what I thought was odd about Rick's proposal was that he gave her money for a down-payment on a house."

Dory glanced at Cam with a smirk. "She might just spend it on shoes."

"Why would they need a house?" Rob Fuller asked with a frown. "He has a condo and he just inherited his dad's place. That makes no sense to me."

Wayne rose to his feet. "We need to get Meredith talking about some of these things. Maybe she'll let her guard down, and we'll learn something about what happened to Chester." He jutted his chin at Ben. "Are you ready?"

Ben stood up. "I am. Cam, will you go ask Hadley if he found anything on the ring from Meredith's apartment? Brooke confirmed that it's hers, so Meredith definitely took it, but maybe there's trace evidence from the attack." Cam nodded and quickly left the room.

"George, please go get Meredith from her cell and put her in the interrogation room."

Suddenly everyone's attention was riveted to the door and the sound of Sophie Coffin's raised voice, saying, "You can't go back there!"

Ramsey Tremaine stood in the doorway. His office manager, cheeks flushed, was hot on Tremaine's heels.

"I tried to stop him, Sheriff Bradley, but he wouldn't listen."

"Don't worry about it." Ben winked at her. "Listening isn't his area of expertise—too busy running his mouth."

Dory snickered and Sophie Coffin gave Ben a grin before turning on her heel and heading back to her desk. George squeezed past the momentarily speechless attorney.

"Perfect timing, Tremaine." Ben gave him a big smile. "Saves us the trouble of calling you. We're just about to question Miss Flynn."

Ramsey stepped forward as the rest of the sheriff's office staff filed out of the room. Somehow Dory and Rob both managed to step on his foot, but Mr. Tremaine didn't yield an inch. Rather than leaving the room, Wayne stopped and stood nose to nose with the attorney.

"You're in my way," he growled.

Ramsey took a tiny step back. "Call off your dog, Bradley."

Ben gave him an even bigger smile. "He's just trying to leave the room. From over here, it looks like you're the problem. Would you agree with that assessment, Wayne?"

The big detective never took his eyes off Ramsey Tremaine. "He's the problem, all right."

"Oh, fine. This is ridiculous." He stepped aside and Wayne strolled out of the room, muttering something under his breath. Ben couldn't be sure, but it sounded a lot like "little prick."

"Like I was saying, perfect timing. Would you care to join me in the interrogation room?"

"You just don't get it, do you? I told you that you better leave the Willis family alone or we'd be filing a harassment suit. Meredith is a fine young woman and a wonderful member of our community. If you think persecuting her and people like her is the way to keep your job, you are sadly mistaken."

Ben gave him a warning glare. "Watch yourself." He walked out, leading the verbose attorney toward the interrogation room. "You were right about one thing," he said over his shoulder. "Rick didn't do it."

"I know he didn't," Ramsey blustered. "I told you he was with me."

Ben paused with his hand on the doorknob of the interrogation room. "That's right. But while he was celebrating his engagement, his fiancée was assaulting Brooke Piper." He opened the door and waved the attorney in. "After you."

Meredith was already seated at the table, looking a little the worse for wear after her night as a guest of Rose County. Her white blouse was wrinkled and sweat-stained. Her mascara had run, accentuating the dark circles under eyes. She looked ten years older as she raised her head toward Ramsey.

"I need a moment with her."

"Certainly." Ben backed out, pulling the door shut behind him as Ramsey Tremaine put a comforting hand on Meredith's shoulder.

The sheriff walked down the hall to Wayne's office. His chief detective looked up from his cellphone. "Nothing on the ring," Ben said. "Cam just texted me. Hadley says it looks like it was cleaned with a jewelry cleaning fluid."

Wayne shook his head. "It's going to be Brooke's word against hers on the assault, but there's no denying Meredith took the ring. That's the only real piece of evidence we have."

"Yeah, it is," Ben said, blowing out a puff of air. "And it's not for the murder—although Meredith does have a prescription for Xanax."

"That was at Rick's condo," Wayne reminded him. "He could have given that to Chester just as easily as she could. They both had opportunity."

Ben took a seat opposite Wayne. "That reminds me," he said, "I called Rick this morning before the staff meeting. He knew about Meredith's father, so that couldn't be what she and Chester were talking about the night he was killed."

Wayne frowned. "Well, this one has me baffled. Maybe she has some answers. How do you want to play it?"

"Tremaine's in there with her right now," Ben told him. "I'm thinking that Cam and I will go in and the rest of you will observe, at least for the first part."

Wayne looked a question at him. "Cam is non-threatening, and I'm less intimidating than you are," Ben said. "I want to lull Meredith to start with and then I'll take a break—maybe send you in to take Cam's place if we aren't getting anywhere."

Chapter Forty

—

Sheriff Ben Bradley

SHERIFF BEN BRADLEY and Deputy Cam Gomez were facing Meredith and her attorney across the table with their backs to the one-way glass of the interrogation room. Meredith stared straight ahead. Other than Sophie Coffin and the lab techs, the rest of the sheriff's staff were on the other side of the glass, invisible witnesses to the interrogation. So far, no one had learned much. They had been at it for almost an hour.

Ben's patience was at its limit. He stood up, stretched and walked around the table to stand behind the suspect. Speaking low and close to her ear as he had seen Wayne do on many occasions, Ben hoped to rattle her composure.

"Since we know you attacked Brooke before you took the ring whether you admit it or not, let's leave that for now. We need to talk about the night Chester died." Meredith stiffened in her chair. The acrid smell of her sweat rose in Ben's nostrils. He leaned in closer. "According to Marina Hernandez, you and Chester were talking about something he wanted you to tell Rick—something he wasn't comfortable knowing."

"Is there a question in there somewhere?" Ramsey challenged.

"What were you and Chester talking about that night?"

Meredith glanced at her attorney, who gave a small nod. Ben took the chair to her left.

"I have no idea what she thought she heard." Meredith sneered and directed her remarks across the table at Deputy Gomez. "When I was growing up, the help knew better than to eavesdrop, but if you're going to listen to some Mexican maid, you're going to hear a lot of lies."

Cam's nostrils flared and she took a deep breath. She looked at Ben, and then at Meredith. "If you're trying to make me mad, or impress us with your background, don't bother." Cameron Gomez rose to her full height of 5'2" and leaned both hands on the table, staring into Meredith's eyes. "We know all about your spoiled childhood and your criminal father. You just spent the night in jail, which is something Marina Hernandez has never done in her life. I'm not impressed, and unlike you, I'm free to leave, so that's what I'm going to do." Straightening up, she glanced at her boss once more.

"I could use a break," Ben said. He got up and walked to the door, holding it open for Cam, who marched out into the hall. "You two sit tight. I'm going to get some lunch. Be back in an hour or so."

"What about lunch for us?"

"You're free to leave, Mr. Tremaine. You can bring something back for her."

Ramsey shook his head. "I don't think so. You'll just come back in here while I'm gone and intimidate my client."

"Up to you. I'm sure we have some frozen meals for the county prisoners—someone from my staff will microwave them and bring them in with some water."

Ben let the door bang shut behind him. Wayne Nichols was waiting in the hallway. "I've never seen Cam like that, have you?"

Ben laughed. "No, pretty impressive. What do you think about Meredith's demeanor in there?"

"She's very measured in her responses for someone in her position, except for that little flare-up just now. I get the feeling Miss Flynn can keep a secret."

"I get the feeling she's a total bitch," Ben said. "And I'm getting nowhere."

Wayne looked at him, a little grin playing around the corners of his mouth. "I just heard from Mark on something I asked him to run down for me a few days ago—he's working on the final puzzle piece. Watch for a text from Emma, okay? And put me in, coach."

AN HOUR LATER, after Ramsey and Meredith had finished their microwaved lunches and the sheriff and his staff had enjoyed barbecue that Sophie Coffin brought in, Ben sent his two detectives in to continue the interrogation. He and the rest of the team went into the observation room.

"I insist that my client be allowed a bathroom break," Ramsey Tremaine demanded as soon as Wayne and Rob entered the interrogation room.

"Not a problem," Wayne said. "Detective Fuller will escort her to the ladies' room and wait outside."

"Can I have my purse?" Meredith asked. "I'd like to freshen up a bit."

"No, I'm sorry. You can't have your personal belongings until you bond out, if the judge grants bail." Rob actually sounded regretful, Ben thought. *Is he acting, or does he truly feel sorry for her?* He turned to Dory. "Would you meet her in the restroom and show her where we keep the extra toiletries, please?"

"Sure thing, bossman." Dory was out of her chair and out the door in a flash. Ben watched Rob leave the interrogation room with Meredith while Wayne and Ramsey continued to stare each other down from opposite sides of the table. He felt oddly removed from the scene, almost as if he were watching a crime drama on TV. No, Ben realized, it was more of a nature documentary. Wayne Nichols, with his commanding size and predatory ways, was the lion waiting for his prey. Ramsey Tremaine, smaller but possessed of a mean streak, would be the hyena, fattening himself off the lion's kill.

Dory sat back down beside him. "She'll be out in a minute. I gave her a comb and a toothbrush and some toothpaste. Girl needs a shower, though." She fanned her hand in front of her nose.

"She does. It's fear sweat." Cam spoke up. "She's going to break soon."

MEREDITH CAME BACK with Rob and they resumed their seats. Ben watched intently as Wayne Nichols' posture changed from his stare down with Ramsey to a milder, less threatening presence. "Are you feeling better?" he asked Meredith in a soft voice. She gave a tiny nod. Wayne gave Rob Fuller a quick glance.

"I looked up your work for the foundation," Rob said. "It's really very impressive, what you've accomplished there. Were you inspired by your mom?"

"I was." Meredith's chin came up. "I was only twenty-six when she lost her battle with pancreatic cancer. We were very close and I went into fundraising to defeat this horrible disease."

Ramsey Tremaine frowned at the young detective. "She's an impressive woman who's been through a lot. That's not why we're here today, though, right?"

Wayne Nichols leaned back in his chair. "Maybe it is. I know that the loss of her mother after being abandoned by her dad must have been extremely difficult for a girl who was raised in such a wealthy and sheltered environment."

Meredith was nodding vigorously. She started to speak, but her attorney put his hand on her arm to forestall her.

Ben's cellphone buzzed in his pocket. He took it out and saw a text from Emma, the lab tech. He stood up and left the room, quickly walking to the interrogation room. The sheriff entered without knocking. "Was this what you were waiting for?" he asked, bending down to show Wayne and Rob the text.

"Yep. Didn't take our favorite geek very long." Wayne's smile broadened. "This won't either. Care to join us, Sheriff?"

Ben sat in the chair to Wayne's right and looked across the table at the nervous attorney. He put his hand on Wayne's shoulder.

"It's going to be all right now, Meredith. You don't have to lie for him anymore."

Meredith swallowed, the long elegant line of her throat convulsing.

"The FBI's closing in. He'll be in their custody before you know it. Chester was going to tell Rick about seeing you with your father, wasn't he? That's why he had to die."

Her defenses crumbled, and for just a second, Ben could see the little girl she once had been. Meredith put her hands over her face and spoke through her long fingers. "I just needed a little more time and he wouldn't …. Considering Rick's line of work, I knew he'd go straight to the FBI if Chester told him and I just …." She put her hands down, looking at Wayne with a ravaged face.

"So your father came to Rosedale and got in touch with you sometime in June, right?" Wayne Nichols went in for the kill. "I think he leaned on you for a big chunk of money to help him flee the country. I know your savings account was emptied out around the time of Chester's death. Between the pressure from your dad and Chester pushing you to tell Rick about your father, you were losing your best shot at a rich husband. You got desperate, didn't you?"

"I just couldn't face … being poor again." Her words were almost inaudible in the quiet of the interrogation room.

Ramsey Tremaine put his arm around her shoulders. "Don't say anything else, Meredith."

Ben shook his head. "She's said enough. We're going to add

Murder One to her other charges. Go get the cuffs, Rob."

Ben and his chief detective watched as Meredith leaned, sobbing, into her attorney. Ramsey Tremaine was silent, patting her and staring into space.

Chapter Forty-One

—

Mae December

MAE WAS OUTSIDE with all four of her dogs at nine o'clock on Thursday morning, when she got the call from Brooke's friend. Her cellphone buzzed in the pocket of her shorts and she answered it with a quick, "Hi, Channing."

"Hi there, Mae. I wanted to let you know that they're probably going to send Brooke home tomorrow," the nurse said. "She's undergoing some more tests today, but the doc up in neuro told Dr. Ingram that she's probably ready to go. Any luck with her parents?"

"Good girl," Mae said to Cupcake, who had done her business and ambled back over to sit at Mae's feet. She gave the puppy a treat from her pocket stash.

"What?"

"Sorry, Channing. I was talking to our puppy. I did get through to Brooke's mom, and she said she would work on her husband and try to get him to come see Brooke in the hospital. I haven't heard back from her, but I'll call her again."

She heard a short sigh. "All right, let me know. Thanks."

Channing was gone. Mae put her phone back in her pocket and led the dogs inside, out of the hot, steamy morning and into the cool of the old farmhouse. She filled their water dishes and put Cupcake in her crate after letting the puppy have a quick drink. The three older dogs went to the laundry room, presumably to lounge in their beds. Mae poured herself a tall glass of sweet tea and took it upstairs to drink while she bathed and got ready for the day.

Ben had kept her up late last night, regaling her with his account of the day's events. Mae's report on Meredith had been pivotal in solving the case. Thinking that something must have happened recently with Eli Carnton, Meredith's father, Wayne had put Mark Schneider to work. The computer whiz, who worked for the East Nashville Police Post, had found searches in Chester's computer history for information about Eli Carnton that led him to believe that he had resurfaced. Mark had then gotten in touch with a contact at the FBI, who confirmed that Eli Carnton had been spotted in Rosedale with his daughter. By last night, Meredith's father was either in their custody or about to be. Wayne's suspicions had been correct. Mark alerted his girlfriend Emma, who sent Ben a text. Wayne had used the information to extract what amounted to a confession from Meredith.

Ben had left for the office before eight this morning, saying he had some final details to take care of on the case and would probably be home after lunch. "You can officially start as my campaign manager today," he added, after giving her a goodbye kiss. "Or whenever you like."

Mae ran a bath in the claw footed tub in her bathroom. Painted robin's egg blue, it was the first room she had redone in the farmhouse and still one of her favorites. She undressed, set her tea glass within reach, and gratefully sank into the water. Although Tammy had not yet been given the green light to go back to barre class, she had guilted Mae into going without her. Mae had the sore muscles to prove it. As she took a long soak, she sipped her tea. When the water cooled, she climbed out, toweled off, and slipped into a long, turquoise tank dress. She misted her hair with an anti-frizz spray, applied mascara and lip gloss, and went back downstairs, mulling over ideas for Ben's campaign as well as what she would say to Brooke's mom.

Walking out to her screened porch, Mae took out her cellphone and found the number for Brooke's mother, Callista Piper. Then she sat down on the glider and pressed the call button. The phone rang five times before going to voicemail. She left a brief message, simply asking Callista to call her back, and put the cellphone down on the seat beside her.

Rocking the glider back and forth with her feet, she looked around at her screened porch. July Powell, a gifted interior designer who also happened to be Mae's sister, had suggested using a cowhide rug to anchor a "rustic chic" look for the porch. Mae had originally planned on a more traditional design, but the distressed metal finishes and neutral colors July chose made for a surprisingly restful contrast to the lush greenery outside. Mae was about to get off the glider and go get Cupcake for a little training session when the phone buzzed against her leg.

"Hello, Callista," she said. "Thank you for calling me back."

MAE AND BEN were seated in Brooke Piper's hospital room. She seemed more energetic than last time they had seen her, sitting up in bed with some color in her face. Ben told Brooke that Meredith was in jail and she didn't need to worry about going back to her apartment.

"That's a relief," the young woman said with a half-smile. "Channing said I'm probably going home tomorrow and I was a little nervous about it." Brooke turned her face toward Mae. "Did you ever, um, talk to my mom?" she asked hesitantly.

Mae glanced at her phone. It was almost three o'clock. She smiled at Brooke. "I did. And Ben—I mean Sheriff Bradley— talked to your dad earlier today. He also had Jim Warwick, the man who administered your lie-detector test, give your father a call."

Brooke drew a quick breath, almost a gasp. Her dark eyes widened as she looked at Ben. "What did my dad say when you talked to him?" she asked, her voice shaking in the quiet of the room.

Mae tapped on Ben's arm. He glanced at her with a smile. "I'm going to let him tell you about our conversation himself." Ben stood up and went to the partly open door. He pushed it open the rest of the way and stepped back, allowing Frank and Callista Piper to step inside. Callista went straight to her daughter's bedside. Mae saw the tears shining on the woman's cheeks as she bent to embrace Brooke.

Frank Piper watched them for a moment, a smile slowly transforming his thin face. Taking Ben's hand, the tall, brown-haired man shook it vigorously. "I can't thank you enough, Sheriff Bradley." He nodded in Mae's direction. "Or you, young lady. I made a terrible mistake ten years ago—not believing my own daughter. If your fiancé hadn't reached out to Callista, and you hadn't insisted I speak with Mr. Warwick, I might have gone to my grave without seeing my," he stopped, closed his eyes and cleared his throat, "my own sweet child again."

Brooke's father went to the other side of her bed and stood there, his large hands dangling at his sides. Brooke and Callista turned identical profiles up to him, and Brooke reached out a tentative hand. Grasping it between both of his, Frank Piper fell to his knees with a stifled sob.

"Can you ever forgive me?" he asked, his voice breaking.

"I forgave you a long time ago, Daddy."

Frank reached out to hold his daughter, squeezing like he never wanted to let her go. Realizing that their presence was no longer necessary, Mae got out of her chair and walked over to Ben.

"Time to go?" he murmured. She nodded, and they walked

out hand in hand, leaving the Pipers to enjoy their reunion in privacy.

Brooke's friend Channing was waiting for them in the hallway. Smiling, she pulled the door of the room closed and stood with her back to it. "That went very well," she congratulated them. "You two do good work together" She winked at Mae. "Guess I can't steal him from you after all."

"Are you on a break?" Ben asked the irrepressible nurse.

"My shift already ended." She batted her eyes. "I just happen to be free for the rest of the day."

"What about Lucy, is she around?"

"She's already left. Why?"

"Because my lovely fiancée and I are having a little get-together at the house to celebrate closing the case, and to thank everyone. We'd like you to come by."

This was news to Mae, but she was glad to hear it. "We'll invite Wayne and Lucy too, of course," she told Channing. "Six thirty sound good?"

"Sounds great. Where do you live?"

"We're across the street from Lucy. I'll text you the address. See you later," Mae said.

She took Ben's hand as they left the hospital. "How about a campaign kick-off as well as a celebration for closing the case?" Mae asked.

"You ready to get to work as my campaign manager today?" Ben's eyebrows went up and he gave her a little grin.

Mae squeezed his hand. "Sure am. Let's gather the troops."

Chapter Forty-Two

——

Dr. Lucy Ingram

LUCY WAS RUNNING errands after leaving the hospital. She walked out of the grocery store into the parking lot and took a deep breath. It was nice to be outside. There had been unexpected rain earlier in the afternoon and the oppressive heat of the previous two weeks was somewhat relieved. She loaded two bags into her car and had started to climb into the driver seat when she heard her cellphone ringing. She pulled it out of her purse and clicked the "accept call" button.

"Hi, Mae."

"Hi, Lucy. We're having a party at the house tonight. Can you and Wayne come around six thirty?" her neighbor asked, in her usual soft, sweet voice.

"I know I can, but I'll have to check with Wayne." Lucy shut her car door and started it so she could roll the windows down. From Mae's end of the line she heard a muffled male voice.

"Ben says not to worry about Wayne's schedule. He'll be free."

Lucy laughed. "All right. We'll see you tonight then. 'Bye."

She clicked over to hear the message that Wayne had left her when she was in the store. "Call me." His voice sounded positively elated. "The Chester Willis case has been turned over to the DA. They're moving forward with prosecution."

Listening to him, Lucy felt her own spirits rise. She was looking forward to the party and seeing Wayne tonight. Pulling the car out of the parking lot, she put the phone on 'speaker' to get the full story.

"What happened?" she asked Wayne as soon as he picked up.

Wayne explained that, with the assistance of computer expert Mark Schneider, he had obtained enough financial information on Meredith Flynn to corner her into a confession for Chester Willis' murder. Lucy could hear the satisfaction in Wayne's voice that was always present when a case had been closed successfully.

"Did you hear that Ben and Mae are hosting a party at their place tonight?" Lucy asked.

"Yes, I got a text from Ben about it."

"They're ready to celebrate, thanks to your hard work," Lucy said. "You sound so happy."

"I didn't solve this one on my own, that's for sure. Ben and the rest of the staff were really on their game. Mae also did some background research that made a big difference, and I couldn't have done it without Mark Schneider. This one's going to go a long way toward getting Ben reelected. And Ramsey Tremaine will be defending a killer, which isn't going to help his popularity."

"If she confessed, what defense could he even offer?"

"He'll just try to get the jury to feel sorry for her. Her father ran out on the family and her mother died of cancer when she was young. But everyone has tough times; it doesn't excuse murder."

"Feeling pretty good today, aren't you?" Lucy teased.

"You bet. And now that the pressure is off, how about I drop by before the party? I have a little something for you."

"A present? Cool. I don't think you've gotten me anything since Valentine's Day. The party starts at six thirty, so if you want to get here around five, we can walk from my house."

"See you then. 'Bye."

Lucy clicked off her cellphone. Turning on to her street, she could see that it had rained harder in the valley than in town, and there were little puddles in low spots along the road. The parched look was gone from the shrubs around her home. She pulled into her garage and shut the car off.

Reaching for her purse, she grabbed the two grocery bags and went into the house. It was very quiet and the silence was a relief after the hectic day she had endured in the ER. Setting her purse and keys on her stainless-steel kitchen countertop, she quickly put the food away and headed to her master bathroom, kicking off her shoes on the way. She removed her earrings and put them on her dresser before stripping off her scrubs and throwing them in her hamper. Lucy turned on the shower and stepped in with a grateful sigh.

She was climbing out of the shower and reaching for one of her fluffy white towels when she heard Wayne's voice calling her name.

"In here," she answered, pulling the towel around her.

"Hi gorgeous," Wayne said, grabbing her to give her a hug. She had rarely seen him so happy. His usual phlegmatic demeanor had vanished and he seemed almost boyish. He was holding one hand behind his back. He gave her a long look, reached for the towel, and pulled it off her slowly.

"Quit that," Lucy said, reaching for the towel and laughing. "I'm getting all fancied up here, so either behave yourself or get out."

"Okay, okay." Wayne backed away and sat down on her bed, one hand still behind his back. "I'll just observe you in my usual close and attentive manner."

"Now you're going to make me self-conscious." Lucy grabbed

another towel and rubbed her long brown hair with it as she followed him into the bedroom. He grinned but showed no sign of departing. With a shrug, she walked into her closet to select an outfit. After putting on black undies and slipping a slim sleeveless black dress over her head, she walked back into the bedroom and stood in front of the mirror that hung over her dresser. Opening her jewelry box, she chose a silver and turquoise necklace and put on silver hoop earrings.

"I thought you said something about a present," Lucy said and then glanced behind her in the mirror to see Wayne holding a large bouquet of white roses.

"Oh, thank you," Lucy said, pleased. "They're absolutely beautiful. What's the occasion for the gift?" She reached for the cellophane-wrapped bouquet, tied with a white ribbon. "I want to get these into water. Come into the kitchen."

Wayne walked behind her into her kitchen, watching as she got a large cut-crystal vase down from an upper cabinet. Lucy filled the vase with cool water and tossed the packet of flower-life extender that came with it into the trash.

"You don't use that stuff?"

"It's not as effective as a touch of bleach and a quarter teaspoon of sugar." Lucy pulled out her sugar bowl and added a carefully measured teaspoon. Locating a small bottle of bleach from under the sink, she poured a bit into the vase. "So you were telling me the occasion for the flowers."

"I bought you the flowers to thank you. On the way over here I was thinking about how much I owe you on this case, Lucy. If you hadn't had your diagnostic instincts set on high, Chester Willis' killer would never have been brought to justice, and his death would still be classified as a suicide. You're the real hero this time, not me."

"Thank you," Lucy said. "I only did the diagnostic work, but with my history, I'm not about to let a murderer go free if there's any way in the universe to make him or her pay."

"I'm with you on that." Wayne gave her a kiss.

Walking back toward the bedroom, Lucy said, "I know Meredith injected Chester under his large toenail with insulin, but how exactly did she accomplish that? In my ER we would've sedated any patient for such a procedure, not that we would inject insulin under a toenail anyway."

"And that's what Meredith did: she sedated him, slipped one of her own Xanax in with his meds."

"That would definitely have knocked him out," Lucy said, stepping into her black and white high-heeled sandals. She opened a dresser drawer and pulled out a lightweight, knitted shawl that was white with silver threads. The dress was sleeveless, and she thought she might want something around her shoulders, given the cooler than usual evening. She gave her hair a quick brush. Almost dry, it curled just at her shoulders. "But why did she kill him?"

"I'd like a beer before we go." Wayne left the room, looking back over his shoulder at her he asked, "Do you want anything?"

She checked her reflection once more in the mirror before answering, "A glass of white wine might be nice. I'll be right there."

Lucy put on some lipstick and dabbed her wrists with perfume before joining Wayne at her kitchen table. She took a sip of the wine he had poured for her and gave him a direct look. "What was Meredith's motive?"

Wayne drained his beer in one long gulp, then went to toss the can in her recycle bin. He looked out the window and then back at Lucy. "Looks like the party's starting. Let's walk over, and I can tell you the rest of the story on the way."

"Good thing you poured me a small glass." Lucy took another sip of the chilled wine, then set her glass beside the sink.

As they walked out the door, Wayne gave her a sidelong glance. "I find myself telling you more than I'm usually comfortable sharing. We're supposed to be close-mouthed about our cases."

"I think, at least in this case, that I'm entitled to know, Wayne.

After all, without my picking up on the unnatural death …" Lucy's voice trailed off as she looked at him.

"Of course, but all my training has taught me to keep criminal information to myself."

"Perhaps I can give you some reassurance," Lucy said as they walked down her driveway toward Little Chapel Road and across the street to Mae's driveway. She took Wayne's arm. Walking in heels on the gravel road was an unsteady business. "You certainly recall doctor/patient privilege? It's unbreakable, even in a court of law."

"Right, but I'm hardly your patient." Wayne looked at her, smiling.

"True, but what I'm trying to say is that I've also been trained to keep my mouth shut. You can tell me anything, and if you ask for confidentiality, you can be sure my lips are sealed." She pinched her thumb and first finger together, touched them on her mouth and turned them as if locking her lips with a key.

Wayne nodded. "All right, then. Meredith's father left his family after being indicted for white collar crime. It was years ago, but he came to Rosedale recently and talked Meredith into giving him her savings. He cleaned her out. Chester found out about her father being in town and was pressuring Meredith to tell Rick about her past. The fact that Rick's share of the estate was increased after Chester died was a bonus for her, of course." Wayne stopped walking and turned toward her.

"I finally put the whole thing together after questioning both Rick and Marina Hernandez again. The night Chester was killed, Meredith was late getting to the Willis house. She arrived after Leonard went to bed. The housekeeper, Marina, was doing the dishes and Rick and Chester were sitting at the kitchen table when Meredith got there. Chester said he needed an insulin shot. When he got his insulin out of the fridge and gave himself a shot, according to Marina, Meredith watched him carefully. Chester then asked Rick to get his pain meds and a sleeping pill from upstairs, said his leg was hurting.

Meredith offered to go get it for him. When she came back, what she handed Chester was his pain pill and a Xanax, not an Ambien. The pills are similar in appearance and in the dim light, Chester would have never noticed the difference."

"Let's keep going. We need to get to the party," Lucy said, but then she stopped. "I just remembered something. Chester's medical record indicated an extreme sensitivity to Xanax. In fact, he'd developed breathing problems once when taking it to have an MRI for back pain. He was claustrophobic and couldn't be put in the MRI tube without sedation."

"Turns out Meredith knew that," Wayne said. "Rick teased his brother once about being a wimp and needing drugs to get through an MRI. Chester told both Rick and Meredith about the sensitivity. He said he couldn't have the drug again because of the reaction."

"So, poor Chester went off to bed with a Xanax in his system and without a clue." Lucy shook her head. "I liked Chester, you know. He was a very upbeat person. That's why I was so sure he hadn't killed himself. Chester was going to be there for his father, for however long his life lasted." Lucy shuddered.

By then they had reached Mae's front yard. They paused beside a border of sunflowers blooming near her house, their yellow faces with dark centers turned toward the lingering sun.

"Rick and Meredith were going to the fireworks that night, and Rick went out to the car. Meredith said she'd forgotten her purse, which she actually left behind on purpose. She went back into the house. While Rick was waiting for her to return, Marina Hernandez came outside and Rick had to move his car so she could leave. It gave Meredith just enough time to grab a syringe, fill it with insulin, and tiptoe into Chester's bedroom. He kept a night light on because sometimes he got up to have an orange juice or give himself a needle stick to test his blood sugar."

"I can just see it … Chester's asleep. Meredith's in the bedroom and pulls the covers aside. She holds Chester's foot in her hand as she injects him under his toe. He's so out of it he doesn't even flinch. Then she leaves her boyfriend's brother to die alone. Oh, Wayne, it's just too horrible." Lucy turned away as tears sprang into her eyes.

When she turned back, Wayne was watching her closely. She pulled a tissue out of her purse and wiped her eyes.

"I'm sorry this is so upsetting to you, Lucy."

"As a physician, I try so hard to keep people alive. To think of that sneaky little bitch killing Chester .... It's evil, just monstrous."

Wayne pulled Lucy to him in a hug, then released her. "We still need to talk about our living arrangements," he said. "I know you don't want to leave your home, but you're right, I'm not sure about living this close to my boss."

Lucy sniffled. "Maybe we need to get something new for both of us where we can start our life together. What would you think about that?"

"I think that might be a really good idea." Wayne smiled.

She took his arm again and they walked over to join the party.

Chapter Forty-Three

———

Mae December

MAE WATCHED AS Channing approached their front door promptly at 6:30, the first of their guests to arrive. Out of her scrubs, she was quite stunning in a sky-blue, sleeveless dress that was short in the front and brushed the ground behind her. Sky-blue streaks in her hair and silver earrings that almost reached her shoulders completed her ensemble. She handed Mae a bottle of Sauvignon Blanc. "Thanks for inviting me tonight," she said.

"Come in, Channing. Thank you for the wine. You look amazing, doesn't she, Ben?" she asked her fiancé, who couldn't seem to stop staring at their guest.

"She does," he agreed enthusiastically.

Mae handed him the bottle. "Why don't you go open this and pour a glass for us?"

Ben hurried off, bottle in hand, just as Wayne and Lucy walked in. They were followed closely by Rob Fuller and Dory with her boyfriend, Al Peckham. Mae led everyone to the kitchen, where Ben handed her two glasses of wine. She took a sip of the crisp, grapefruit-tinged Sauvignon Blanc and handed the other glass to Channing Soldan.

"Thanks. Who's the cutie over there?" Channing tilted her head toward Rob, who was talking to Wayne Nichols.

"That's Rob Fuller. He's the other detective for the sheriff's office. Single, as far as I know. Wayne," Mae called out after the doorbell rang, "would you introduce Channing to everyone she doesn't already know? I need to get the door."

After greeting Tammy and Patrick as well as Deputy George Phelps and his wife Annabelle, Emma Peters and Mark Schneider, Mae directed them back to the kitchen. "Ben will get y'all something to drink. I'm waiting on a few more people." *I can't believe we rounded up this many guests on such short notice.*

Mae closed the door behind her and stood on the front porch, enjoying the balmy evening air and the view of the valley. A car she didn't recognize parked in the field to the right of the driveway. Cam Gomez got out of the driver's side and a woman she had never seen before climbed out on the passenger's side.

"Hi, Cam, c'mon up!" Mae called out, and Cam waved back. She and the other woman walked up the driveway side by side and climbed up the front steps.

Mae hugged Cam and held out her hand to her petite, short-haired friend. "I'm Mae December."

"Paula Crowley," she answered with a smile. "Good to meet you."

"You too. Glad you both could make it." Mae opened the door and led her last two guests down the hall and into the kitchen, where the party was in full swing.

Ben looked from Cam to Paula; then his eyebrows went up and he hurried over. "Hi, Cam. Good to see you, Captain Paula."

"Please just call me Paula, Ben. It's good to see you too." Mark Schneider waved at Cam and Paula from across the room, and the two women walked over to join him and Emma at the long counter where Mae and Ben had set up appetizers and a cooler with drinks.

"Help yourselves to whatever you want," Ben called after them. "There's more drinks and food on tables out in the backyard, too." He turned to Mae and in a quieter voice said, "I thought Cam asked you if she could bring a date."

"She did." Mae looked at Cam and Paula, standing close together and obviously comfortable with each other. "I'm pretty sure that Paula is her date."

"Well, okay." Ben gave a little shake of his head. "Didn't see that one coming. Rob's not going to be happy about it, that's for sure. He has a huge crush on Cam."

"Oh, I think he'll be fine." Mae cut her eyes toward the other corner of the kitchen, where Rob Fuller was whispering in the ear of a flushed and giggling Channing Soldan.

Ben glanced their way, smiled and put his arm around her. "Looks like Noah's Ark—everyone's paired off around here."

"Are your parents coming?" Mae asked.

"Yes, my brother and his wife too. They're going to be late though—going to a soccer game for one of my nephews first."

Dory and her boyfriend came in from the backyard. "Al, this is my boss, Ben Bradley."

"Al Peckham, nice to meet you." The tall, broad-shouldered man smiled, his teeth very white against his dark complexion. "Good to see you again, Mae. How're your folks?"

"Oh, Mama and Daddy are just fine. We invited them tonight but they're keeping my sister's kids while she and her husband are on vacation." Mae looked around her loud, crowded kitchen. "Besides Sophie Coffin and her husband, they were the only ones who turned down our invitation. Not sure we could've fit four more people anyway."

"I like a crowd for a party." Dory nodded her head decisively. "And I know Sophie's husband isn't feeling well right now. So we've got friends and family here, not just staff from the office.

I'm guessing this soiree is about more than closing the case. Am I right?"

"Aren't you always?" Ben looked at Al Peckham. "Good luck keeping up with this one."

"Oh, don't I know it!" the big man replied. "Trust me, I don't even try."

"You learn much faster than I do apparently. Anyway, Mae has agreed to manage my reelection campaign, so we want to get ideas from everyone as well as celebrate. We'll wait until my family gets here to talk campaign strategy, though."

"Oh, I've got *lots* of ideas," Dory said, "but they can wait a little longer. Where'd you put your three dogs for the festivities?"

Mae laughed. "We're up to four again, since we got Matthew's puppy. Her name's Cupcake, and she's up in our room with the other three. Want to meet her?"

Dory did, but Al said his knee was giving him trouble on stairs, so they left him chatting with Ben. Mae announced that she was taking Dory up to meet the puppy and Tammy, Patrick, Cam, and Paula all followed her up the stairs.

"I just love your house, Mae. How long have you lived here?" Cam asked.

"Thank you. A little over four years now. Ben moved in this spring, after we got engaged." Mae opened her bedroom door and flipped on the light switch, and her guests all started to laugh. The three dog beds that she'd carried upstairs were on the floor, empty. Tallulah, the black pug, raised her head from Mae's pillow where she reclined. Squinting in the overhead light, she gave a little squeak. Titan and Tatie, her two corgis, were curled up in the center of the yellow star on her quilted bedspread. They were both snoring.

"Did I mention that I also train dogs?" Mae said with a laugh. "Not necessarily my own, of course." She walked over to Cupcake's crate and unlatched the door. Cupcake, ears held together by an orange ribbon, ambled out to a chorus of "aww, so cute!" from the guests.

Cam sank down in front of Cupcake. "I used to have a basset when I was younger. He always tripped over his ears when he was a puppy. Is that why hers are pulled up like that?"

"Yes, otherwise she stands on them and gets stuck. Do you want to hold her?"

Cam nodded and rose fluidly to her feet, cradling Cupcake to her chest. Everyone else crowded around and Mae stepped back. She went over to the bed and sat down, petting her young female corgi Tatie and watching her friends fuss over the little basset. Tammy came and sat down beside her.

"Kind of like having a new baby, isn't it?" Her best friend winked. "Except your nipples don't hurt and you actually get to sleep all night. I'm jealous."

Mae shook her head. "You're not fooling me with all this 'I'm tired, my boobs hurt' stuff. I've known you since the sixth grade and you've never been happier."

Tammy's dark eyes sparkled as she looked at her husband Patrick, who was taking his turn holding Cupcake. "You're right. I love Patrick and little Benny so much. But you know what else makes me really happy at this stage of my life?" She bumped her shoulder into Mae. "Seeing how happy you are. There was a time when I wasn't sure you'd ever recover from losing Noah, and just look at you now."

Mae blinked back tears. "Yeah, I made it to the other side of that … awful time. Thanks to you and Patrick." Her handsome fiancé stuck his head in the door, curly hair rumpled and blue eyes shining. "And Ben, of course." She squeezed Tammy's hand and got off the bed. Walking over to Ben, she slid her arm around his waist. "Sorry to leave you in charge of the party by yourself. Do you need my help with anything downstairs?"

"No, babe." Ben pulled her close and brushed his lips against her cheek. "I just need you next to me."

"Don't worry." Mae smiled up at him. "I'll be right here beside you for the rest of my life."

Lia Farrell is actually two people: the mother and daughter writing team of Lyn Farquhar and Lisa Fitzsimmons.

L YN FARQUHAR TAUGHT herself to read when she was four years old and honed her storytelling abilities by reading to her little sister, Susan. Ultimately, her mother ended the reading sessions because Susan decided she preferred being read to rather than learning to read herself.

Lyn fell in love with library books when a Bookmobile came to her one-room rural school. The day the Bookmobile came, Lyn decided she would rather live in the bookmobile than at home and was only ousted following sustained efforts by her teacher and the bookmobile driver.

She graduated from Okemos High school and earned her undergraduate and graduate degrees from Michigan State University. She has a master's degree in English literature and a PhD in Education, but has always maintained that she remained a student for such a long time only because it gave her an excuse to read.

Lyn is Professor of Medical Education at Michigan State University and has authored many journal articles, abstracts, and research grants. Since her retirement from MSU to become a full-time writer, she has completed a young-adult fantasy trilogy called *Tales of the Skygrass Kingdom. Volumes I and II (Journey to Maidenstone and Songs of Skygrass).* Lyn has two daughters and six step children, nine granddaughters and three grandsons. She also has one extremely spoiled Welsh corgi. Her hobby is interior design and she claims she has the equivalent of a master's degree in Interior Design from watching way too many decorating shows.

LISA FITZSIMMONS GREW up in Michigan and was always encouraged to read, write, and express herself artistically.

She was read to frequently. Throughout her childhood and teenage years, she was seldom seen without a book in hand. After becoming a mom at a young age, she attended Michigan State University in a tri-emphasis program with concentrations in Fine Art, Art History and Interior Design.

Lisa, with her husband and their two children, moved to North Carolina for three exciting years and then on to Tennessee, which she now calls home. She has enjoyed an eighteen-year career as a Muralist and Interior Designer in middle Tennessee, but has always been interested in writing. Almost six years ago, Lisa and her mom, Lyn, began working on a writing project inspired by local events. The Mae December Mystery series was born.

Lisa, her husband and The Rock, their Siberian husky, currently divide their time between beautiful Northern Michigan in the summertime and middle Tennessee the rest of the year. She and her husband feel blessed that their "empty nest" in Tennessee is just a short distance from their oldest, who has a beautiful family of her own. Their youngest child is in school in Texas. Life is good.

Four Dog's Sake is the fourth book in the Mae December Mystery Series, which began with *One Dog Too Many*.

You can find Lyn and Lisa online at www.liafarrell.net.

The Mae December Mystery Series, 1-3

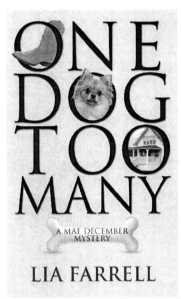

Mae December runs a dog boarding business in Tennessee. When her neighbor, Ruby Mead-Allison, fails to pick up her Pomeranian, Mae discovers the woman's body. While delving into the mystery of Ruby's death, Mae and handsome Sheriff Ben Bradley find no shortage of suspects. Meanwhile the killer wants to put a permanent stop to Mae's meddling.

On the eve of the opening of the historic Booth Mansion in Rosedale, TN, a man is shot and left for dead on the nursery floor. He is found by his former lover, the sister of Mae December, local kennel owner and girlfriend of Sheriff Ben Bradley. Ben's relationship with the family complicates an already complex case involving many of their friends and neighbors.

It's a bitter cold January in Rosedale, Tennessee. Mae December finds yet another body, this one on the banks of the Little Harpeth River. Another murder for her boyfriend, Sheriff Ben Bradley, to investigate. Mae's broken wrist makes helping with the case difficult, but that's okay, because evidence points clearly to the owner of a nearby puppy mill.

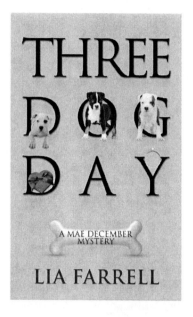

THREE DOG DAY

A MAE DECEMBER MYSTERY

LIA FARRELL

CPSIA information can be obtained
at www.ICGtesting.com
Printed in the USA
LVOW12s1620270916
506409LV00004B/667/P